Music of the Spheres

Valmore Daniels

MUSIC OF THE SPHERES

The Interstellar Age Book 2

Valmore Daniels

THE INTERSTELLAR AGE

Forbidden the Stars

Music of the Spheres

Worlds Away

The Complete Trilogy

For a complete list of available books, visit:

ValmoreDaniels.com

INCEPTION

Copán :
Honduras :
Central American Conglomeration :

My shame is unimaginable.

For years my grandson believed I was just a silly old man. I had hoped he would change his mind and grow to respect me and my knowledge when Colop—the Sky Traveler; the one they call Alex Manez—returned from the stars to thank me for helping the scientists.

I know my grandson never truly respected me, and he has proved to me that I am unworthy. I can no longer bear to face the people in my village.

Perhaps I was too prideful after Colop told me that they needed my help to discover the key to the fifth world so that we may become one with the People of the Stars. He told me the path to the stars was still clouded, and only I could unlock the secrets of the ancient scroll. I had to help him complete his journey.

He is the only one who can hear the Music of the Spheres, but it is not enough. He must also be able to hear the Song of the Stars.

It has been two summers since I spoke with Colop last, but I have worked very hard to translate the scroll for him.

They sent translators to help me when I refused to let them take the scroll away, but since they came to our village, they have been more than useless. They try to find English words to match the ancient Mayan symbols, and they do not listen when I tell them they are traveling down the wrong path.

I told them Colop should be here to learn the story, but they say it is impossible; they will send him images and recordings instead. They do not understand that their machine will only strip the meaning from my story, and so I declined their offer.

Frustrated with me, they took images of the scroll and sent them back to their labs; they used microscopes and chemicals to tell them if the secret was in the paper; they entered the Mayan symbols and pictograms into their computers.

Afraid of damage to the sacred scroll, the translators encased it in a plastic cover for me; for this contribution I am pleased, and I have hung it on the wall in my home.

All their efforts produced nothing more than gibberish, however. After a time, their irritation led them to threats, and then bribes, and then to more threats.

When they demanded to know if I am keeping the secret from them, I told them I have nothing to hide. I can only tell them what my grandfather said to me: true understanding lay not with the story, but in the telling of the story. I offer to tell them the story again, but I don't think they are capable of listening.

One week ago, my grandson, who has also been frustrated with me for a long time, asked me to tell him the story one more time. I had hoped that my telling would give him understanding, but he ran from my house before I finished the Song.

Yesterday, he brought a friend he said he had met on his

city adventure. The stranger asked me plainly why I would not help the scientists learn the secret. If I made them happy, he said to me, perhaps the knowledge could help raise the status of the Mayan people in the eyes of the world. At the very least, they would send us wealth.

I told my grandson's friend we did not need any more computers or machines. Such conveniences are secondary and unimportant in the great plan. Our status is not necessary, either. Our purpose should be to help Colop complete his journey and become one with the stars; that is all that truly matters.

My grandson said that his friend would like to listen to me tell the story once more. I hoped, perhaps, that their young ears would hear more than the old ears of the scientists from the north.

We sat on the long couch in front of the scroll and I told the story to my grandson and his friend one last time. I was very careful to tell it in the manner it was told to me by my own grandfather.

When I finished, I looked at them expectantly. At first, the other man's face was clouded over, but my grandson was excited.

"Do you not hear it?" he said to his friend.

After a moment, the stranger nodded. "Yes. I think so. I think you are right."

My heart swelled with pride. Finally, my grandson understood something in the tale. It was his destiny to hear the story. My grandfather had passed the legacy to me, as his grandfather had passed it to him. And now my grandson will become ambassador to the People of the Stars.

"You know the secret?" I asked him. I was hopeful.

My grandson nodded. "Yes, Grandfather, I believe I do. Thank you."

"Good." I closed my eyes with satisfaction. When I opened them again, I said, "Then you must find Colop and reveal the secret to him so that he also may hear the Song of the Stars."

He smiled at me in a way I had never before seen. "Oh, Grandfather. No, I will not find Alex Manez. And no, I will not give him the secret."

"I do not understand," I said.

He stood, and I saw that he clenched his fist at his side. "It is now *my* secret. It is *my* destiny to conquer the stars, not his."

My grandson tore the plastic-sealed scroll from the wall. When I stood to protest, his friend pulled out a gun and pointed it at me.

"What is this? What are you doing?" I demanded of my grandson.

"Sorry, grandfather. You have to come with us."

Two more men entered my house, then. They had rifles. I had no choice but to go with them.

How could I have been so blind? How could I not have seen all these years how my grandson despised our humble life in the village, and envied the power of Colop?

There is no use left for me. I have failed the gods, and must surrender myself to their mercy.

2

Selected EarthMesh Forum Excerpts
keyword search: *Quanta*

September 2103

"…think the mission was a total fail. Now they're touting him around on the newsfeeds as if he's a conquering hero. He didn't even see any aliens or anything. The *Quanta*: ship of fools. What a waste of money and time…"

October 2103

"…was on a liner to Luna Base last week. Someone said Captain Alex Manez was on board. I tried to get a look at him, but the security was too tight. NASA's meshsite said they're gearing up to launch another one of those *Quanta* ships…"

November 2103

"…you hear about the *Quanta 5* test flight yesterday? The quantum drive lasted about two seconds before it blew the ship right into the cosmos. This is—what?—the eighth astronaut they've either killed or maimed trying to get this right. Not to mention how many billions each of those ships cost. When are they going to give up? There are more important things to think about…"

January 2104

"…I guess it was my own fault. I sank our life savings into USA, Inc. stock before the *Quanta* flight, and I kept it there even when they missed the scheduled return date and the value started to sink. Now they've put Quantum Resources on the auction block because their stock is at an all time low and they don't have any more money to spend. I just hope that stops the devaluation. It's going to be a tight Christmas…"

February 2104

"…saw a report that NASA and CSE officially released Captain Alex Manez from their active roster. He was the pilot for the *Quanta*. Now that they've scrubbed the interstellar program, I guess they don't need him anymore. I can't seem to find any pictures of him…"

March 2104

"…and after fifteen years, now I'm out of a job. USA, Inc. needs a new CEO. First he spent trillions on *Quanta* ships, all of which either blew up or just didn't work, or the pilots died in training exercises. Now he's sold all Quantum Resources stock to Canada Corp. for pennies on the dollar. Didn't he think about all the people who worked in the Houston office? I'm fifty-two; with the economy in a shambles, who's going to hire me now…?"

August 2104

"…finally getting their heads out of the sand. I just read a press release from Canada Corp.'s SMD stating that they're no longer actively searching for that Kinemet element. I mean, without a working *Quanta* ship, the stuff is far too costly to mine. We can use iron ore; that'll get people building again, jumpstart the economy and create some jobs..."

August 2105

"...you guys remember that position I was applying for with Quantum Resources? They were the ones spearheading the first *Quanta* missions ten years ago, but they're more of an applied astrophysics think-tank operation now. Heavy into theoretical research—right up my alley. Well, I got the job! I start orientation in four weeks..."

3

Canada Station Three :
Lagrange Point 4 :
Earth Orbit :

December 2105

Alex Manez sat in the cockpit of the *Quanta*. All on-board electronics were dead, the heads-up displays were blank, and the only sound he could hear was the soft beating of his heart in his chest.

To the side of the pilot's chair, a pull ring hung from a short length of wire. All he had to do was to reach for that ring and give it a sharp tug. The reaction would switch on the generator and charge the battery, which would in turn power the computers and other electrical systems, including the Kinemetic dampers.

Alex reached out for the pull ring, and his fingers—the slender fingers of a teenager—touched the cool thin metal. The last time he had done this, his hand passed through the ring, as if he were a ghost caught between the living and spirit worlds.

The last time, the ship had exploded.

Now, there was no urgency in his actions. With minimal effort, he drew the ring back until it clicked, and watched as the holoslate in front of him flickered to life.

A green light indicated that all systems were operational and ready for normal navigation.

Disinterested, he brushed a thin strand of hair out of his eyes and longed for the time when he had a full head of hair. It seemed like a lifetime ago.

He looked up when a short, high-pitched binging sound came out of the holoslate.

Superimposed on the screen over a schematic display, a sour-looking face appeared, and narrowed eyes stared directly at Alex as if looking straight through him.

"And then what happened?" asked Kenny Harriman, the newest physicist to join the Quantum Resources research team on CS3. He was considered something of a whiz at the University of British Columbia, from where he had been recruited.

Biologically only a few years older than Alex, Kenny acted like a tenured professor. It was as if he had something to prove. From the moment he arrived in the lab, he had insisted on reading every report concerning the *Quanta* missions, reviewing every diagnostic ever run on Alex, and making sure he was supervising every simulation exercise.

He also had an annoying habit of making every question or statement a challenge. Kenny was a very excitable young man who obviously loved the pursuit of knowledge. At the same time, he was on a personal mission to drag Quantum Resources back into the spotlight of the world's scientific community.

In contrast to the physicist, Alex was the epitome of calm. "I told you. Nothing happened."

"Nothing!" Kenny tapped something on his haptic console, and the canopy of the life-sized flight simulator snapped open.

The hydraulics lifted the top up and away from Alex. He blinked to adjust his eyes to the brighter light of the simulation room. Through a large pane of glass, two analysts hunched over computer schematics in the adjacent room.

The light continued to sting Alex's eyes, but he watched as Ellen Yarrow adjusted the rim of her glasses over her pert nose.

Once, when Alex had first arrived on CS3 after his interstellar flight, he had tried to strike up a conversation with Ellen. She'd acted like she was uncomfortable, and excused herself. Since then, she had gone out of her way to avoid him.

Alex had no idea why he tortured himself over her, or over the possibility of any relationship. Even if he looked as old as his birth certificate stated, he was still a freak of nature, a science experiment gone awry.

He was doomed to solitude.

"What do you mean, 'nothing'?" Kenny demanded.

Alex fixed the physicist with a smile of innocence. "I don't mean anything by it. Nothing happened when I pulled the ring on the flight."

Kenny seemed completely unaffected. "Tell me why I don't believe you."

"It wasn't enough of a kick to turn the *Quanta* back on." Alex explained. "I had to provide the charge to initiate the systems."

"Right. This 'electropathic' ability, which you've failed to demonstrate to us time and again." The physicist pulled a disbelieving face. "All we have is your say-so you have the ability to manipulate electrical systems ... oh and the questionable reports from the crew of the *Orcus 1.*" He waved his holoslate in front of Alex.

Alex had had the same argument for the past two years with every scientist, technician and administrator Quantum Resources and Canada Corp. had sent up to Canada Station Three.

Before the real *Quanta's* first interstellar voyage, Alex had judged that the Kinemetic influence on the electrical systems of the ship would far surpass initial estimates. The shielded battery would not hold nearly enough power to start all the shipboard computers. And he had been correct. The pull ring had done absolutely nothing.

The longer Alex had been in proximity to the kinetic metal, the more of a charge he had built up. Once the *Quanta* had reached Centauri space, there was enough electrical current at Alex's disposal for him to start the computers and bring the life-support systems back online. That effort—among other things—had completely depleted him for a very long time.

Alex said, "I will be more than happy to show you how it works. I just need an adequate amount of Kinemet to replenish me."

Kenny gave him a cool gaze filled with disbelief.

Alex repeated himself, and there was a tone of quiet desperation that slipped into his voice. "I need it."

Without Kinemet, Alex was not only powerless to control electrical currents around him, but the longer he spent away from it, the faster his physical body deteriorated.

As with all living things, there were certain vitamins, minerals and amino acids an organism needed in order to maintain and sustain life; with Alex, it was as if exposure to the kinetic metal had added one more required element to his biological makeup when he had been irradiated on Macklin's Rock.

The physicist shook his head. "Even if I could authorize a small quantity—which I can't because we don't have any—I'm not convinced that mere exposure to the element will suddenly infuse you with some kind of supernatural power."

"It's not a sudden effect."

"Besides," Kenny said, narrowing his eyes, "according to these reports, when they were still building *Quanta* ships, they allocated half a milligram of Kinemet here for testing purposes. You were in contact with it."

"It wasn't enough," Alex said. "A drop of water for a man dying of thirst." Without the influence of Kinemet, his health had deteriorated drastically. The doctors couldn't prove that lack of exposure to Kinemet was causing his issues, and without a substantial quantity of the metal, he couldn't prove that it would help.

Kenny waved his hand in the air frantically. "We can go around in circles forever on this. It wasn't the question I was asking, anyway."

"I know," Alex said.

"I know you know!" Kenny was not as capable of hiding his frustration as his predecessor. He took a long, deep breath. "You say you were able to start the generator."

Nodding, Alex said, "I was."

Kenny sighed. "Then why did it explode, and why didn't you die in the explosion?"

"It's in my report," Alex said, his voice weary. "I got the systems up, but it was too late to engage the dampers. The secondary Kinemetic reaction had started; there was no way to stop it from exploding. I barely had enough time to eject the escape pod."

Kenny blinked. "It's too bad the flight recorder can't corroborate your story."

"I told you, when I used the electropathy to start the generator, I pushed too hard and it wiped the storage drive."

"Convenient," Kenny said.

Alex frowned. "You should have shielded it better."

Kenny flicked his hand dismissively. "Never mind about that. You had rations for one week—two if you pushed it. So how did you survive *after that*? What happened in the almost two-and-a-half months between when you arrived in the

Centauri system and when you made the return trip. You just—what—floated in space all that time in the pod?"

"It's a little foggy," Alex said. "I think I was suffering some aftereffects from being quantized. Time didn't really flow in an ordinary way." He wasn't a very good liar. From the look Kenny gave him, the physicist didn't believe him on that point.

In his debriefing to Quantum Resources—when it was still a joint venture between USA, Inc. and Canada Corp.—Alex had reported that his escape pod had detected a star beacon, an identical cousin to Sol System's *Dis Pater,* on the outer rim of the Centauri System. Another huge monument that resembled an electron cloud, the alien structure rested on the surface of a minor planet a fraction of the size of Charon.

Alex repeated himself for the hundredth time in the past two years. "I used the pod's jets to head for the alien star beacon. When I got there, it just … sent me home."

Fixing Alex with a look of frustration, Kenny said, "And if all of the Kinemet blew up with the *Quanta,* how did 'it' send you back to Sol System?"

That was one of the many questions the Quantum Resources scientists kept asking, but they continued to disbelieve any answer Alex gave them; and they were right. It was unfortunate that he was unable to tell them the truth.

He hated that there were things about his story he couldn't share. But if he shared his secret before the world was ready, it would lead to…

He didn't even dare think of it.

The frustration he felt had only sharpened over the past few years. The world needed to develop the Kinemet technology as fast as it could, but they had encountered a brick wall. Coupled with the worsening economy, it seemed no one was that interested in investing in Kinemet.

At times, Alex wanted to scream to get the world motivated,

but he knew he had to bite his tongue.

Time was running out; at the rate of things, it might take decades for the science of Kinemet to get where it needed to be.

Because of his health, Alex didn't have decades; he most likely didn't even have years.

But whenever Calbert Loche or Raymond McGrath sent up a new physicist to Quantum Resources, Alex did his best to help them, hoping they were the ones who could unlock the secret of Kinemet.

Inevitably, due to his reluctance to tell the complete truth, and also because those details he did share were difficult to believe, those newcomers eventually discounted the rest of Alex's story.

Kenny was a little more stubborn than his predecessors, but he was on the wrong track. Alex knew where today's conversation was heading, and the day's events had taken a toll on him. He didn't have the strength to endure an argument, and at this point, he didn't care if Kenny Harriman pitched a fit over it.

Alex said, "I'm tired. I need to rest."

Vibrating with barely suppressed anger, Kenny stormed off and tapped his report into the haptic console. One of the lab assistants approached and assisted Alex out of the simulator's cockpit.

∞

It had been over two years since Alex's return from the first interstellar voyage. The world financial crisis had intensified in Alex's absence. USA, Inc. and Canada Corp. had banked heavily on a successful mission for the *Quanta*. Contact with an alien race would have made the country corporations' stocks soar. New technologies, medicines, and even the possibility of interstellar trade would have boosted shareholder and consumer confidence.

With Alex's report that he had seen nothing out there except the distant flare of the Centauri system's red dwarf star, Proxima, the media had descended on the two country corporations, hungry for blood. They accused the United Earth Corporate Council of wasting trillions of dollars on an empty space fantasy when they should have concentrated their efforts on the realities of increasing population, famine and energy depletion. The UECC had backed out of the *Quanta* trials, and after NASA and Quantum Resources' repeated failures, USA, Inc. decided to follow suit.

Quantum Resources barely survived USA, Inc.'s downsizing efforts by selling all shares to Canada Corp. and relocating its quantum research facility to Canada Station Three.

Without a steady supply of Kinemet for practical trials, Quantum Resources had turned into more of a theoretical analysis laboratory. At the moment, their only solid asset was Alex Manez. Despite his agreement to be their guinea pig— and as his body continued to fail him—he found himself becoming more and more obstinate.

As had happened during his self-imposed exile on the pirate base on Luna, without the direct influence of Kinemet, Alex had begun to physically deteriorate once more. It was as if the radiation emitted from that element, while basically harmless to those who had not been exposed during a transfer reaction, had become a requisite substance for Alex. He fed off it; it replenished him and kept him alive.

He had no idea how long he would live without it.

The harshest side effect of his condition was that he could not tolerate Earth's high gravity anymore. While the main labs, administration areas, and the common and recreation centers on Canada Station Three were all fitted with the latest in artificial gravity technology, the levels in the living quarters were completely adjustable by the occupants. Alex, when home, kept gravity to a bare minimum.

Unable to stand on his own for more than a few short minutes at a time, Alex had purchased a set of hydraulic leg braces which would support his weight. He purchased them with the proceeds from the severance package given to him by NASA.

When not in his quarters, Alex wore his hydraulic braces. Using fluid dynamics, biomechatronics and environmental pressure sensors, the braces were able to compensate for any external factors, such as walking on an incline or stairs, or—if he were back on Earth—snow or rain. They provided him with a more natural gait. From a distance, most people would not be able to tell he wore orthotics. Not that it made any difference: Alex looked pale and sickly; his hair was thin and stringy, and his bones continued to atrophy no matter how many vitamin shots the medical staff administered.

All the researchers and corporate administrators treated Alex like a child. Even Ellen Yarrow looked at him as if he were something she discovered in a Petri dish. Although his body appeared to be that of a sixteen-year-old boy, according to his birth record, he was twenty-five; legally an adult. During the eight or so years when his body had been in a quantized state, he had not aged physically.

Once the assistants secured him in the leg supports, Alex pulled on his loose-fitting trousers and fastened them at his waist.

Out of the corner of his eye, he saw Kenny returning, and steeled himself for a confrontation.

Kenny watched as Alex finished dressing.

The physicist finally said, "Look, I don't want us to be enemies. I want you to trust me. I just want what's best for everyone."

Alex scoffed.

Kenny threw up a hand. "Fine. I want what's best for me, but that can only lead to helping you. So please, can't we start the dialogue over again?"

"If you truly want to help yourself," Alex said, "then you'll listen when I tell you that what you are doing right now is irrelevant—and quite possibly counterproductive."

Shaking his head, Kenny asked, "How can the study of the most advanced technology in the universe be irrelevant?"

Kenny often spoke as if he were in a lecture hall.

Alex sighed. "That's not what I'm saying. It is the most important thing in the world. We need to master it before—"

"Before what?"

Alex shook his head. "First, you need to understand the basics of Kinemet. And we don't even know how to stabilize it. We need to focus on how Kinemet affects people, not how to build a better quantum drive. Everyone keeps looking at the power of Kinemet as if it's just the key to light-speed travel."

"But it is!"

Alex shook his head. "Yes, it can be a trigger for quantizing matter into light and powering a properly equipped vehicle at near light speeds. But that's only the most rudimentary of its properties."

"What are you talking about?" Kenny scanned his notes, but Alex knew none of his predecessors had written anything about this.

Normally, he wouldn't try to explain himself. However, of all the researchers sent up to CS3, Alex had a feeling that Kenny's mind might be open to new possibilities.

Alex said, "It can do so much more than just be a fuel for

light-speed travel."

Voice low, ears alert, Kenny asked, "Such as…?"

Alex pointed to himself. "Human chrysalis, for one. Though we've failed miserably in that regard. And then there's the Grace."

Kenny stared at Alex as if he were speaking another language.

He blinked. "The grace of what?"

Alex cursed himself and said, "Nothing. Sorry, I'm just too tired to think straight. I have to go to my quarters."

4

Interim Report :
Health Status :
Alex Manez :

From:
Dr. Naryan Amma, Ph.D., CS3 Medical Chief of Staff

To:
Canada Corp. Health Services, Dept. of Nutritional and
Metabolic Diseases.

Diagnosis:
The subject, Alex Manez, displays symptoms indicative of
massive vitamin deficiency, particularly D and C, though all
levels of those vitamins are with normal ranges.

Despite bombardment of multivitamins and a diet of citrus and
dairy products, Alex Manez suffers from continued hair loss,
chronic insomnia, pale skin and osteoporosis.

There is indication of onset muscle degeneration, and I expect
other symptoms to become prevalent as his condition worsens.

While his mental acuity remains in the top percentile, his
emotional state has become volatile, and he is prone to
depression and anxiety.

Treatment:
All attempts to correct the subject's condition have failed to reverse or even stall his deterioration. Physical exercise exacerbates his pain, multivitamin injections and supplements show no effect, and growth hormones only serve to cause gastrointestinal distress and may lead to kidney and liver failure.

Prognosis:
Alex Manez has no more than six months to live.

5

Houston Interplanetary Spaceport :
Texas :
USA, Inc. :

It had been over ten years since Justine Turner had seen a sunrise or sunset, since she'd looked upon the face of another person with her own eyes, and since she had even been able to look at herself in a mirror.

She'd gone blind at the edge of Sol System. While she did not regret the events that brought her to that point—and would not trade those experiences for her sight—she found some days more difficult than others, especially in the beginning.

One of the toughest transitions was the loss of her command status. She wanted nothing more than to captain a ship again; to breathe the stale cabin air of a control center; read digital displays and make decisions that would take her vessel out into the vast reaches of space.

The months she had spent on the journey back from Pluto had been the hardest, when she was completely cut off from all sight.

When she got home, she underwent optilink surgery to allow her brain to interpret electrical pulses from an optical-neural translation sensor, which she clipped to the bridge of her nose.

Still, she had struggled with the most basic of daily chores: cooking, dressing and personal grooming to name a few. She had hired an assistant to help her the first year home, but that only reminded her how helpless she was.

Holoslate interfaces were based off haptic technology. It was a perfect match for those who used Braille. After learning the system, Justine was able to read any eBook, manual, or meshmail with the built-in Braille application as easily as a sighted person.

But adjusting to a world where she was blind wasn't the worst part; it was the boredom. She'd had nothing to do.

So once she'd mastered the optical sensor technology, she had pleaded with the officials at NASA to reassign her to the active duty roster.

When they offered her an instructor's position, she jumped at the chance, knowing it was most likely the closest she would ever come again to being in command, or tasting the exhilaration of space flight.

There was a second reason she had so eagerly accepted an instructor's position. The feeling of satisfaction and accomplishment in passing her knowledge on to the young trainees was something she had come to love.

She would never have a child of her own. Biologically, it was still a possibility—there were women much older than her who had children—but at this stage in her life, and with her own personal challenges, she just couldn't see herself making that decision. By the time he or she was a teenager, Justine would be in her late sixties, and she couldn't imagine that she would have enough energy to keep up.

The closest she had ever come to having a child was during those short few months aboard the *Quanta* with Alex Manez. It had given her a fleeting taste of motherhood, and for the first time in her life, she had understood the power of that instinct. To care for and impart her experiences to those who would follow in her footsteps gave her as much of a sense of completeness as she could ever have wanted.

The years she spent as a flight instructor were some of the best in the last decade.

Now, however, that was all behind her.

In the past two years, NASA and USA, Inc. had suffered a great many setbacks—not to mention the loss of many lives on the *Quanta* experiments. That had resulted in the sale of Quantum Resources to Canada Corp. and the shoe-boxing of the entire Kinemet program. There were far too many problems here on Earth to spend any more money on interstellar exploration; or at least, that was the reason the directors at USA, Inc. had given for their decision to sell.

Many of NASA's independent contractors had been released from their contracts, and even many regular staff members had been offered severance packages and early retirement.

They had offered Justine a very generous sum, enough that she could easily have weathered the troubled financial times in relative comfort for many years to come. She had taken the settlement, and wondered what to do with the rest of her life. For a time, she thought about returning to the Lowell Observatory and completing her studies there, but the call of space was too great for her to simply retire.

With her background, she managed to secure a position with Lunar Lines Ltd., who ran their space liners between Houston Spaceport and Luna Base, as a public relations hostess.

It was a one-week round trip, and Justine worked two flights on, one flight off. The position was much more than being an attendant or a tour guide; she was also responsible for the comfort and general safety of the passengers, as well as their peace of mind. While travel to Luna Station and the various space stations orbiting Earth was becoming more frequent, only a fraction of the population had ever undertaken the trip, and for many of those who took a liner it was the first time. They were understandably nervous flying into the void of space.

That morning was the beginning of another of Justine's rotations, and she always looked forward to this leg of the trip for more than just the chance to be in space.

At the Earth-Moon Lagrange 4 point was Canada Station Three, among the Kordylewski clouds. Lunar Lines always had a one-day stopover there before heading to their ultimate destination, and it was Justine's only chance to see Alex Manez.

She worried about him; he seemed to become more pale and sickly every time she visited him. The last time she had stopped there, over two weeks before, he had been significantly more tired than usual and had cut their visit short.

This time around, she hoped to get a word in with someone in charge of the Quantum Resources labs, and find out what they were doing to help him. And if she didn't get satisfaction from them, she would just have to call in a few more favors.

The apartment's home-unit computer system sounded a chime on the main holoslate, indicating there was a vehicle in her driveway.

"Identify," she said out loud.

<Ace Taxi Service,> Hucs informed her. *<Cab Number 3419; the driver's name is Tomas Salenko, four-year taxi license holder.>*

"Oh, he's early. Thank you. I'll be a just another minute."

<Relaying message.>

Justine hurried back to her bedroom and approached the bed. Resting on the sheets were her two travel bags and a specially developed harness.

The optical recognition scanner on her optilink fed her brain rudimentary spatial data. It allowed her to navigate between one room and the next, and even gave her the ability to discern the difference between a fork and a spoon. It didn't have the capability to show her color, texture or patterns. She could detect the frame of a painting hung on a wall, but she had no way of telling whether it was a blank canvas or a Van Gogh.

Meeting people was just as challenging. It was as if she were face blind. Until someone spoke, Justine had extreme difficulty telling one moving biped from another, unless they had very distinct physical traits.

Optimedia Labs, the company she had originally purchased her optilink through, was also the company who had invented the Virtual Tourist.

A few months back, they had released the next generation in recognition software. Intended for the digital mock-reality entertainment industry, the Personal Environmental Recording Suit—PERSuit, as it was trademarked—was a step up from their Virtual Tourist Camera.

It recorded and interpreted over ten million coded shapes, sounds, smells, colors and textures. Thousands of micro-sensors in the fabric of the harness constantly scanned all audio, video and olfactory data within range.

Contestants on game shows or adventure shows would wear the PERSuit while participating, and then viewers could download those episodes into their septaphonic masks and experience those events for themselves, as if they were there in the contestant's place.

While the downloads were relatively inexpensive, the harness itself was pricey, and getting the techs to integrate the PERSuit sensors with her optilink required signed affidavits that she would not sue in the event of a sensory overload.

Combining her body's natural senses with the artificial sensors was not recommended by any of the company's medical staff.

The result was more than she had hoped for, and while she wore the specifically tailored harness, it was as if she had her sight back. There was a major drawback to the garment.

Within a few days of wearing it, Justine began to feel the effect that the company had feared: extended exposure caused her to develop severe migraines. She couldn't wear the harness for more than twelve hours in a day before the pain became unbearable—her mind just couldn't process the enormous amounts of data.

Through experimentation, Justine had also found that if she wore the harness four days in a row, the headaches would start as well.

As a compromise, she never wore the harness at home— she had memorized every nook and cranny in her apartment and didn't need it anyway—and she rarely wore it in public.

For the most part, she wore it when she was working. In her newest vocation as a liner hostess, being able to identify passengers by sight was a valuable ability—especially since the majority of those passengers were country-corporate decision makers, department heads for various science and tech companies, and influential members of the media.

Folding the harness carefully, she packed it in one of her travel bags and headed out to catch her taxi to the spaceport.

∞

Houston Spaceport was bustling with activity. As the taxi pulled up the long stretch of road to the main entry gates, Justine could sense many human forms gathered on the grassy hills in front of the twenty-foot-high fence. While her optilink sensor picked up that the protestors held signs, she could not read any of the slogans written on them; she could, however, hear their angry shouts when she opened the window a crack.

"Feed the people—not your greed!"

"Space is a waste!"

"We need jobs on Earth, too!"

"God gave us Eden; only those who are unworthy seek to leave the garden!"

It was nearly impossible to explain to such protestors that space exploration had opened avenues to new technologies and conveniences which they themselves used on a daily basis. Mining the asteroid belts did provide jobs as the raw materials were shipped back to Earth for processing; it also saved the Earth's natural resources.

There were protestors at nearly every facility in the country that promoted science and technology. If someone suffered a job loss for whatever reason, they often didn't care to look closely at the actual cause; it was easier to point the finger at the nearest target. In the past few years, it was the space industry. Nearly gutting the NASA program was not enough; they wanted to ground all space exploration.

There were also outcries from many of the world's religions, which had started from the day Justine and her crew had discovered the *Dis Pater* on Pluto. Many thought it blasphemous to consider that humans weren't a unique and divine species. To entertain the notion that there were thousands of alien races among the stars was sacrilege.

Some pundits theorized the only reason there hadn't been a full-out religious revolution was because of the failure of Alex's mission. He had come back without any evidence of alien contact; that, to the religious extremists, was proof that the entire affair had been a hoax, and humankind's status as the sole intelligence in the universe was secure.

Over the past year, the crowds of protesters had gradually

dwindled, and their rants had not held the vehemence they once carried.

Security, however, remained tight. Once the taxi arrived at the main entrance, it was scanned before any of its occupants were allowed to exit the vehicle. The taxi was quickly cleared of any harmful substances, such as explosives, weapons, or contraband. Justine got out, gathered her bags, and headed for the main building.

The automatic doors parted for her as she entered the spaceport, but when she stepped in, her way was blocked by a tall, thin figure whose back was to her.

Many first time visitors to the port were intimidated by the size and scope of the main terminal, which also doubled as a kind of museum of space flight. Large reproductions—most life-sized—of NASA's various rockets, shuttles and other craft from its long history were displayed throughout the interior of the large building. Crowds of tourists came just to look at the scale models, even if they didn't have tickets for an outbound flight.

Justine assumed the man in her way was simply taken aback by the scope of the space terminal.

"Excuse me," she said politely.

The visitor turned, and though Justine could not make out his features, what struck her as odd was that he wore glasses. With current technological levels, they could correct nearly everything short of blindness. It was rare to see someone still wearing spectacles. When he spoke, there was a hint of a foreign accent that Justine couldn't quite place.

"My apologies, ma'am. I am not sure where I need to go."

Justine, who had been in the port a hundred times, said, "Are you here for a tour or a flight?"

"Flight."

"Check-in is right over there." She pointed to a bank of

kiosks to their left. "Then you'll have to go through security."

"Thank you," the man said with a slight nod, and then he headed off.

Justine had no need to check in. She went straight to the security gates and said good morning to the ever-watchful guard. She had to remove her optilink so that he could perform a retinal scan. There was a gentle chime as the computer confirmed her identity, and then a second chime indicating she had a personal message.

Justine put her optilink back on and turned in the direction of the holoslate. While any words written in analog format on a sign were nothing more than a blur, the optilink sensor had the ability to receive digital data and feed it directly into her optic nerve—the original purpose of the technology. Her name, position, and other vital information popped up on the floating slate beside the scanner, and the blinking message icon hovered below her name.

She touched the icon, and it transformed into a terse sentence: *Please report to Director Mathers.*

The guard, trying to be helpful, pointed down an adjacent corridor with his neuro-baton and said, "Administration is that way, ma'am." He sat back down on his chair, looking bored. "Director Mathers' office is there."

"Thank you," Justine replied with a smile, though she knew exactly where his office was, and headed off in that direction.

∞

"Sir?" she spoke softly at the entrance of Director Mathers' office.

Behind the large oak desk, a high-backed leather chair swiveled around towards Justine. Director Allan Mathers held up one finger for her to wait. His other hand was touching the comlink on his ear.

"—Yes, she's here now," he said to whoever was on the other side of the call. "—Yes. Consider it handled… All right. I'll brief her and send her right down."

He pulled the comlink off his ear and dropped it on the desk.

"Justine," he said. "Close the door and come in. Sit."

Usually, the director greeted his employees with a smile, but today his face was grave and drawn. He looked out the window into the distance while Justine closed the door and approached the desk.

"What's up, sir?" Justine asked as she eased herself into the small guest chair.

Director Mathers turned back and leaned his elbows on his desk. He touched the tips of his fingers together and leveled his gaze at Justine.

"Did you scan the news this morning?" he asked.

Justine shook her head. "Sorry, sir, I was in a bit of a rush." Then, when the director didn't follow up his question, she asked, "What's happened?"

"Justine, you are aware that with all the cutbacks, quite a few of USA, Inc.'s subdivisions, like NASA, have been outsourcing a number of their flights to commercial lines like ours. We even sometimes provide transport for armed forces troops and military cargo to Luna and the outlying space stations."

Nodding, Justine said, "Yes, of course. Why are you telling me this?"

"I'm not comfortable about it, but the directive came from corporate." He glanced up at her, then looked back at his hands.

"What directive, sir?" Justine wrinkled her eyebrows. "I'm not sure I follow."

The director took a deep breath. "Well, apparently a report just came in that the original Mayan scroll—the one they say was transcribed from alien visitors a thousand years ago…"

"Yes," Justine said, gulping. "I know which one you're talking about."

"Well," he continued, "it's been stolen, and the old man who had it has gone missing. They think he might have been kidnapped."

"Oh?" Justine hadn't heard any news about this. She wondered what the kidnappers thought to accomplish. At last report, translating the document was a bust. That was one of the reasons for mothballing the *Quanta* experiments.

Director Mathers nodded. "That's not all. The Honduran Cooperative passed some intelligence on to the CIA. There's a growing movement within the Departmentals in that country. Many of them consider that, because the aliens"—he made air-quotes—"picked the Mayan people to visit half a millennia ago, they are the 'chosen ones' and should be in the forefront of any interstellar commerce. They've been grumbling for years about being sidelined. The governments, though, now think this group might be behind the kidnappings and theft."

Justine pursed her lips. "I've heard something about them. What do they call themselves?"

"Cruzados," the director said. "But now NASA feels keeping their supply of Kinemet here in Houston is a security risk. They've suffered enough bad press, and don't want to see themselves in any more headlines. They're not doing anything with the Kinemet currently, and so they want to transport it to Luna Station. They feel the rebels don't have the resources to attempt any extra-planetary action."

"How much Kinemet are we talking about?" Justine asked.

"About a thousand kilos."

She whistled. "That's a lot!" They had used about a hundred

kilograms of the kinetic metal on Alex's flight, and they'd overestimated how much they would need.

"We've got the room," he said with a shrug.

Then Justine cocked her head. "So, what does this have to do with me?"

"Understandably, NASA wants to keep this shipment hush-hush until it has arrived safely on the Moon. An army squad is providing protection." He pointed at Justine. "But NASA wants a liaison to go with them. Someone who has security clearance, and apparently yours has never been revoked, right?"

"That's right."

"You were attached to NASA from the Air Force," he said. "Best of both worlds. So they've requested you accompany the security detail."

Justine didn't want to get her hopes up. She swallowed, then said, "Accompany? What does that mean? What do they want me to do?"

"Same thing you always do. Only this time you'll be attending the soldiers they've assigned to the cargo."

"Oh," Justine said, trying valiantly to keep the sharp disappointment out of her voice.

"You're to report to hangar twelve for a briefing with Colonel Niles Gagne before the other flight crew or passengers embark."

Justine got to her feet and sighed.

The director said, "This is not a crap assignment."

"Yes it is," she told him.

"It came from up top, Justine," he said by way of apology. The expression on his face showed his sincerity. "Look, just do this one boring flight—"

"A week in a cargo hold babysitting a squad of soldiers is more than just a little boring," Justine said and headed for the door. She would never be recalled to active duty. No one needed a blind pilot. "It's demeaning. If you recall, my actual position with Lunar Lines is in public relations. Now you want me to serve coffee to soldiers?"

"I'll make it up to you," Director Mathers said.

Justine opened the door, but paused before leaving. "Well, I can think of one thing that would make this worth it for me."

"What?" he asked.

"I have a friend on CS3," she said.

"You mean Alex Manez, don't you?"

Justine nodded. "Yeah."

"What about him?"

"He's not doing so well." Justine pulled at her lower lip. "On the return trip, I'd like to take some shore leave up there; spend a little time with him and see what I can do."

"That can be arranged." The director smiled. "Consider it a bonus. We'll arrange some rooms in the Starwatch Resort. I'll even write it up as a training expense."

Justine smiled. "Thanks, Allan."

She closed the door behind her. Feeling much better about her newly assigned duty, she strode off to find hangar twelve and the colonel.

6

Canada Station Three :
Lagrange Point 4 :
Earth Orbit :

Within moments of entering his apartment, a sudden bursting pain literally knocked Alex off his feet.

That haunting song that he heard whenever he used his *sight* filled his mind, pushing out every rational thought.

How is this happening? he screamed to himself. The Kinemetic radiation had long since left him.

The song was there nevertheless. It urged him—no, *compelled* him—to finish what he'd started over a decade before.

Alex was not whole, and unless he could complete his journey and transform into a full Kinemat, he would die in agony; and very soon. Time was his enemy.

For the rest of the day, hiding in his apartment, Alex floated in and out of consciousness.

Since the first time he had been exposed to Kinemet, Alex had not been able to sleep or to dream. He could do neither, and did not seem to have suffered any of the physiological or psychological effects of sleep deprivation. Apparently, his mind could still shut down.

As if drugged, his thoughts soared and wandered. Images appeared before him, and flittered away before they could fully form.

Always, though, there was the Song, calling to him. No matter what he did—taking painkillers, turning off the lights, lying down—it was always there.

It was difficult for him to think clearly. Like a gas-powered automobile running on empty, he needed an infusion of Kinemetic radiation before he succumbed.

His exposure to Kinemet a dozen years before had begun to transform him, but the change was far from complete. Alex was a hollow shell, a ghost, trapped between two dimensions. The key, he knew, was in translating that ancient scroll. No one had been able to solve the riddle, and they'd given up trying. Alex knew the answer was in the scroll. It had always been right there.

As he thought about it, fighting off the pain of Kinemet withdrawal, the certainty grew.

With great difficulty—and struggling to maintain his wits—Alex commanded the communications system to make contact with Michael Sanderson. If there was anyone who could figure out his puzzle, it was Michael.

But the pain! He couldn't remember if he had connected with Earth and spoken with Michael, but before he could try again, the song filled his head ... and then something happened to him that tore him away from reality.

His body, ill-equipped to deal with the pain, betrayed him.

He began to shut down.

The last thing he heard was the ancient voice calling to him: *Alex, come home.*

7

Sanderson Family Barbeque :
Hull, Quebec :
Canada Corp. :

A cloud of smoke billowed out of the barbeque when Michael's brother, David, opened the lid to reveal half a dozen charred steaks.

"You think maybe they're cooked enough?" Michael asked, standing off to the side.

With his fingers wrapped around the neck of a beer bottle, he lifted it to his lips and tipped the drink up enough to let a stream of golden liquid pour into his mouth. Several drops spilled over his beard, and he wiped them away with the back of his hand.

"Wise-ass remarks will not get you invited back," David said, waving a spatula in a fan-like motion over the burning steaks to dissipate the rising smoke.

"Probably better for my health, anyway." Michael winked at his brother.

"If you're worried about your health, you'd best watch what you say." David lifted one of the barbeque utensils and pointed it at Michael. "I have tongs, and I'm not afraid to use them."

Michael laughed. "I'll go get some plates," he said and headed toward one of the picnic tables scattered around the yard.

Halfway there, he stopped and turned around. David was poking at the blackened meat with a long knife.

"And a fire extinguisher," Michael added in an attempt to keep the banter going.

"Bah!" David made a shooing motion, but he was grinning when he went back to his attempts to resuscitate their dinner.

Laughing, Michael closed the distance between the barbeque and the tables. By the time he got there, though, his smile faded.

His humor never lasted long these days.

After Alex Manez made his miraculous return from Centauri, Michael had returned to Quantum Resources as a consultant to help coordinate the *Quanta* trials. For reasons the technicians could never adequately explain, none of the test pilots who were exposed to the Kinemetic radiation had fully developed the electropathic ability that Alex had. Without that control, they were unable to return the ships to normal space once they were quantized as light. Several of those who volunteered died during the initial Kinemetic irradiation.

Failure after failure caught up to the corporations, both financially—each ship cost in excess of seventeen billion dollars—and from a public relations perspective. Coupled with the continued economic instabilities as more country corporations went into bankruptcy on a global basis, USA, Inc. had decided to mothball most of their experimental sub-companies, including Quantum Resources, which they sold to Canada Corp. at a bargain basement price.

Rather than relocate to Canada Station Three and administer a team of theorists, Michael decided to let them release him from his contract. Although Alliras Rainier had offered him his old position with the Space Mining Division, Michael and his wife opted for retirement. He had enough savings for him and Melanie to live comfortably for the rest of their lives.

But what Michael hadn't expected was that the rest of Melanie's life was cut short a year ago when a city autobus's brake line failed and slammed into her one-seater automobile while she was out on a shopping excursion. She had died instantly. A day did not go by that Michael didn't miss her fiercely.

Over the following months, Michael fell into a deep depression, let his beard grow out, and spent most of his days wandering from room to room in his empty apartment. The only times he ever emerged was for the monthly family dinners his brother held.

No wife, no job, no purpose.

The only thing that held Michael together was the weekly call he placed to Alex Manez; but it was getting harder and harder for Michael to maintain his hope that something would be done to help the boy and his deteriorating health. Without his political contacts, Michael was helpless to prod the medical staff on Canada Station Three to figure out a cure for Alex's condition.

During their conversations, Alex invariably told Michael not to worry; that it would all work out in the end.

"Are you all right?" a voice said, breaking Michael out of his reverie.

He looked up to see Andrea, David's wife, fixing him with two very concerned blue eyes. She was a slender woman with smile lines at the corner of her mouth and eyes. Streaks of silver had begun to flow through her raven-black hair.

Andrea and Melanie had been very close friends, and once in a while she would drop over to Michael's apartment and look in on him, do his laundry and try to clean up the place.

Michael realized he had just been standing in front of the picnic table with a stack of disposable plates in his hand.

He gave her a smile. "Yeah," he said. "Just lost in thought."
Turning around, he brought the plates over to the barbeque.

In addition to David and Andrea, Michael's two nephews, and their wives and kids, were also in attendance. Andrea's sister and her family were also there. David's son was out of town, but his daughter-in-law Debbie and her two children were spending the weekend. All told, David Sanderson's backyard held over twenty people.

Michael was grateful for the crowd. Not just for the company, but because, with so much hustle and bustle, he could blend into the background and not have to interact. He loved his family, but lately he had found himself detaching from human contact. It was good to be around people—it reminded him of his humanity—but he just didn't have the energy to cultivate any kind of relationship with anyone.

David looked up when Michael approached. "Good timing; the steaks are ready."

"They were ready fifteen minutes ago," Michael said, lifting the corner of his mouth in a half-smile.

"Just…" David mimed scraping the burned parts off with a knife. "And smear it with sauce."

Michael laughed. While David put steaks on the plates, Michael carted them over to the tables. While he trucked back and forth, he noticed he had picked up a little shadow.

He looked down to see his six-year-old grand-nephew staring up at him with a grin. "Hello, Carl," he said.

"Hello, Great-Uncle Michael." Carl waved his hand in a sweeping motion.

"Just call me Uncle Mike—I haven't felt great in a long while. Did you want to be my helper?"

"Sure, Great-Unc—sure, Uncle Mike."

Michael handed him a plate with a thick steak hanging over the lip, and watched while Carl balanced it and carried it over to the tables. All the while, he stuck his tongue out of the corner of his mouth in concentration.

Michael and David smiled while they watched him go.

"Grandkids," David said. "They'll keep you young."

Then his smile faded. "Sorry, Michael. I know you and Melanie tried hard."

"I guess it's for the better," Michael said after a while. "I was always working fourteen-hour shifts. Barely had enough time for Melanie. If I had kids they'd probably have grown up strangers, full of resentment."

When Carl came back for his second load, Michael said, "You okay, sport?"

"Yeah. Aunt Ginny says she only wants a half. And one that isn't a burnt offering."

With a laugh, David quickly sliced a steak in two and put the slightly smaller portion on a plate, which Michael handed to Carl.

"There you go. Steady now," he added when Carl overbalanced the plate.

"You know," David said, and there was an uncomfortable quaver in his voice, "if you're not doing anything, why don't you swing by next weekend? Andrea and I are going to a bridge tournament. There's a lot of single people our age there."

"I'm not ready."

Dave held up his hands. "Hey, don't mean to push."

Michael shook his head. "I'm just not sure what to do with myself is all. I always thought this would be my chance to travel the world with Melanie."

"You can still travel." David prepared another steak for Carl when the young boy returned. "There are chartered tours for practically every destination."

"Wouldn't really be the same."

"You've got to get out of this funk," David said. "I'm saying this as your brother and your friend."

"I know. I appreciate it, really. I guess I just need to figure things out. I can't explain it."

David put his hand on Michael's shoulder. "You don't need to explain a thing. Just know we're here for you."

"Thanks, bro." Michael didn't need to force the smile he gave David.

When Carl came back for the last time, he said, "It's just you and Grandpa left, Uncle Mike. —And me."

"Well," Michael said. "Looks like your grandfather saved the juiciest steak for you, a reward for all your hard work."

Carl beamed as he took his prize back to the picnic tables, shouting at his mom, "Look what I got."

David served the last two steaks, and he and Michael headed to the table to fill their plates with potato salad, pickles and buns.

While everyone ate, they shared jokes, gossiped, and just basked in the familiarity of family.

Michael's appetite wasn't what it used to be, and when he had only finished half of his supper, he excused himself from the table to use the washroom.

"Don't fall in!" someone joked, and Michael waved a hand in the air as he went into his brother's house.

On the way to the facilities, he passed by David's front room. A large DMR casement was playing the highlight reel of the last Roughriders football game. At the bottom of the flat screen was a scrolling newsfeed, and it was one of the sentences there that caught his attention.

He quickly moved in for a closer look, but only caught the last part of the announcement:

"…NASA spokesman discounts the impact of the missing Mayan scroll." Then the newsfeed went on to other political matters.

Michael sat on the couch next to the control pad and typed in a command to flip the screen to his favorite bulletin board. He cursed when he had to physically toggle back and forth between pages.

Within a few minutes, however, he had the entire story—the kidnapping of Yaxche and the theft of the ancient scroll—and his face grew dark.

"What's wrong?" asked his brother from the doorway.

"Who uses a damned DMR casement anymore? Why don't you upgrade to a holoslate with an organic user interface?" Michael asked. "You know, haptic consoles have been around for five years now."

"I really don't need to multitask while watching the Jays get beat by the Cubs," David said matter-of-factly. "I'm fine with one screen at a time."

Taking a deep breath, Michael said, "Sorry."

"Hey, no problem. You okay?"

Michael looked up. "Looks like the Cruzados kidnapped that Mayan translator, Yaxche. He was the one who helped us interpret the Mayan text from Pluto." He flipped a page on the casement. "And they also stole the scroll that was supposed to help us figure out how to use the Kinemet."

"Oh?" David blinked. "I thought they had given up on that."

"Yeah. They had." Michael glanced back at the casement. "And it looks like they won't be doing anything about this either." He sighed.

"Well, if NASA and everyone else thinks the document is a dead end, why would the Cruzados go to all this trouble?"

"I don't know."

David spoke again, and Michael could tell his brother was trying to make it sound casual. "Why don't you call up that Calbert Loche fellow? Get your info straight from the horse's mouth."

For a moment, while Michael had read the boards, there had been a spark there, a hint of the passion that had fired him throughout his forty-year career. David was obviously trying to fan those flames.

Michael had to admit that his natural curiosity had gotten the better of him for a moment.

He said to his brother, "You know, I think I might do that."

∞

Most nights Michael couldn't sleep. His thoughts troubled him: how much he missed Melanie; his lack of purpose; his growing disconnection with everyone who had been a part of life.

That night, however, he couldn't sleep for another reason. His mind kept working over and over again about why, after so many years and after NASA and Quantum Resources had devalued the worth of the Mayan scroll, that anyone would go through the trouble to steal it. Or kidnap Yaxche. Did they want to hold him for ransom? Who was going to pay?

Unable to sleep, Michael threw on a thin robe and went to his computer. Although many of his files were classified and confiscated when he 'retired' from Quantum Resources—both as director and as a consultant—he maintained a folder of his own collected data and musings. Shorthand notes that held no meaning to anyone but himself were added to various documents he had downloaded off the mesh. He also kept a copy of all the declassified material that had been on his computer when he left the company.

Michael began the long and arduous task of sorting and filtering through every file on his computer. He hoped, somewhere in the morass of information, there might be something they had missed. Maybe someone else had stumbled on a vital piece of datum that would reopen the doors to interstellar travel.

It was three in the morning when Michael finally noticed the time. He yawned and rubbed his eyes. He needed a couple of hours sleep to process all the documents he had read, and he had only gone through a small percentage of the notes.

Michael laughed to himself about how much his brother would applaud the change in him, the sudden purpose. He went to the refrigerator and poured himself a tall glass of milk. There was no way he was going to get to sleep with a full mind and an empty stomach. At least if there was something in his gut he had half a chance of getting a few precious hours before morning rolled around. He wanted to be alert when he contacted Calbert Loche.

No—he thought suddenly to himself—when he *met* with Calbert. Michael decided right then and there that he needed to speak to his former colleague in person.

He went to his computer and logged onto his travel account and purchased a ticket for Toronto, where Quantum Resources maintained their earthbound administrative offices.

Calbert would see him; Michael's strong endorsement had launched him into the director's chair. And if anyone in the industry had an inside track on what was really happening, it would be Calbert, who always had both Raymond Magrath and George Markowitz nearby. The trio were an intellectual powerhouse when they put their respective heads together. Since the restructuring of Quantum Resources, the three had been delegated to more of a public relations and administrative role.

Satisfied in his plans, Michael headed for his bed. His empty bed...

He had an unexpected pang of loneliness and loss when he

approached the bed he had shared with his wife for more than forty years, and he had to choke back the tear that welled in his eye.

Melanie…

He lay down and was on the cusp of sleep when the comchime sounded and gave him a start.

Looking at the clock again, he willed his lungs to pump air in and out once more. Every time someone called unexpectedly, Michael had a flashback to when he answered the phone to a somber but officious voice asking him if he was the husband of Melanie Sanderson.

Regaining his composure, he said, "Who is it, Hucs?" to his apartment's home-unit computer system.

<Voice chat from Alex Manez,> was the answer.

"Oh?"

That was odd. Usually it was Michael who initiated contact with Alex. Michael hoped there was nothing wrong.

"Put him on."

The call came through, and at first Michael thought the link had been disconnected because all he got was static.

"Hucs, can you amplify?"

But there was no need because Michael heard Alex speak then, and the boy's tone sent a chill through him.

"Michael." Alex's voice was hollow and haunted.

Michael asked, "Alex, are you all right?"

"It's getting harder," Alex said. "The Song is in my head but I can't hear it because it's too loud. They want me."

"Alex? What are you talking about?"

"I don't know how much longer I can hold out," Alex said, and Michael wished he could look at the young man. Over a year ago, Alex had disabled the video feed on his communicator. He had said he didn't want anyone to see him looking the way he did.

"Alex, do you need me to come up there?" Michael hadn't been up to CS3 since before Melanie passed away.

"No," Alex said. "But I do need you to do something for me."

"Anything. What do you need?" Michael asked.

A silence stretched out for an impossible length of time and for a moment Michael thought they had been disconnected. But then Alex said, "Find him."

"Find him? Find who?"

"He has the answer. He's always had the key; he just never knew it." Alex's voice was becoming thin, and Michael could sense that the conversation would not last very long, and neither would Alex.

He said, "Tell me who you mean, Alex. You need to help me if I'm to help you."

When there was no immediate answer, Michael barked out a command. "Hucs, get the communications officer of Canada Station Three—"

"Yaxche," Alex said, interrupting Michael. "You have to hear him tell you the story."

And then the link went dead.

Michael repeated his command to Hucs to reestablish communication. After several minutes, he managed to connect with a CS3 operator.

"This is Michael Sanderson," he stated. "Former Director of Quantum Resources. I need to get in contact with Alex Manez. It's an emergency."

"Right away, sir," the woman said.

While he waited, Michael pondered the emotions running around inside him.

In the space of a day, he had gone from a lost soul to someone with purpose. Was it the thrill of a scientific mystery, was it the promise of untold wonders, or was it the concern he held for this young man who was at the heart of the matter? Or a combination of all three?

The operator came back on. "I'm sorry, sir, but Alex Manez has been admitted to our care facility. He's had some kind of episode. I'm afraid he will be unable to take your call."

"Of course," Michael said. "Who is attending him?"

"Dr. Amma. She's the top neurologist in her field."

"I'm sure she is. Listen, I know it's not really your job, but if you could do me a favor and transmit updates to me at this link, I would appreciate it."

"Yes, sir. I understand your concern."

Michael hung up. He sat on the bed.

Find Yaxche?

How odd that earlier in the day Michael had learned about the old man's kidnapping, and now he'd received a message from Alex—almost four-hundred-thousand kilometers away in space—telling him to get to the bottom of this mystery.

One option Michael had was to chart a flight with Lunar Lines and go see Alex. The rational side of him knew that there was nothing he could do except stand vigil beside his young friend, and in the end that might be the only course of action that would do either of them any good.

But Michael had to hold on to the hope that there was, indeed, something that could be done. If finding Yaxche and figuring out why the Cruzados had kidnapped him—and what key he unwittingly possessed—gave Alex any chance of surviving his disability, then Michael really had no choice when it came down to it.

Resolved in his sense of purpose, he slipped inside the bed sheets and forced himself to fall asleep.

He had a very busy day ahead.

Canada Station Three :
Lagrange Point 4 :
Earth Orbit :

When Alex came out of his trance, a nurse hurried over to him, looking concerned.

"What happened?" he asked her in a groggy voice. He couldn't focus. The lights hurt his eyes.

"It's going to be all right, Alex," the nurse said. Her voice was muffled, as if she were speaking to him from a great distance.

"Where am I?" he asked.

The nurse put a cold pack on his forehead. "You had a minor cerebrovascular attack—probably just a side effect of your condition coupled with stress. You've developed a fever, but Dr. Amma told me you would be fine in a day or so. Just rest."

He lay back and closed his eyes, not to sleep, but in an attempt to get back to that superconscious state and figure out what it all meant.

Exhaustion, however, prevented him from reaching that transcendent plateau. He opened his eyes once more, but the nurse was gone.

Alex lifted an arm to press the call button, but his muscles were far too weak to respond.

Despondently, he remained in the hospital bed the rest of the night, struggling to recapture his thoughts, but finding them as elusive as his long-gone dreams.

∞

Dr. Amma visited Alex early the next morning.

"How are you feeling, Alex?" she said. "You gave us all quite a scare last night."

She was middle-aged, very thin and short. With her hair pulled back in a tight bun, she took on a vague ferret-like semblance. Of all the people on Canada Station Three, and all the Quantum Resources staff, Dr. Amma was the only one Alex thought truly wanted to help him. Everyone else treated him as a lab rat or an untapped gold mine.

"I'm fine," Alex said.

"Did you get any sleep?"

"I don't sleep." Alex smiled when he said it. Dr. Amma often asked him questions like that, as if trying to trip him up. There was a touch of the psychologist in her, he thought.

"Ah, yes. One can always hope." Dr. Amma looked down at her holoslate and read from her notes. "Well, it looks like your electrolyte count is back to normal. Vitals are stable."

"I'm fine," he said. "It wasn't a coma and it wasn't a stroke."

Dr. Amma leveled her gaze at him. "All the readings indicated you were presenting symptoms of a hemorrhagic event. We couldn't take a tomography scan because of your pre-existing condition, but it resembled a stroke."

Although Alex's electropathic ability had been reduced to a shadow of its former power, there was a minute amount of residual radiation in him, enough to skew the results of any X-ray or electroencephalograph. Lack of proper testing reduced any medical diagnosis to nothing more than an educated guess.

"I was aware through the entire incident," Alex told her. "Though it was clouded."

Dr. Amma narrowed her eyes. "And how would you describe the incident?"

Leaning back into his pillow, Alex stared at the ceiling. "I was separated from myself, but at the same time I went deeper into myself than I ever had before."

"A dissociative fugue?" Dr. Amma guessed.

"No. It was more of a trance. I think … I belong in a different place, or a different state, and my consciousness wanted to go there."

"Do you know where that is?" she asked.

"No," he said. "I lost the connection."

"I hope you won't be sending the medical teams into a panic again."

Alex smiled. "No. And I'm sorry if that frightened everyone. It was unintentional."

Dr. Amma pulled the holoslate to her chest and folded her arms over it.

"Alex, I want to help you. I need to know everything. If you have any idea how to make you better—"

He said, "Get me next to a supply of Kinemet."

"You know I can't," she said. "They stopped mining it, and whatever they have left over they're hoarding like it was the key to the gate of heaven."

Proposed Holocommercial :
Lunar Lines PR Transcript :

The sun slowly settles over the crescent of Earth's horizon. As the sun meets the Earth, it's corona explodes in a flash of light.

ANNOUNCER

From the Earth…

The sun disappears to darkness, and a full moon, bright and silver, rises in its place in the night sky.

ANNOUNCER

…to the Moon

Cut to:

Several passengers lounge on large seats and at a bar in the luxurious interior of a Lunar Lines vessel. They are laughing and smiling.

ANNOUNCER

Why not travel in style?

Cut to:

A female passenger lays her head on a pillow on a contoured bed and pulls a comforter blanket around her.

ANNOUNCER

Lunar Lines – We'll get you there.

Normally, Justine would be circulating around the cabin of the *Diana* once the space liner reached escape velocity and the passengers were free to roam about.

Like a minor celebrity hired to mingle with customers at a restaurant or political event, Justine's primary job description was to socialize, tell stories of her days as a pilot, and offer technical explanations for every aspect of their voyage; anything to put the travelers at ease.

Her position as flight guide didn't give her the rush of actually captaining a ship, but at least she was in space and talking about the things which held her passion.

This particular trip, however, was going to be excruciatingly boring for her.

The cargo bay itself encompassed nearly the entire length of the liner and the lower half of its height. From a fiscal standpoint, Justine knew, most of the company's profits came from freight rather than fares. Taking on passengers was more for the public relations exposure than anything else.

Since a good deal of the cargo was perishables intended for either Canada Station Three or Luna Station, they kept the heat in the bay at minimum. Justine needed to wear a thick sweater over her PERSuit harness to keep from freezing, and this severely hampered the sensors. Unfortunately, the harness was tailored to fit snugly, and wouldn't fit on top of a sweater or jacket.

Not having the harness on made her job navigating through the maze of containers something of a nightmare, especially when she had to cart drinks and snacks from the kitchenette one floor above to the soldiers guarding the insulated crate of Kinemet at the back of the cargo hold.

It was ridiculous to think only someone with security clearance was permitted to serve the guards, but she was determined to make the best of it.

The eight uniformed men took their jobs extremely seriously. They were a very tight-lipped crew, and when they were on duty, they held their post in complete silence. At all times, two of them stood guard on either side of the container holding the Kinemet. They had M72 ion pulse rifles at the ready. A third and fourth soldier walked the perimeter of the cargo bay. Every three hours, they would relieve each other in rotating shifts.

When she first arrived in the cargo bay and was introduced to the squad members, they were very formal and would only address her as Major Turner, even after she repeated to them, "Just call me Justine."

Once they were in space, Justine asked them for their orders, and they stared at her in frozen terror. Here was a retired NASA major fetching drinks for them.

"Guys," she had said, "if you don't tell me what you want, it's going to be a very thirsty trip."

Having grown accustomed to putting people at ease with her former celebrity, Justine cracked a few jokes and made sure to ask them questions about their family back home in order to get to know them. After a few hours they relaxed around her, though they all remained very respectful and polite.

They would respond to direct questions from Justine, but the only one who went out of his way to engage in conversation with her was the squad leader, Lieutenant John Jeffries. He was quite young—all the soldiers were—and Justine could tell he was trying to set an example for the men under his command. Soon, however, he truly warmed to Justine and there were moments she was certain he forgot her former status as a major.

When the soldiers were off shift they snoozed, read books or watched vids on their holoslates. Lieutenant Jeffries had brought an old-fashioned crib board and challenged Justine to a game when he wasn't on duty. It killed the time.

Ordinarily, with her optilink sensor, she was unable to discern standard print on paper or cardboard. When the optilink was hooked to the PERSuit harness, however, she could interpret changes in color and translate the two-dimensional images to her mind.

The only problem was, while she played the game, she had to take off her sweater, so she usually had to stop after a few games before she got too cold.

During Lieutenant Jeffries' second stint off-duty, they played for about an hour. Justine was up six games to five over the lieutenant, who had won most of their previous matches. She was on a winning streak, and didn't want to quit, despite the fact that she was shivering.

Lieutenant Jeffries was five points behind the skunk line, and Justine needed six points to win. She kept her pegging cards, since it was his first count.

He played his first card. "Three," he said. "Try to 'fifteen' that."

Justine laid down a 'three' of her own. "Six for two." She took her points while Lieutenant Jeffries pondered his next play. It was obvious he had kept his small cards as well in an attempt to avoid being skunked. He played what Justine assumed was his highest card: a seven.

"Thirteen," he said.

She dropped her deuce and smiled. "Fifteen for two. Two to go."

He hesitated and took a second look at her harness. "You sure that thing doesn't have X-ray vision or something?"

Justine laughed. "No excuses. Get ready to be humiliated."

"Okay," he said. "Here's my other 'three'. Eighteen."

With an exaggerated motion, Justine placed her own 'three' down. "Twenty-one for two. And game."

Clicking his tongue, the lieutenant flipped over his last card. "I had a 'five'."

"I had you either way." Justine showed him her 'four'.

Throwing down his card in mock outrage, the lieutenant said, "I can't let you get away with that. One more?"

"I wish I could, but you won't have much competition against an icicle." Justine chuckled and slipped her thick sweater over her head, reducing her vision to the regular optilink level. "It's time for me to make a round anyway. Did you need anything?"

"No thanks," he said. "Hey, I know this must be the worst assignment you've ever had."

"Not the worst," Justine said with an equivocal smile.

"Compared to flying to Pluto?" he asked while packing up the crib board. "Working as a hostess must be difficult."

Rubbing her hands together to get the circulation flowing, Justine gave a half-shrug. "It may not be as exciting," she said, "but at least at I get to tell tall tales, and they pay me for it."

She got up and, after polling the other soldiers for their orders, made her way to the elevator and up to the kitchenette.

Besides the flight crew and the hospitality staff, no one else knew Justine was on board. She was recognizable, and if any of the passengers saw her, it might lead to questions NASA and the military didn't want to answer.

While she was loading a cart with snacks and drinks, one of the stewardesses, Brandi, popped into the cramped room and walked directly toward her. Justine couldn't see the look on her colleague's face, but the woman's voice was a mix of concern and puzzlement.

"There's a call for you," Brandi said.

Justine shook her head. "No one knows I'm here. Are you sure it's for me?"

Brandi nodded.

"Who is it?" Justine asked.

"Don't know. It's encoded."

Thinking it might be Director Mathers checking in with her, Justine nodded to Brandi. "Thanks."

After securing the food cart in the walk-in cooler, Justine made her way toward the cabin, outside of which there was a tiny communications cubical.

It was a video chat, so there was no need for Justine to take her sweater off. The regular optilink sensor could translate the digital images on the screen as if she had normal vision.

She stepped inside the cubicle, closed the door and turned on the holoslate.

A familiar but unexpected face appeared, and Justine was momentarily taken aback.

"Clive?"

When Alex had returned from Centauri, Justine had wanted to be there on the Moon when Alex got back, and had spent a few hours catching up with him. After Alex was whisked off by NASA officials back to Earth, Justine had remained for a few days for a debriefing with Clive Wexhall, who was still NASA's liaison on the Moon.

The first evening, he had invited her out for dinner. Justine didn't know whether it was her euphoria at having Alex back safe and sound, or her own sense of isolation because of her blindness and demotion from flight status, or if it was just too many glasses of wine, but she had ended up spending that night—and every subsequent night during her visit—with Clive.

Once she had returned to Earth, she had chalked it up to nothing more than a brief fling, but Clive wanted to see her again.

Despite his regular calls to her afterwards, she had tried to keep her emotions in check, and keep their relationship on a casual level.

When she had secured her job with Lunar Lines six months ago, Clive had somehow found out and had been waiting for her the first time she docked at Luna Station.

They had spent every moment of the two-day layover together as if they had never been apart. Justine had told herself not to let her feelings get the better of her. She had explained to Clive that she wasn't ready for anything more serious in her life. He said he was perfectly fine with that.

Whenever Justine was away, they remained friendly and platonic; but whenever she was on Luna Station, she would stay with him at his apartment. They had fallen into a routine, and Justine didn't want to change their arrangement.

She had not had time to contact Clive before the space liner took off, and normally he wouldn't call her while she was on duty, so she was surprised that he managed to track her down. No one was supposed to know about her presence on the ship.

"Nice to see you, too," he replied with a playful smile and a hint of sarcasm.

When Justine didn't respond right away, Clive pretended to look hurt.

"Sorry," she said. "Of course, I'm happy to see you. You

know that. I just wasn't expecting you to call me here."

"You don't like surprises?" he asked with a smile. "I would have called before you left, but I've been up to my neck in paperwork, arranging for the transfer and storage of your, ahem, precious cargo."

"You know about the shipment?" she asked.

"Who do you think suggested you for the assignment?"

Justine's eyes flared. "You! You're responsible for me spending the last ten hours in a freezing cargo bay? And you didn't give me a heads-up?"

His smile grew wider. "Sorry about that," he said, not sounding apologetic at all. "But I figured it would be a great opportunity for you."

"What?" Justine couldn't believe her ears. "And how is this a great opportunity for me? It's so secret I didn't know about it until a few moments before I came on board. And it's so tedious, I'm about to go crazy from the boredom. And did I mention," she added, "that I'm freezing my extremities down there?"

Clive laughed. "I have some news that might warm you up."

She pointed a warning finger at him. "It had better be good."

"I've arranged to escort you—and the shipment—from CS3 to Luna Station."

"You have?" Justine felt herself flush. Then she blinked. "Where are you calling from?"

"I just arrived on CS3 about a half hour ago. I've also made reservations for a private booth at the Terra Vista Restaurant, and I have balcony tickets to *La Danse Des Étoiles.*"

"I've always wanted to see that," Justine said, her voice softening.

"There's no sense in spending the eight-hour layover—as you say—freezing our extremities on the liner's cargo bay.

There are plenty of things to do on CS3."

"Clive, if I didn't know any better, I would think you were trying to butter me up for something."

He laughed. "It's all for purely selfish reasons, I assure you. I just want you to start thinking of me as more than a bi-monthly boyfriend." Clive's tone turned serious at that last part.

Justine balked at his declaration. She was comfortable the way things were. There had been far too many changes in her life over the past few years, and she was just starting to get her feet under her and adjust to her circumstances.

She truly looked forward to spending a couple of days every other week with Clive on the moon. With his busy political schedule and her traveling, Justine didn't know if there was any way they could bring their relationship to the next level. Or that she wanted to.

The thought of anything more than what they had already scared her. Justine's long-ago marriage to Brian had been a disaster, and it hadn't been his fault. She had always been a career-minded woman, and had her eyes—and heart—set on the stars.

Even now that she could no longer captain a ship, deep down she held the desire to return to space as something more than a tour guide. She did not want to be bound to Earth or the Moon. It was a ridiculous notion, but she hoped technology would advance to the point where it could either completely restore her sight, or provide her with a less cumbersome prosthetic device than the PERSuit.

"Hey," Clive said. "I didn't mean to bring you down."

"No, not at all." Justine smiled to show she wasn't upset. "But while you're in a generous mood, maybe I can get you to do me a very special favor."

He raised an eyebrow.

Justine said, "Maybe you can help me with Alex Manez."

Clive made a gruff sound in his throat. "Not this again. Since Quantum Resources is under full Canadian ownership, I don't even have clearance to *ask* if they have any Kinemet, let alone get them to allocate any for—"

Then he suddenly figured out what Justine was getting at.

"No way." Clive's face turned red and he dropped his voice. "I seriously hope you're not suggesting we smuggle any of our Kinemet off that liner."

Justine shook her head and clicked her tongue. "Clive, you know I would never ask you to do anything like that."

"Then … what?"

"How about the exact opposite?"

Clive stared at her for more than a few seconds, confused.

"But—" Then he sighed. "Oh, I see." He sounded reluctant, but said, "Yes, I think that can be arranged."

11

Quantum Resources :
Toronto :
Canada Corp. :

Toronto was vastly different from Ottawa, both in architecture and culture. While the city planners in the nation's capital tried to keep the city's expansion spread out over a large area, Toronto was home to some of the most impressive skyscrapers in the country. Where Ottawa was a hub for politics, Toronto's focus was commerce.

When Quantum Resources was first chartered, its mandate had been to develop Kinemet into a usable fuel source for interstellar flight. Since the *Quanta* missions had consistently failed, and Alex's mission had turned into a public relations disaster, Quantum Resources' ability to capitalize on the new technology had been severely hampered. After Canada Corp. bought all outstanding shares and put Quantum Resources under the umbrella of the Space Mining Division, the Director of SMD had changed QR's mandate in order to put the company back on a profitable basis.

In their early years, Quantum Resources had attracted some of the best thinkers in the field of astronomy and physics, and it would be a shame to put their collective brain-power to waste. While some of the company's resources were reserved for analyzing what they knew about Kinemet in the hopes of one day turning it into a viable fuel, the main thrust of their efforts was to improve existing technologies and increase their efficiency.

As a former employee, Michael was still subscribed to their quarterly meshmail reports. In the last two quarters, and for the first time since its incorporation, Quantum Resources was in the black.

When the autotaxi dropped Michael off at a high-rise office complex he didn't recognize, he rechecked the destination he had entered into the navigation screen. The directory confirmed this was the location for Quantum Resources.

It had been several months since Michael had spoken to Calbert, but at that time his former colleague had not mentioned any upcoming relocation.

Michael authorized the debit charge, and with his overnight bag in hand he stepped out of the vehicle and entered the building.

In the foyer, he approached the reception kiosk and skimmed the list of companies. Quantum Resources offices were on the thirtieth floor.

When Michael got out of the elevator, he stepped out into a scene of chaos. Construction engineers and electricians were putting up walls, stringing power lines, and setting up computer workstations.

Stepping up to a foreman, Michael said, "Hello, I'm not sure if I have the right place. Is Calbert Loche here?"

The foreman pointed down a half-built hallway. "Yeah. His office is back there."

"Thank you." Michael smiled and let him get back to work as he picked his way through the piles of ceiling tiles, steel frames and scattered tools.

When he reached the end of the hall, he heard the unmistakable voice of his former second-in-command.

"I don't care how you do it," Calbert Loche said as he stared out the window, his back to the door and to Michael. "We need that meshlink up and running by tonight."

Calbert turned as Michael stepped inside the incomplete office, and the clouded look on his face disappeared as he recognized his old boss. He motioned for Michael to take a seat while he finished his conversation.

"Yes, there'll be people here all night. I don't care about overtime, just get your guys to have the link hot by morning." He paused while listening to the response, then nodded. "Good. That's what I want to hear."

Calbert gently touched the comlink sensor at his temple to disconnect it. His smile widened as he reached across his desk to shake Michael's hand.

"Long time no see," Calbert said, and pointed at Michael's chin. "Looks like the weeds are taking over the lawn."

Michael chuckled, and rubbed his fingers through his graying beard. "It's from the stress of dealing with all my sassy employees over the years," he said with a grin.

Gesturing to a guest chair on the other side of his desk, Calbert eased himself into his seat and leaned back.

He regarded Michael with a convivial smile. "How've you been keeping?"

Michael nodded. "Good. Good."

"Staying busy?"

"Doing a lot of reading." Michael motioned his hand around the office. "I didn't know you guys had relocated."

"Expanded."

"What?"

Calbert's eyes widened. "We're keeping the main labs where they are and just moving administration here."

"Oh? Breakthrough?"

"Ha," Calbert said. "I wish. No, without any Kinemet, we're

just spinning our wheels. About six months ago, our grant money ran out, and we all thought that was it. But then the Chilean Corp. found out about our experiments with 'steam cracking'. As it turns out, it's totally useless for quantum purposes, but there are other possibilities. They approached us about using the technology to increase the efficiency of their hydrogen plants. We applied some of our theories on their systems and nearly doubled their production with only a marginal increase in expenditure. Since then, we've secured contracts with a dozen other power plants around the world. It ain't glorious work, but it does pay the bills."

"That's fantastic," Michael said.

"And the extra profit keeps Ottawa off our backs, and allows us to maintain our labs on CS3, which," he said, his voice measured and careful, "is why you're here. Right?"

Nodding, Michael said, "Yes. I got a strange call last night from Alex."

"I know. I received the report this morning." Calbert stood up and looked out the window. "You know my hands are tied. SMD holds our charter and they call the shots. I'm just a pencil pusher, as far as they are concerned. I wish I could help."

Michael cleared his throat. "Maybe you still can."

"How?" Calbert asked. "I know you've tried to go through Alliras, but since USA, Inc. stopped funding us, SMD isn't willing to spend resources actively looking for more Kinemet. We don't have any in our possession, and if NASA has any left over, they're not fessing up."

"I know."

Calbert, sounding defensive and frustrated at the same time, said, "I've got some contacts on the SMD survey teams. If anyone uncovers even a hint of Kinemet, you can be sure I'll know about it in two shakes."

"I know," Michael repeated.

"I'm sure things will turn around in a few years and we can begin mining Kinemet again."

Michael shook his head. "Alex doesn't have that long. But that's not what I want to talk to you about."

"It isn't?"

"Do you have a transcript of the call I received from Alex?" Michael knew Calbert did. Alex was a very well guarded and unique secret, and anything and everything he said was catalogued, charted and analyzed.

"Yeah…?"

Michael cocked his head. "He asked me to find Yaxche."

"I heard about the kidnapping and the theft. I feel bad for the old man, but as far as that scroll is concerned, it's a lost cause. I'm not sure why anyone would go to all the trouble."

"But someone did." Michael leaned back in the chair. "Alex obviously thinks there's more there than what we've uncovered, and the thieves also think so as well. And, I'm not sure if you noticed, but Alex asked me to find the man, not the scroll."

Calbert slowly sat down again. "I did notice that. What do you think it means? Do you think Alex knows something we don't?"

"If he does, he's not conscious of it. But it feels like there is some validity to this, even if there's no concrete evidence. Maybe there's something that's been lost in translation."

"All right," said Calbert. "Let's say there's some merit in finding Yaxche—outside of the humanitarian reasons. What makes you think the Honduran Conglomerate isn't already doing its best?"

"Maybe they don't think he's as high a priority as I do," Michael answered. "Or as important as Alex does."

Rubbing his upper lip, Calbert said, "Not saying I agree or disagree, but even if I did, what can I do?"

"Is George Markowitz doing anything important for the next couple of weeks?"

"George?" Calbert sat forward, looking genuinely surprised. "What does he have to do with this?"

"I'm going to Honduras to look for Yaxche. I'd like George to come with me. More specifically, I'd like you to *assign* him to come with me."

"Why?"

Michael lifted his hand and ticked off a finger. "First of all, he's the only person I know who's met Yaxche. George has been down there a few times. He knows the area. Besides, he's extremely good at research and these kinds of practical puzzles."

Touching his next finger, Michael said, "Secondly, if you give him this assignment and put it on paper, it will give us a certain amount of legitimacy with the Copán Departmental. We can say we're on official business. Otherwise I'm just a nosy tourist."

Calbert took a breath. "This is all a bit much before I've had my second coffee, Michael. Have you even given any consideration to the Cruzados? If they are indeed the ones who kidnapped him, do you think they'll just hand him over to a retired desk jockey?"

"I'm not planning a guerilla incursion," Michael said. "Once we track down where he is, we'll call in the Honduran authorities to take over. I know they consider the document a national treasure. They'll take action. Besides, I'm getting arthritis in my knees; I'm no hero."

Calbert leaned back in his chair. "I'm still not convinced."

"Tell you what, give us a couple of weeks. If we end up with nothing but dysentery, then we'll come home. Unless, of course, you need George for anything…?"

"No, we've got him analyzing hydro fluctuations; any intern

can do it."

"Well, then?"

Calbert shrugged. "All right. Fine. Let's go talk to George and see how he feels about it."

∞

Calbert fought traffic all the way across the city as he drove Michael to the Quantum Resources labs.

As one of the few country corporations that still operated on a profitable basis, Canada Corp. attracted immigrants from all over the world. The national policy had always been to welcome the influx of people, but in the major cities the infrastructure was strained to the limit. In the past two years, the government had issued a moratorium on new visas.

Population and overcrowding had always been a concern. Space stations and moon colonies were far too expensive to provide a feasible solution to overcrowding. In the back of Michael's mind—as with others, he was sure—the possibility of life-sustaining worlds in other solar systems would become a primary consideration once they made contact with the alien culture that had built the star beacons.

When the first *Quanta* mission was announced, there had been a swell of hope for the future, and as a result there had also been something of a population explosion as people anticipated interstellar trade, commerce, and migration.

That hope had been dashed when Alex returned with the news that he had not made contact, and that there were no signs of life in Centauri. The failed attempts to develop the electropathic ability in other pilots, and the subsequent mothballing of the *Quanta* projects only served to decrease worldwide confidence. As markets plunged and country corporations fell, there was an increase in civil unrest and crime rates around the world.

In his mind, Michael felt as if he had a responsibility for the direction in which humankind was going, since he had been involved from the start. Perhaps some of his discontentment in the past few years was because he considered the entire affair unfinished business.

He wanted to help Alex, there was no doubt of that; but at the same time he felt reinvigorated now that he had renewed his purpose.

"I've been thinking," Calbert said as he swerved to avoid hitting a courier drone. "With our current expansion, we're going to be recruiting more technicians and researchers. They're going to need someone grounded in science in an administrative capacity."

"Oh?" Michael's interest was piqued.

"Maybe when you get back you might consider taking a position with the company. I was going to ask you a few months ago, but…"

A few months ago Michael would have said 'no'; he had been too torn with grief over his wife. Melanie had always been supportive of his career, and he knew she would not have wanted to see him wallow in a directionless existence. Now, things were different.

"That sounds perfect," he said immediately, unable to keep from grinning like a boy.

"We'll work out the details later. Of course, there are a couple of conditions."

Michael nodded. "Shoot."

"First, you would have to be able to take orders from me. It's a bit of a role-reversal from the last time we worked together."

"I have no problem with that," Michael said, and he meant it. He had always had complete faith in Calbert, otherwise he would never have recommended him for his current position as CEO of Quantum Resources, Inc. "Anything else?"

"Just one more thing," Calbert said in a drawl.

"Yeah?"

Calbert pointed. "Get rid of the beard."

∞

They arrived at the Quantum Resources labs without incident, and went in search of George Markowitz. When they found him, he was sitting inside a sealed glass tank filled with water. He wore a wetsuit and a complex mask that looked like something out of a science fiction novel. Inside the green-tinted lenses, lights flashed as sensors picked up data and transmitted it to a computer off to the side.

When he spotted Michael and Calbert, George surfaced and pulled the mask off.

"Michael!" he said. "Long time."

"It is. I hope we're not interrupting."

"Nah. Just testing a new compound sealant against stress. Some of the tropical countries are a lot hotter and more humid than others and sometimes the standard sealant breaks down." He had a wide smile on his face. "I'd shake your hand but I don't want to get you wet."

Calbert said, "Actually, if you don't mind taking a break, we'd like to talk to you about another project."

"Yeah, sure." George lifted himself out of the tank and climbed down the step ladder in lively fashion. For a man in his fifties, he remained in very decent shape. Laugh lines at his temples counterbalanced the shock of silver running through his dark hair.

Michael missed George's boyish enthusiasm for all things scientific. The man had completely changed from his bitter days at NASA working under his vindictive brother-in-law. Even with his current mundane task, he flourished at Quantum Resources. It was nice to see people in their element.

George stood there looking back and forth between the two new arrivals expectantly.

"Maybe you should change," Calbert suggested. "This might take more than a few minutes."

Michael said, "Or we could all go to an early lunch."

∞

They went to a pub down on the corner to eat. While George decimated a Reuben sandwich, washing it down with a frosted glass of beer, Michael related what happened with Alex, and the request to find Yaxche.

"I heard about the kidnapping," George said. "He was a very nice old man. I hope he's all right."

Michael grimaced. "I'm sure he is. The Cruzados must believe he knows something more about the scroll than what he told us."

Shaking his head, George said, "You don't think he misled us all this time? I only spoke with him a few times, but deception isn't in his nature. I don't believe he'd lie."

"Neither do I, but maybe something just kept getting lost in the translation. I believe we've reached a pivotal point in all this," Michael said. "Alex—and the rebels, obviously—think the scroll will provide the breakthrough we've been looking for. I think so, too."

George wiped his fingers on a napkin. "All right. Sign me up."

"You sure?" Michael asked.

Glancing at Calbert, who nodded, George grinned like a kid with a new robocycle. "You know, in a way, I always felt like I was one of the pioneers, discovering the scroll in Yaxche's possession. It pained me that no one could figure it out. I've spent hours looking over the reports and studying the simulations and recordings, but I would love to take a crack at this in person."

Calbert finished tapping a few commands into his portable holoslate and said, "All right. I've sent in the orders to head office, reinstating Michael to active duty and informing them of your field assignment. You're both booked on a flight to Tegucigalpa." He nodded at them and winked. "You'd better get packed!"

12

Canada Station Three :
Lagrange Point 4 :
Earth Orbit :

Alex sat at a table by himself in the mess hall. He was alone in a crowd of adults. A few familiar faces would nod and smile when he looked up, but no one invited him to eat his meal with them.

In a way, he couldn't blame them. He was an anomaly. History's first and only interstellar traveler, Alex looked nothing like a pioneer or a hero. He looked like a sickly boy, and most people shied away at the sight of him.

Picking at his plate of fries, Alex sighed and turned his mind back to his memories. Since the night of his collapse, he hadn't been able to achieve that transcendent state again. It had been exhausting, and Alex had felt extremely weak for several days afterward.

But there was something out there that he needed to understand. Some metaphysical connection had been made when he was quantized. Was it that haunting voice? What did it want?

Earlier that morning he had tried to message Michael to let his friend know he was all right, but he only got the answering service saying Michael was out of town, but would check his messages periodically.

"Mind if I join you?" someone said, interrupting his thoughts.

Alex, surprised, looked up to see Kenny smiling at him.

"Uh, yeah. Sure."

Kenny sat down and arranged his lunch on the table. It was some kind of vegetable soup and a toasted sandwich.

"Are you feeling any better?" Kenny asked as he broke some salted crackers into bits and sprinkled them in his soup.

"I guess." Not knowing what motivated Kenny to sit with him, Alex was reluctant to say much.

"You gave everyone a pretty good scare."

"Did I?" Alex spoke in a dramatic voice. "That's good."

Kenny stared at Alex for a moment and started to say something, but Alex smiled to show he was being facetious.

Using his spoon to dunk the more stubborn cracker pieces under the soup, Kenny said, "I guess everyone tends to walk on eggshells around you. No one really knows what you can and can't do. I'm sure it makes you feel less than human sometimes."

"Or more than human."

Kenny took a deep breath. "I'll say it again. I think we got off on the wrong foot, and that's my fault. I'm new and I just wanted to impress the hell out of everyone. I'm sorry if it felt like I was using you as a stepping stool. I'm really a nice guy when you get to know me."

"Thank you."

Motioning to Alex's lunch, Kenny asked, "You not hungry?"

"I'm starving," Alex said. "But not for food."

"Look, if I could do anything about that..."

Alex offered him a conciliatory smile. "I know."

Twirling his spoon in his soup absently, Kenny drew his face into a look of concern.

He said, "I wanted to talk to you more about what you mentioned in the lab."

"Chrysalis." Alex picked up a fry and bit it in half.

"For starters, yeah." He stared into Alex's eyes. "I went through all the reports. I only found one where it's mentioned, and Dr. Hoit, who was head of the *Quanta* experiments at that time, basically dismissed the notion. I'm reluctant to repeat his exact words."

"You don't have to. I read the report."

Kenny looked startled.

Alex said, "Back then I still had my abilities. I could *see* beyond my normal range of vision."

"Uhm." Kenny looked uncomfortable. Not everyone could accept that Alex had once had those powers, unless they saw it with their own eyes. "Okay. So, let's pretend I have a more open mind than some of the others. Do you want to tell me about this chrysalis?"

"There's not really much to tell," Alex said. "Both NASA—when it was in charge of the project—and Quantum Resources have been going about this the wrong way from the start. What they don't realize is that I should not have survived my first exposure to Kinemet. I tried to warn them, but they classified everything I said. Sometimes people get a notion stuck in their head and they're unwilling to believe anything that goes against that."

"I have to admit, it comes with the territory," Kenny added. "Scientists can be the most close-minded people you've ever met."

Alex laughed without humor. Then he said, "The entire *Quanta* project was doomed to failure from the start. One of the reasons I involved myself early on—"

"By hijacking the *Quanta*," Kenny added, twisting his lips in a half smile.

"—was because they assumed that the pilot, once exposed to Kinemet, would automatically return to a material state and turn on the electrical systems when they arrived at their destination, and in turn be able to dampen the reacting Kinemet."

"And you knew there would be a greater delay than what was required? The report said it was several seconds—too long, as it turned out—before you rematerialized."

"I didn't know there would be a delay in my returning to normal space, but I knew there wasn't enough time to start the generators, charge the battery and engage the dampers. The first time I was exposed to Kinemet I was far too disoriented to be of any use. Any pilot in that situation would take too long remembering what they had to do before being able to do it. It was also foolish of the physicists at NASA to think they needed to irradiate a pilot *during* a quantized flight to transform him."

Alex took a deep breath. "But that's not the only thing they were wrong about."

"The only thing?" Kenny was obviously struggling to understand what Alex meant.

"Light-speed travel is important," Alex said. "But the way they're going about it is all wrong. You have to learn to crawl before you can walk, and you need to learn to walk before you can run. From the moment Kinemet was discovered, everyone wanted to go straight from the crib to flying through interstellar space. They've skipped a number of necessary steps before they can understand Kinemet, let alone master it."

"Steps?" Kenny asked.

"To begin with, like with any radiation, radical exposure will result in death. That's why they scrubbed the *Quanta* projects— nearly every pilot who they exposed to the element died, and those that didn't die are in comas."

"But you were exposed," Kenny said. "Twice."

"The second time I was already partially transformed. Additional exposure had no effect. The first time I was exposed I was partially shielded by the TAHU, and I was also far enough away from the point of origin that the effects were somewhat lessened. It was a fluke; I should have died … like my parents. But I believe there was some kind of catalyst that changed the nature of Kinemet before it irradiated me."

Kenny chewed on his lower lip. "You mean how we charge it with hydrogen particles to initiate the quantum reaction?"

"Yes," Alex said. "And I tried to tell them when I got back to Earth, but either I didn't explain it correctly or they were so focused on other things they weren't prepared to listen."

"So … what's your theory?" Kenny asked.

"I think there is a connection between anyone irradiated by Kinemet and those alien monuments. Because I'm only partially changed, the connection is not clear, but nevertheless, I feel it. It's like a voice in my head calling me. It was very strong when I was in Centauri, and I have to believe if I had been fully transformed I would now know the answer. There would have been no need to cool the Kinemet because it wasn't supposed to be used like it was, and the *Quanta* would not have exploded as a result."

"Do you think…" Kenny struggled for the words. "…that voice was a broadcast from any aliens in that system?"

"There were no aliens in Centauri," Alex said, his voice tight. He carefully avoided looking at Kenny. "Just me."

Taking in a deep breath, as if absorbing all the new ideas that way, Kenny slowly let it out again. "So that brings us back to the original conundrum. What is the proper procedure to become … whatever it is that you would become?"

"Kinemat," Alex said.

Kenny raised his eyebrow. "Kinemat?"

"Someone who has been fully transformed by Kinemet.

They started to call it 'the Manez Effect' but I hate that."

"I'm still not clear on what becoming a Kinemat means."

"Part of the problem," Alex said, "is that I don't know either. I don't know the correct method to become transformed by Kinemet, and I don't know for certain what the result is supposed to be. It's difficult to convince someone they're wrong, when you can't prove that you're right."

"Forget what you can prove," Kenny said. "What do you think?"

"I think I'm in a transitional state that should only have lasted a very short time. Days, maybe, or hours. My transformation is incomplete. That's why my health is deteriorating. I need to finish changing."

"I'll say it again: changing into what?" Kenny asked. "And how?"

"I don't know the answer to either of those questions," Alex told him, starting to grow frustrated.

"Do you have a theory?"

Alex took a deep breath to calm himself. "I'm not completely sure, but I believe there are instructions on how."

Kenny made the connection. "The stolen Mayan scroll."

"Yes."

Pulling a disbelieving face, Kenny said, "We had every cryptographer, programmer, and analyst in NASA picking it apart for years. Their conclusion was it's a nice story, but there's nothing there that gives us any more information about Kinemet or the ancient races who built the monuments on the edge of the solar systems."

Alex shrugged. "Just because we don't know how to read the scroll properly at this time doesn't mean it doesn't hold the information we need." Alex absently popped a fry in his mouth and chewed without tasting.

"So," Kenny said, his voice measured, "what you are saying

is, we can't truly begin to understand how to use Kinemet for superluminal travel—at least the way the aliens do—until we are able to complete your transformation?"

"Right."

Kenny picked up his spoon and stirred his rapidly cooling soup. "And our only manual is missing."

"Yes."

∞

Although Justine had not sent Alex a message, he knew she usually worked on the *Diana,* and wanted to come and see her when the ship docked. He'd tried to call her from his apartment, but the Lunar Lines receptionist said they couldn't connect him for some reason. But he wanted to take the chance she would arrive today.

Promising Dr. Amma that he was feeling much better, he got her permission to go. It was an excruciating trip to the main terminal of the space port, but he made it with time to spare. Exhausted from the effort, he sat down on one of the benches.

He didn't have to wait long before he spotted a familiar face.

Clive Wexhall approached with a warm smile. "Alex, how are you?"

"Hello, sir." Alex stood up. "I'm good. It's been awhile."

"Yes it has." He shook Alex's hand. "They don't let me off the Moon very often."

Alex found that he developed an ache in his knees if he stood too long. His braces, designed more for walking, didn't take any of his weight off his joints when he was standing still. If he shuffled his feet or subtly walked on the spot, the biomechatronics would kick in. When he made the motion, though, people looked at him strangely or asked if he was all right.

Alex sat back down on the bench. "Are you waiting for Justine?" he asked.

There was a slight flush to Clive's skin. He said, "In a way, yes; but I also wanted to see you."

"Me?"

"Yes. Unfortunately, Justine won't be disembarking today. She has to stay on the liner."

Alex scrunched up his face. "Oh?"

"But," Clive said, "she asked me to get you clearance to go aboard for a visit while the *Diana* is in dock."

It didn't take any mystical powers to see there was more going on here than the liaison was letting on. Although Alex hadn't had a lot of dealings with Clive, he knew Justine trusted him, and that was good enough for him.

"All right. That sounds fine." He stood up and followed Clive to the security office.

∞

The cabin of the liner was completely empty of passengers when Alex and Clive entered. There were a few members of the cleaning crew there. Bypassing the workers, Clive led Alex to the kitchen area and to the elevator.

Clive motioned for Alex to go into the one-person lift first.

"Where are we—" Alex began to ask, but Clive winked at him and put a finger to his lips.

"I'll be right behind you," the liaison said.

Without another word, Alex entered the elevator. The door shut and it descended to the storage area. When it stopped, Alex stepped out and looked around. He didn't see anyone, and for a brief moment he wondered if he'd been tricked, but then he heard muffled voices.

Without waiting for Clive, he walked down the aisle of containers and spotted a group of soldiers at the opposite end of the storage bay. One of them looked up and grabbed his ion rifle, but then someone said, "It's all right. He's with me."

Alex recognized the voice. Justine beckoned him down, and he waved as he made his way to her.

The soldiers looked at him with a mixture of wariness and curiosity, but Justine didn't offer any explanations to them or to Alex.

She was wearing her PERSuit harness and looked like she was cold. She gave Alex a wide smile, and he quickened his pace as fast as his braces would let him.

Alex was always surrounded by people, but he usually felt alone except when Justine stopped in on her visits. He always looked forward to his voice chats with Michael, but it wasn't the same as seeing someone in person.

As he neared, he felt a change come over him. At first, he thought it was a feeling of happiness at seeing his friend, but by the time he was halfway to her, Alex knew what he was experiencing was something different. He could sense it.

Kinemet.

It was like a ray of sunshine to someone who had spent months in the dark. He could feel it radiating through him, replenishing him. Like a homing beacon, it called to him.

Everything else became peripheral to Alex, and with a renewed energy, he made directly for the large container in the middle of the group. He was barely aware of Justine or the others, and only peripherally registered their presence.

"This is Alex, my friend," Justine said to the group with a lightness in her voice. "I hope you guys don't mind, but he's going to spend a couple of hours here with us during our layover. Don't worry, I've cleared it with the higher ups. Ah," she continued after a moment, "here's the NASA liaison now."

Clive appeared from behind the containers and waved as he spied Justine. As if completely understanding Alex not greeting her in the traditional manner, Justine waved back at Clive and met him halfway down the hall.

Alex couldn't hear what Justine and Clive said to each other. He knew he should at least make the effort to pull himself away from the container of Kinemet and say something sociable to Justine. She had obviously gone out of her way to arrange this for him. But the kinetic metal was a siren's song for him.

When it was not in the midst of a reaction, Kinemet was only mildly radioactive—less than a percent of ultraviolet radiation from the sun. A person who had not been altered by exposure to reacting Kinemet would need to be exposed to the dormant form in close proximity for several months before starting to feel any effects, and then it would most likely only be about as harmful as a sunburn.

Dormant Kinemet did, however, give off enough radio waves to play havoc with some electronics in close proximity. As a precaution against causing any shipboard disasters, the Kinemet on board the liner was encased in a thick container lined with titanium—the same material used in Kinemetic dampers.

Even through the sealed container, Alex could feel the waves penetrating through to his core.

A few hours? If that was the limit to his time, he would need to get closer. He turned around and said, "Can we open it up?"

With Clive in tow, Justine returned to the circle of guards and nodded. "Go ahead, Lieutenant."

As the lieutenant unlocked the main opening by tapping a code into the magnetic lock, Justine grabbed one of the cots and dragged it closer to the aperture.

When the door opened a fraction, a wave of Kinemetic energy poured over and through Alex, and he basked in it.

Justine gently guided him to lie down on the cot, and at that moment, she made an odd face.

"Well, there goes my optilink," Justine said with a laugh. "Might as well put my sweater back on."

"It is safe for us?" asked the lieutenant.

Justine turned toward the sound of his voice, but she appeared to be looking past him. "If you have a digital watch, it probably won't tell the time correctly. And forget watching any vids unless you go to the other end of the cargo bay," Justine said. "But, yeah, the rays are mostly harmless."

The lieutenant called out a few orders to his men to patrol the area, and told the ones off-duty they could go up to the main floor kitchens.

"I'll pop back down to check on you in an hour or so," Lieutenant Jeffries said. With that, the soldiers made themselves scarce.

Whatever Justine and Clive talked about over the next few hours, Alex was completely oblivious to it.

As his body re-energized from the proximity to Kinemet, he found himself once again entering something very similar to that fugue state…

The ancient voice called to him: *Alex, come home.*

13

Lunar Lines Vessel, *Diana* :
Dock Seven :
Canada Station Three :

Leaving Alex next to the Kinemet, Justine and Clive moved as far down the cargo bay as they could while still being able to maintain line of sight.

The Kinemetic radiation continued to interfere with both Justine's PERSuit harness and the optilink; the sensors gave her such static feedback she thought her head would overload with the influx of scrambled data. Even though it meant she was once more plunged into complete darkness, she disabled her optilink and put her sweater back on. At the very least it helped keep away the chill of the cargo bay.

She was fine with her loss of electronically enhanced sight, because she had Clive there; he held her tightly in his arms as they sat on a turned over crate and spoke in soft tones.

"I meant it, you know," he said.

She didn't have to ask what he was referring to, and she was never one to play coy; she would not pretend ignorance and make him repeat himself.

Over the past few hours she'd had some time to think about what he'd said, but she was still torn. On the one hand, she was acutely aware that she wasn't getting any younger, and she wasn't looking forward to spending the rest of her life alone.

On the other, her twilight years were still far away, and there was so much more she wanted to do with her life.

Justine couldn't have asked for a nicer man than Clive. He was understanding, compassionate and kind. Although he could be a bureaucrat both at work and off duty, and could be a stickler for doing things the 'proper' way, he also had a singular wit and could make her laugh. The thought of giving her future over to him and making a life on the Moon together was not unappealing. At the same time, she had this fire in her belly that told her she wasn't ready to settle down just yet.

"I know you meant it," she said to him. "But it's been a very complicated couple of years."

"So that's a 'no'?" he asked, but he said it with a half smile, as if he'd been expecting the answer all along.

"It's not a 'no'," she said. "It's not a 'yes'; but it's not a 'no'." She squeezed him a little tighter and buried her head in his shoulder. "I just need to get a little more comfortable with who I am now before I can make that kind of decision."

After a moment, he spoke in a quiet voice. "You won't mind if I ask again at a later date?"

Justine laughed and gave him a playful slap. "I'd be upset if you didn't."

They held each other in silence for long minutes.

"This is nice," he said after a time. "Not quite *La Danse Des Étoiles,* but it's still cozy."

She playfully slapped his arm. "You're such a liar!"

"Ha." He laughed. "So, what's this supposed to do anyway? To Alex?"

"I don't really know how this works for sure," Justine said, "but I think it has something to do with how he was exposed to Kinemet the first time. It imbued him with its inherent radiation which changed his physiology. Now he needs it like we need Vitamin C."

Clive said, "I'm not sure I completely understand."

"No one does. That's why he's gone so long without it; why he's deteriorating physically. No one believes he needs Kinemet to survive."

"He seems content now."

Justine couldn't see anything. "Does he?"

"Yes. He looks like he's sleeping, but there's a serenity about him."

Justine could feel herself smiling. "That's good."

"How much longer do you think he'll need?" Clive asked. "The liner is set to reload passengers in a couple hours. We'll have to get him off before anyone sees him."

∞

They sat together for two more hours, enjoying one another's company and talking about nothing and everything.

Though she just wanted to rest in Clive's arms forever, Justine finally squeezed his hand, indicating it was time to go. They had things to do.

She stood up and headed back to Alex, and could hear Clive following.

Alex sat up on the cot. "Thank you so much, Justine."

"You're welcome, but really, Clive arranged it all." She felt around for the door of the container and pushed it shut. It locked automatically, and Justine quickly removed her sweater.

As the Kinemetic radiation was cut off once more, Justine's main optilink connection came back online, and she immediately turned on her harness. At last she could look on Alex and Clive's faces with those electronic eyes, courtesy of Optimedia.

Putting his hand out for Clive to shake, Alex said, "Thank you, Clive."

The two shook, and Clive stepped back and put an arm around Justine. "Not a problem, young man. I just wish there was a more permanent solution for you."

"This was good enough," Alex said. "I feel much better."

"How long will it last?" Justine asked.

Alex shrugged. "I don't know. But one thing I do know: I won't be needing these braces for the time being."

Justine watched as he undid the biomechatronic device from his legs.

Alex stood to give Justine a hug, and she blinked away tears. "If I could find a better way," she said.

"I know."

Justine heard footsteps approaching.

"Are we about wrapped up here?" asked Lieutenant Jeffries.

Nodding, Justine said, "Yes. We need to escort Alex out before the passengers embark. Thank you, Lieutenant. You have no idea how much I appreciate this."

"Uh, I really didn't do anything," he said to her in a modest voice, and checked the lock on the container.

"Sometimes," she said, "that's more than enough."

Justine put her hands on Alex's shoulders, and then pulled him close for a hug. It was difficult to explain to people why she cared so much for this boy. Although she never had any children of her own, that maternal instinct was still there.

Alex was like a foster child to her in some ways, and she didn't realize how much his deteriorating health had affected her until this very moment. Seeing him looking hale and happy brought a sudden torrent of tears to her eyes, and she hugged him even tighter.

"I feel much better," he said to her in a low voice. "Thank you."

Justine gave him one more squeeze, then stepped back, but still kept one hand on his shoulder.

"We need to figure out a way to make it permanent."

Alex smiled. "Working on it. Now I have a little more time. And," he added, "now I have something that might help Kenny."

"Kenny?" she asked.

With a subtle glance at Lieutenant Jeffries, Alex spoke in a low voice. "Kenny Harriman. He's the new physicist they sent up from Vancouver. He's trying to figure me out. Since I haven't been able to use any of my gifts, I don't think he fully believed my story. Maybe now if I demonstrate, it might give him some ideas."

Justine was one of the few people who had witnessed firsthand Alex's ability to manipulate electricity and his uncanny capability to see far beyond the normal range of human vision.

It had not occurred to her until that moment that those gifts would once again be restored to Alex once he was recharged with the Kinemetic radiation. He was connected to that element in a fundamental way. As Alex said often, he needed it.

For the past few years, as Alex's capabilities diminished along with his health, it had been harder and harder to convince the corporate governments to take an interest in Alex. Justine hoped that this new physicist, Kenny, would be able to help in time; she had no idea how or when Alex would have access to more of the superluminal metal.

Wiping away her tears, she said, "I'll be interested in hearing about it all when I come back. Speaking of which, I have one more surprise."

"Oh?"

"I've arranged to take a few weeks' vacation time, and on the return trip, I'll start them here on CS3."

Alex's smile stretched wide. "That's great!"

His delight in the news touched a chord in her, and she realized that she had just as strong a connection to Alex as he had to the Kinemet. It was a good reason to reconsider Clive's offer. If she took a position on Luna, she would be much closer to Alex on CS3. There were daily flights between the Moon and the space station.

"Maybe we'll go on a tour of the Kordylewski clouds or something," Justine suggested.

"I would love that."

Clive tapped Justine on the arm and repeated, "We should get Alex off before the passengers embark."

Justine nodded, and the three of them started back toward the elevator. She mouthed a silent thank you to Lieutenant Jeffries, who gave her a salute in return.

Justine noticed that Alex was no longer walking like an old man. Once again, he seemed to be an energetic youth.

When they all got to the upper level and reached the gangway, Alex stopped and turned around.

"Thank you both again. I don't know how much longer I would have been able to last if not for today."

"No need to thank us," Justine said. "I just wish we could do more."

They hugged and, as Alex left the liner, Justine felt an acute pang of guilt. She had spent the past few years clinging to the hope that she could once again recapture the glory of her days in NASA. She had nothing to prove to anyone in that regard, and it was time for her to make some realistic choices.

She followed Clive back to the elevator, and as he gestured for her to go first, Justine hesitated.

"What's wrong?" Clive asked.

Shaking her head, Justine smiled at him. "Nothing. I think I've made up my mind."

Justine and Clive returned to the kitchen area and she enlisted his help to restock the refreshment cart with cold beverages and snacks. She brewed an urn of coffee and liberated a couple plates of fresh pastries for the soldiers.

When she and Clive had descended to the cargo area and distributed the snacks, the men expressed their gratitude as they helped themselves to the donuts, Danishes, and crullers. Their morale seemed high.

Lieutenant Jeffries, flicking icing residue off his uniform as he finished a bear claw, approached Justine.

"Thank you for this."

"No problem," she said. "I'm just sorry none of you got a chance to visit the station."

"Goes with the territory." He held his smile for a moment, then turned serious. "Do you mind if I ask what that was all about, with the boy?"

Justine hesitated to answer. Any explanation she offered would only raise more questions, and she wasn't certain how much she should reveal.

The lieutenant added, "I will have to make a report. I just want to be sure to get my story straight."

She glanced at Clive, who nodded his assent. Clive had cleared the visit with administration, but Alex's status was still classified.

To Lieutenant Jeffries, she said, "Do you remember the news a few years back about the pilot who returned from Centauri System?"

The lieutenant blinked in surprise. "From the *Quanta* flight?"

"Yes. You just met him."

He looked back and forth between Justine and Clive,

disbelieving. "But he's only a kid."

"It would appear so," Clive said in a low voice, "and that information is strictly on a need-to-know basis. When you make your debrief, you can report that Captain Alex Manez, retired, performed an unscheduled inspection of the cargo. Make no mention of his apparent age."

"Yes, sir," the lieutenant said, and if he was uncomfortable with that, he kept it to himself.

A soft chime sounded, indicating the liner was beginning launch procedures. A pre-recorded voice came on the loudspeaker and encouraged everyone to find their seats.

Justine and Clive found their way to the temporary webbed seating that had been installed for the troops, and buckled themselves in opposite Lieutenant Jeffries.

Justine knew she owed the lieutenant more of an explanation, if for no other reason than plain courtesy.

As the liner fired its engines and eased out of the docking bay, Justine told Jeffries how exposure to the Kinemet had affected Alex on a cellular level, and now he required a certain proximity to the element to maintain his health.

She also explained that, because of the shortage of Kinemet, obtaining it for Alex had been near impossible. Justine and Clive had understandably taken advantage of the situation just to help out a friend.

"Most of your superiors are aware of Alex and his condition," Justine said. "However, I would suggest you keep this information in confidence. I don't think it's something you want to be drawn into."

" 'Unscheduled military inspection' sounds good to me," Lieutenant Jeffries said, one side of his mouth turned up in a half smile.

The voice that suddenly spoke through the cargo hold's holoslate was not pre-recorded, and was not recognizable by

Justine as one of the crew; it had a thick Spanish accent.

"Attention American soldiers. Remain calm. Because of the corruption of the corporate countries who have kept humankind in ignorance for far too long, the Cruzados have liberated this vessel and its cargo.

"Cooperate, and you will not be harmed. Resist us and you will be ejected into space."

14

Tegucigalpa :
Honduras :
Central American Conglomeration :

His Mayan name was Te'irjiil, but only his grandfather ever addressed him as such. Most Hondurans spoke only Spanish and had difficulty pronouncing his given name, so he went by the name Terry Fernandez. That was the name he gave to the desk clerk of the hostel in Tegucigalpa, the capital of Honduras, after he ran away from home in Copán Departmental.

That first night away was the most frightening experience in his life. He had to share a room with three others, one of whom looked pale and sickly and coughed throughout night. The second resident of the room snored heavily, and the third occupant wouldn't stop talking about how he was going to plunge a knife into the next person who crossed him.

It was the first time Terry had ever been alone, and the strangeness of the city was overwhelming. The pungent stink of the streets, the hard faces of the citizens, and the screams of police sirens and honking of horns all together nearly sent him running home with his tail between his legs.

He had never seen a group of more than a hundred people in one place at one time before. Now in a city of millions, Terry felt incredibly small and insignificant. He told himself to be strong, and was proud that he survived the night.

The next morning, as he stood on the sidewalk outside the hostel, he counted the few lempira he had saved over the past six months. He calculated the cost of the hostel and meals; he knew his money would not last him more than a week, even in the poverty-stricken barrios of the city.

At twenty years of age, Terry's only viable trade skill was as a laborer in the coffee plantations that employed more than half the population in his home departmental. He had no idea what he would do in the city, but when he spotted a truck with the name of Ruiz Coffee, the company he had worked for back home, he followed it to their warehouse and asked to speak with the foreman.

"I'm young, strong and healthy," Terry said after the foreman—an extremely grumpy-looking man with grizzled grey hair—initially told him they weren't looking for help.

"We already have too many workers," the foreman said and flicked his hand at Terry. "Every day we turn good men away."

"I will work for free today," Terry offered. "Just to prove myself."

The foreman sized him up and pressed his lips together as if tasting something sour. Finally, he said, "All right. We have a truck that needs to be loaded on dock three. Start there. See if you can keep up with the others. We'll see how you do."

With a grin, Terry headed down to the loading docks and pitched right in.

While waiting between trucks, one of the other laborers struck up a conversation with Terry.

"I'm Humberto," the man said. He was middle-aged and stocky, with short-cropped hair and a thick moustache. He sized Terry up a moment before extending his hand. They shook.

"My name is Terry."

Humberto asked, "First time in the city?"

Terry wasn't sure whether he should reveal too much about himself, but he didn't think he could come up with a believable fiction. "How can you tell?"

Humberto pointed at his clothing. "I used to wear homespun outfits when I lived in the country, too."

Looking down at his rural-style clothing, Terry felt suddenly conspicuous. The other workers wore denim pants and factory-made shirts with logos and slogans on them.

At first he suspected Humberto was making fun of him, but the other man did not have a smirk on his face. Instead, Humberto looked concerned and maybe a little sad.

"Yes," Terry admitted. "I don't have enough money to buy new clothes. Yet."

"I know a place you can get jeans cheap, some sneakers and a shirt that doesn't scream 'country'. After the shift, I'll take you there, if you like."

"I don't know…" For a brief moment, Terry wondered if he should trust someone he'd just met. He'd heard stories about criminals in the city who preyed on unsuspecting victims.

Humberto shrugged. "Offer's open if you want."

A new truck arrived, and then they were too busy loading to talk.

At noon break, Terry went and sat by himself to eat some fries he purchased from a lunch truck. He listened to the other workers joke and laugh, and though he wanted to join in, he kept to himself.

Deep down he knew running away from home the way he had was childish. Though he wasn't sure if he could make a life in the city, he knew there was nothing for him back in his village.

For the longest time he had courted Itzel, whose

grandfather, Artec, was friends with his own grandfather, Yaxche. Both of the old men had conspired to arrange the union, and Terry had been smitten from the start.

His parents—who both worked long hours—had delegated Terry's upbringing to his grandfather, and usually deferred to his authority. They approved the marriage, but that was the extent of their involvement.

Terry and Itzel had spent many evenings sitting on the porch making plans for their future. Then Itzel became feverish with typhoid seven months ago.

Honduras continued to be one of the most impoverished country corporations, and Copán Departmental was severely lacking in medical facilities and supplies. Within two days of the first symptoms, Itzel had succumbed to the disease. With her death, all hope Terry had for a future died as well.

His anger, at first, was without direction. As the lonely days piled up, he realized that there had been a chance of Itzel's survival had the village had proper sewage, treated water, or a qualified doctor—amenities that many other countries in the world enjoyed.

Their village had had its chance. With so much interest from USA, Inc. and NASA in that ancient document, the leaders of the community could have negotiated access to it for better medical care, infrastructure and a better way of life. They also could have sold it outright, as the NASA officials had first wanted.

Instead, his grandfather had chosen to keep the old scroll with him as a cultural and religious artifact, and he basked in the self-importance he received from his new status. It would be blasphemy to charge admission to view the relic, his grandfather had told Terry one time. The ancients had intended for all humankind to benefit from the knowledge contained within.

But no one had figured out the meaning of the inscrutable words, and so no benefit had come from it, only a continued lack of medicine and technology that could have saved Itzel.

Terry's traditional upbringing would not let him direct his rage at his grandfather or the leaders of the community for not bargaining with the scientists. And so, the only option he could think of was to abandon the people who had failed him and make his own way through life. He had spent the past half a year planning and saving.

But now he was alone, friendless and more than a little frightened. The rudimentary education he had received in the village was enough for him to read and write, but Terry did not even have basic computer skills. The village only had one computer and it didn't have an EarthMesh connection. When the scientists from USA, Inc. left, they took all their machines with them.

At one end of the spectrum, humankind had traveled to another solar system, and at the other end, there were millions of people who lived in squalor. This was the inequality that kept Terry going. He had no idea how he would do it, but he vowed to set things right and bring balance to the world so that no one would have to suffer and die needlessly, like his darling Itzel.

With renewed passion, Terry threw himself into his work that afternoon, enough so that at the end of the day the foreman invited him back.

"You're not union so you'll work on a day-by-day basis." With that, he gave Terry his first day's pay.

"I said I would work today for free," Terry protested, holding the lempira in his hand uncertainly.

The foreman shook his head. "You need proper clothing. That outfit you have on makes you look like a beggar. If any of the supervisors came around, they would write me up for it." He made it sound as if Terry were doing him a favor by accepting the money.

The foreman shooed Terry off and he immediately went in search of Humberto, who was walking toward the main gate.

"Is it too late to go to the store with the cheap clothes?" he asked the larger man.

"Change your mind?" Humberto didn't break his stride, and Terry matched his pace.

"Yes, you were right. I need to look like I belong."

"So old sourpuss is keeping you on?" Humberto jerked his thumb back in the direction of the foreman's office.

"Just as a day worker," Terry said. "For now."

"All right. Let's go."

As he led Terry off the factory grounds towards the city centre, Humberto surprised him by saying, "I know who you are."

"You do?"

"Yes." Humberto glanced at Terry out of the corner of his eye. "I saw you on the news a few years back."

Terry answered in a sullen voice. "Oh, that."

"The way the reporter told the story, your village was host for all those rich NASA men. Good fortune for you."

"It could have been," Terry said. "But it wasn't."

As if measuring Terry up, Humberto took a long while before prompting him to tell his story.

"It's all right if you want to keep yourself to yourself," Humberto said finally. "But I left a village very much like yours because I was angry at how poor our conditions were. I didn't want to live like that anymore. No one should have to live like that."

Sensing he finally had someone who would understand him, Terry started at the beginning and told Humberto about his grandfather and the ancient scroll, about NASA and Alex

Manez, and when he ended his story with the account of how Itzel had died unnecessarily, there was a catch in his throat and a tear in his eye.

Humberto clapped his hand on Terry's back. "After we get you some clothes, there are some people I want you to meet. They all have a story like yours," he said. "They also have a plan to put things right. I think you'll like hearing what they have to say."

∞

Terry was nervous about going to a secret meeting. He had heard the stories of criminal organizations operating in the city, recruiting ignorant farmers and villagers into their operation and either corrupting them into their way of life, or using them up and discarding them in the most unpleasant ways.

The only thing that kept him steadfast was Humberto. He seemed perfectly at ease as the two of them wound their way through the narrow barrio alleyways to a ramshackle building. It looked like an abandoned storage warehouse.

"Don't worry," Humberto said. "I called ahead to let them know we are coming."

Upon entering the building, Terry was surprised to see only two people waiting for them. He had imagined a gang of cold-eyed men brandishing weapons. Instead, the first man was scrawny and wore glasses. His pock-marked face was split in a wide grin as he stepped forward to shake hands.

"Hello, I'm Jose Arroyo."

Uncertainly, Terry shook the man's hand as Humberto introduced him.

"His first day in the city," Humberto said to Jose, "but I feel he is the very person we have been waiting for."

Jose nodded. "You're from the village with the alien scroll?"

"Yes," Terry answered. There was no use trying to hide it. If he had been on a newsvid, he would be recognizable to many. "But the scroll is not alien. It's ancient Mayan. My grandfather is its caretaker. He believes it is the story of the end of our gods; the NASA people thought it was the story of an alien visit."

"Ah, yes." Jose gestured to a table with four chairs. "Please sit. Would you like something to drink?" He nodded to the other man who dug into a picnic cooler and withdrew four bottles of beer.

When the man popped the cap and offered the drink to Terry, he said, "Pleased to meet you. My name is Alberto." Though his voice was deep and rich, there was a hardness in his eyes. Terry noticed a scar that ran from Alberto's left ear to the corner of his mouth.

Being polite, Terry tipped the beer to his lips and drank deeply. They all sat down.

"First off, I want you to know that Humberto, Alberto and I all have Mayan blood running through our veins to some extent. In that, you are like our brother. That is one reason we have arranged this meeting."

That was unexpected information, but Terry immediately felt a little more comfortable and trusting of these men.

"I believe in being honest with my friends and family, and I believe in coming straight to the point," Jose said. "Do you mind if I am blunt with you?"

Terry shook his head. "No. Not at all."

Jose leaned forward and smiled. "We want you to go back home."

∞

At one point in pre-Columbian history, before the colonial

invasion, the Mayan civilization had been more advanced than any other culture in the Americas.

Along with art, music, and architecture, the Mayans had also been the first in that part of the world to develop a written language. They studied mathematics and astronomy, and in some ways their development rivaled those who lived on the other side of the world.

"It is no wonder," Jose told Terry, "that the alien visitors chose the Mayan people as the custodians of their technology. If history had progressed as it should have, the Mayan culture would today be the dominant force on Earth."

Unfortunately, the wars with the northern tribes, the arrival of the conquistadors and the flood of aggressive Europeans over the last thousand years had drowned out the Mayan culture and reduced their civilization to small pockets of communities.

Jose's mother, he told Terry, was a half-blood Mayan, and had married into a reasonably wealthy Honduran family. Growing up, Jose's mother had told him stories of his culture. "My legal name is Jose, but my Mayan name is Huehuetlotl."

It was while Jose was in university studying law that the story of the discovery of Kinemet had broken. For years, he followed the story with interest. After the first interstellar mission, NASA had tried to acquire the ancient scroll for themselves.

A legal aid by that time, Jose and a few sympathizers had organized themselves into an activist group. At the time, they had called themselves the Mayan Spiritualists, and they tried to put pressure on the Honduran government to restrict, or at least regulate access to the scroll.

"NASA was spending a lot of money in the area and in the capital region," Jose said. "Too many government officials were lining their pockets with bribe money from businesses and contractors who wanted to work for the wealthy Americans. Our movement was denounced, and those same politicians instead pressured my law firm to have me fired and blacklisted. The only work I've been able to find in the past year has been as a tutor to university students."

Jose gave Terry a very intense, impassioned look. "For centuries our people have been taken advantage of, when all along we were meant to lead the way to the stars."

His words stirred similar emotions in Terry. The Mayans had been stepped over by those with money and power, and kept poor and ignorant. If the Mayan people had continued to be a power in the Americas, tragedies like the death of his darling Itzel would never have happened.

Jose continued. "It was then that my friends and I began our work in earnest. There are more than a hundred of us now, and our numbers are growing. We even have a rich benefactor—unfortunately not Mayan, but he believes in our cause."

Terry asked, "And what is your cause?"

"We now call ourselves the Cruzados, and our mission is to restore the Mayan people to their rightful place as ambassadors to the people of the stars."

"How will you do that?" Despite his initial misgivings, Terry was becoming intrigued. If he joined a group who shared his beliefs, the possibilities were limitless.

"The world will not simply grant us the status we deserve. They have already shown their disdain for us. Therefore we must make them give it to us." There was a hard edge to his voice and fire in his eyes.

Terry balked momentarily. "Make them? You mean, by force?"

"If necessary," Jose said, his hand balled into a fist. Then he relaxed his hand and opened it; the smile returned to his face.

"But it will be better if we secure our position with a different kind of power: knowledge. If we have something no one else has, then they have no choice but to deal with us."

"The secret of the scroll," Terry guessed.

"That's right."

"But their scientists have been working on that for years. They've given up. No one knows how to decipher it, not even my grandfather. What can we do?"

Jose put his hand on Terry's arm. "We can have faith in our destiny. The secret will be revealed when the time is right. And when that time comes, we must be prepared."

∞

Over the following weeks, Terry met with the Cruzados a dozen more times, often talking or arguing late into the night. They formulated a number of plans, and by the end of Terry's first month in the capital, he had thrown his full support into the cause.

∞

Terry returned to Copán Departmental in a rented pickup truck four weeks after leaving. The bed of the truck was filled with food, clothing, and medical supplies. In his pocket, he had more lempira than he could make in a year working the coffee fields.

When he arrived in his village, he recounted to his grandfather and parents how he had made his small fortune at a casino one night, and his first thought was the welfare of the village. He told them he had contracted with an engineering company to rebuild the village's water processing and sewage system, and had arranged for a doctor to visit the village once a month. Regaled as a hero, Terry spent the better part of the year working to improve conditions in their community.

Terry also brought a pocket-sized holoslate with a mesh connection. Jose had supplied it to him, and instructed him to keep this device secret from his fellow villagers.

Every night, when he was by himself, Terry used the computer to learn to read and write English. He also took courses in math, history and science. Jose believed firmly that knowledge was power, and insisted that all Cruzados had the benefits of an education. As a side benefit, Terry also discovered world music, and spent hours listening to everything from classical to rock to the latest progbeat rage.

Jose had insisted that Terry also spend as much time as he could learning the customs and culture of USA, Inc. and Canada Corp. and the history of the NASA space program— the *Quanta* missions in particular and every scrap of information they could find out about Kinemet.

During the day, his task was to find out as much as he could about the ancient scroll. Though he still found himself with unresolved feelings of anger towards his grandfather's stubborn and backwards ways, Terry forced himself to ask after the history of the document and pressed his grandfather to speculate about the secrets it held.

Once a week, Terry would check in with Jose or Humberto to exchange updates, and once every two months Terry would leave the village for a weekend. He told his grandfather he was going to visit the friends he made in Tegucigalpa. In reality, he went into the countryside at a secluded camp where he would train with the Cruzados in combat techniques.

Initially, Terry resisted the idea of military action.

"Sometimes, in order for your voice to be heard," Jose told him the first time Terry picked up a weapon, "you may need to raise it."

∞

The months rolled by without any new developments until the day when, in frustration, Terry demanded that his grandfather repeat the story of the ancient scroll over and over again.

Listening to the words his grandfather spoke, the key to unlocking the secret of the document came to Terry as if it were preordained.

Running back to his own house, Terry contacted Jose on his holoslate.

That call set in motion a whirlwind of events that ultimately brought Terry to where he was today: standing on the bridge of a Lunar Lines ship with an ion pulse rifle in his hand while Jose announced their takeover to the passengers.

To Terry, the past year seemed more like a dream or a nightmare, and it was then that he realized he had lost control of his own destiny.

15

Tegucigalpa :
Honduras :
Central American Conglomeration :

The virtual tourist flicks on to show a city bathed in heat and humidity. The sky is a clear blue with barely a trace of clouds behind the skyline of the airport.

A cacophony of noise from the loading trucks, taxis and passenger vehicles outside the terminal is loud enough that Michael—who is framed in the two-dimensional image—has to raise his voice to be heard.

He looks cranky and tired.

"What are you doing?" he asks after tapping a request for an autotaxi into a kiosk.

George's voice comes from off-screen. "Documenting our trip."

"We're still at the airport," Michael says. "I'm not sure they care whether we can get an autotaxi or how much we paid."

"Well, you never know. Don't worry, I'll edit out the boring parts before I submit the recording. But I think our arrival in Tegucigalpa is a good bookend."

Michael presses his lips together. "You look conspicuous. We need people to trust us before they'll talk to us."

The image bounces. "The only fieldwork we do is looking at reactors. Calbert never saw any reason to upgrade us to the new PERSuit system. Now that's a toy I'd like to get my hands on."

Shaking his head, Michael says, "We'll just have to make do with what we have. Let me do the talking when we get to the consulate."

"You got it, boss."

Michael grimaces as he waves down a cab. "Sorry I barked at you. It was a long flight."

"No worries."

An autotaxi pulls up and they throw their bags in the storage compartment. The image jostles dizzyingly as they enter the vehicle.

The computer personality prompts, *<Destination?>*

The image pans to Michael, and George says, "Why don't we go to the hotel first, check in and get cleaned up?"

"That sounds good." Michael scratches his beard. "Maybe I'll shave, after all. I didn't think it would be so hot down here."

"The Ambassador Arms," George says to the computer, and the autotaxi pulls out into the street.

∞

The virtual tourist image turns back on outside the glass doors of an office on the third floor of the Centro Financiero Banexpo building. The frame zooms in on the sign of the Canadian Embassy.

Michael, who looks energetic and confident, stands at the door and pauses. With a clean-shaven face, he is dressed in a loose-fitting white shirt and brown pants.

He removes a wide-brimmed hat and faces George and the camera eye.

"All right. I guess if we're documenting everything, I'll narrate." Michael clears his throat. "We're here at the embassy office to get our travel papers, maps, and to meet with John Markham, who is the consul's aide. We hope he can give us some additional information on the theft of the Mayan scroll and the kidnapping of Yaxche, the translator."

Michael enters into the reception area where a smartly-dressed woman smiles a greeting.

"Hello, I'm Michael Sanderson and this is George Markowitz. We have an appointment."

"Mr. Markham is expecting you. Go right in." She points down a carpeted hallway. "It's the office at the end."

Michael nods and then proceeds to the consul's office.

Inside, John Markham stands up from his desk and comes around to shake Michael's hand. Deeply tanned skin stretches around his mouth as he greets them. His eyes glance at the VT camera.

"We're recording our progress for our report," Michael says.

"Oh, that's fine. Come in. Have a seat." He returns to his side of the desk.

The image briefly flashes on George's hiking boots as he awkwardly finds his chair and sits down. As he points the camera back up, John is handing Michael a thin memory card.

John says, "After your supervisor called to let me know you were coming down here, I took the liberty of compiling some local newsvids that reported the incident."

"Thank you." Michael takes the card and inserts it in his holoslate to transfer the files. "Every little bit will help."

"I'm afraid there isn't much there. Whoever these Cruzados are, they've kept a very low profile up until now. They've never taken part in anything more serious than a protest at the Office of the Interior when NASA first tried to purchase the document. For the past year, they've been so quiet we assumed they'd disbanded."

"Do we know the names of any of their members?"

"Just one. Jose Arroyo, who we believe is their leader. I talked to my counterpart at the US embassy and he forwarded a copy of all the data they've gathered on the Cruzados, and a timeline of their activities. Like I said, it's not much."

"Do you have any contacts with the *policía?* Someone we can talk to about this?"

John frowns. "Yes, but I'm not certain they will tell you anything useful."

Michael looks up from the holoslate. "Oh?"

"Well, for one thing, the government of Honduras doesn't think the theft and kidnapping are much of a priority."

With a glance at George, Michael says, "They don't?"

"The only reason the National Department of Investigations even opened a case file is because of pressure from USA, Inc. and the Honduras Office of Tourism."

"They don't think kidnapping is important?"

John shakes his head. "It's very important, but it happens so often in this part of the world that unless there is a ransom demand or an imminent threat to a VIP, the authorities simply don't have the manpower or resources to investigate. And so far, the Cruzados are only *suspected* of this crime. They haven't taken responsibility or communicated any demands yet. As a matter of fact, according to the consul in the U.S. Embassy, the only reason we know the Cruzados are involved is because of an unsecured EPS to a contact in Houston."

Michael and George share a grim look between them.

John shrugs apologetically. "I want to help you as much as I can, but I have to tell you I think you're wasting your time. Until the Cruzados surface on their own with a list of demands, you're just spinning your wheels."

Michael has a thoughtful look on his face. "I appreciate where you're coming from, but we have to follow through on this."

"Of course."

With a quick look to George, Michael says, "We thought we would begin our investigation in Copán, where it happened. Interview some of the local residents."

"I can certainly help you with travel arrangements. There's a bus that runs daily between Tegucigalpa and Santa Rosa de Copán. From there, perhaps you can hire an autotaxi. I believe Yaxche's village is less than an hour away."

George shakes his head, causing the image to move side to side. "When I was there last, I rented a truck from the owner of the hotel where I stayed. The autotaxis won't run rurally."

John smiles and stands up. "Excellent. I'll call down for some bus tickets while you get your travel documents from my receptionist." He walks around the desk again and shakes both George's and Michael's hands. "And if you have a few extra days while in Honduras, you should visit Copán Ruinas. It's quite astonishing. If you're a history buff, it's a must-see."

∞

There are a series of images of the landscape looking out from inside a bus. The noise of the vehicle's engine is too loud for anything to be heard other than garbled audio.

∞

A short nighttime shot of a hotel in Santa Rosa de Copán slowly pans to a busy sidewalk filled with pedestrians. On the street corner opposite the hotel an old beggar holds his hand out while gumming his teeth and staring into the distance.

∞

The morning sun casts shadows on the dirt road of a small village. A couple of barefoot kids kick a partially deflated soccer ball back and forth near a well which serves as their central plaza.

Michael steps into the frame. "We're here in the village where Yaxche and the document were taken. What's the village's name again?"

George says, "Pueblo de Santa Brio, but most everyone here just calls it the *pueblo.*"

Michael makes a motion with his hand for George to follow him. "We're going to try to find one of Yaxche's relatives and see if they can give us any more information than what we already have."

"If I remember correctly," George says off-screen, "his house is the last one on the end. Maybe his daughter or his grandson is there."

Michael heads towards the far side of the small village. As he walks, a few of the residents stop and look up at him and George in passing curiosity.

There are no more than two dozen ramshackle houses in the village, all looking in dire need of repair. The front of one of the homes has a few tables set out. On one of the tables are baskets of fruit, bread and two dead chickens. On one of the other tables a number of handcrafted trinkets are arrayed. A plump woman smiles at them and says, *"Comprar?"*

Michael glances at George with a helpless smile. "I forgot to pack my translator."

"She wants to know if we want to buy something."

Michael shakes his head. "Maybe later."

To the woman, George says, *"Más tarde. Gracias."*

She smiles and waves at them as the two make for Yaxche's house.

The home itself is of typical construction: the walls are

made of adobe, and the roof is constructed with clay tiles. Unlike many of the other houses, this one has a small porch and the floor is made of wood rather than packed earth. The front door is partially open.

George calls out into the house. *"¿Hola?"*

There is no answer, but one of the soccer-playing children trots over.

"La casa está vacía," he says.

"Do you know what happened?" George asks in Spanish, immediately translating the conversation for Michael's benefit.

The boy shakes his head. "They were taken by men with guns."

"They?"

"The soldiers came and put Terry and his grandfather in a truck. They drove off. This was many days ago."

"Have you ever seen those soldiers before?"

"No. I know nothing of them." The boy pointed to a house two doors down made of thatch and clay. "Terry's mother is there. She waits for them to return."

"Thank you," Michael says and passes the boy a twenty lempira bill.

Yipping with joy, the boy runs off to show his friends the money.

Michael turns to the camera. "This is news. We had no idea Yaxche's grandson was abducted as well."

The two of them cross the packed dirt street to the house the boy had indicated and knock on the flimsy door made of wood planks bound together with a weaved rope.

A middle-aged woman opens the door. Worry lines stretch across her face; her eyes flick back and forth fearfully between Michael and George. Recognition blossoms when her gaze settles on George, who had been to the village over a decade earlier wearing similar headgear.

Behind her are two pre-teen girls who look on with curiosity.

The woman speaks in Spanish, and George translates between them.

She says, "Please come in." She turns to her children and tells them to go play outside.

Michael smiles politely and nods as he follows the woman into her sparsely furnished house. Handmade chairs surround a carved table. A shelving unit holds plates and glasses, and on the mantle over a rudimentary fireplace is a photographic portrait of a young man.

Michael points to it. "Is that your son?"

"Yes," the woman says, wringing her hands. "He and my father have been missing these past days. Taken by the bandits, for what reason I do not know. We have nothing of value." She glances at Michael and George out of the corner of her eye. "You are not the police. Why have you come?"

"We want to help find them," Michael answers. "Though we only found out today that your son was also kidnapped. Can you tell us about him?"

"Yes." She sits down on a chair at the table. "He is my only son and I love him, though this past year he has grown apart from me and his father. Terry was engaged to be married, you see. Itzel was beautiful and brought joy to him and our family, but she was struck down by sickness and died. Terry ran away from us in grief and did not return for a month. He left a boy but came back a man. He brought a great many supplies and ideas to our village."

When she spoke, she did not look proud, and Michael shot a quick look at George before saying to her, "You don't look happy about that."

"Something happened to Terry when he was away. My husband does not hear me when I say that he is not the same;

he and the other villagers only see the improvements to the village and the wealth he brought back with him. But where did he come by this money? He says he won it gambling, but I think he may have done something shameful. I think—"

She falls silent and stares at her hands. "It is not my place to say."

Michael puts a hand on her shoulder. "You can tell us. It might help us in our search for him and your father."

There is a tear in her eye as she looks back up at Michael. "My husband tells me I am being foolish, but I think my son may have … stolen the money from the banditos. That is why they have taken him and my father. They will either ransom them to the village, or they will take their anger out on them."

She grabs Michael's arm. "Please. I beg you. Find my son and my father before something terrible happens to them."

With a grim face, Michael says, "We will do everything we can. Is there anything you can tell us about these bandits?"

"No one saw them closely. They drove a black truck and had hunting rifles. That is all I know."

Michael turns to George and says, "Maybe we can track the Cruzados by their truck? It might be a long shot, but if there was a satellite in the area the night of the kidnapping we might be able to see which direction it went."

George taps his holoslate. "On it."

Michael pats the woman's hand. "Thank you," he says. "We will do our best to bring your family back to you."

∞

Inside the rented truck, George punches several commands into his holoslate while Michael drives.

"Anything yet?" Michael asks.

George nods. "Talk about a needle in a haystack. There was

a geological satellite in this section of the departmental looking for mineral deposits. They pick up all kinds of heat signatures. It looks like there were three hundred vehicles traveling on the main road between Santa Rosa de Copán and the Copán Ruinas that night—maybe even double that."

"Double? What do you mean?"

George shakes his head. "The satellite tracked in a zigzag pattern, so there are dozens of gaps in the record. The three times it passed over the village, there was no thermal activity."

"Damn."

George taps a few more commands. "Maybe I can run a filter. Eliminate any commercial vehicles or transports. Autotaxis. That kind of thing. Maybe we'll get luck—"

"You don't have to search any further, George," Michael says. "I think they found us."

George looks up. In the camera view is a large black van traveling towards them at high speed, kicking up a cloud of dust behind it.

Michael edges to the side of the road. The truck veers to cut them off, so Michael slows the vehicle to a stop.

"What are you doing?" George asks, his voice rising.

"Well," Michael says. "It's not like we can outrun them. After all, this is what we want, isn't it? If these guys are Cruzados, maybe they'll tell us where Yaxche and his grandson are. And the scroll."

The black van skids to a stop a dozen meters away and four men with rifles jump out, pointing the weapons at Michael and George. The men have kerchiefs covering their mouths.

They yell in Spanish, and George translates: "Get out of the truck with your hands in the air. Do not try to run."

Michael says, "We'd better do as they say."

The two of them open the doors and step out. They put their hands up as Michael calls out, "We mean you no harm.

My name is Michael Sanderson from Quantum Resources in Canada."

"We know who you are," one of the men says in English. "Keep your mouth shut."

Another Cruzado walks purposefully toward George. He commands, "Turn it off."

George says, "Turn what off?"

The armed man reaches out and grabs the Virtual Tourist. He pulls it from George's head.

"The camera," he says, as the image bounces around showing the dirt road, a pair of booted feet, the sky, and then complete darkness.

16

Lunar Lines Vessel, *Diana*:
Unknown Transit :

Justine could feel the *Diana* pulling out of the Canada Station Three dock. The massive ion pulse engines gave off severe vibrations when initially engaged, and the first jarring motion of the ship as it uncoupled from the dock was enough to knock someone off their feet if they weren't safely fastened in their seats.

Both Justine and Clive clung to each other for balance as they quickly made their way to the canopy seats and strapped themselves in.

Lieutenant Jeffries' men had taken up defensive positions around the cargo, in case the hijackers decided to come down to the cargo bay. When the engines shuddered, two of them grabbed on to the container's handles to stabilize themselves while the other two, who had dropped to one knee, lost their balance and fell over.

Two of the men who had raced toward the elevators after the announcement—ion rifles up at the ready as if expecting the hijackers to burst into the cargo bay with guns blazing—were thrown from their feet into heavy metal boxes when the liner jerked into motion. One of them got right back up, but the other took a very long time to recover.

Once the liner stabilized, Lieutenant Jeffries and his

corporal hurried over to the man to check his condition. He looked back and gave Justine a nod that told her, although battered and bruised, he was otherwise fine.

Justine had been through an attempted hijacking before, though the assailants had been successful in their main purpose: kidnapping Alex Manez. But Alex wasn't on the *Diana*. He had disembarked safely.

Fighting back the panic welling inside her, Justine clung to Clive's arm. His face was set in a stoic mask, but his eyes betrayed his fear.

"It's the Kinemet." Clive stated the obvious. "They want it."

"Why are they letting them take the ship?" Justine asked through clenched teeth.

"CS3 isn't really designed to stop a ship from *leaving*," he said.

Justine shook her head. "I mean the flight crew. All liners have protocols against this. The cabin is self-contained and sealed—in which case they would never initiate takeoff procedures. And even if someone were to manage to get in and hold the pilot at gunpoint, the system is designed to disengage electrical if there are any other biometric readings in the cabin besides the captain and navigator."

Clive glanced at Justine. "Unless they are a part of it."

A dark look settled on his face and he called out, "Lieutenant Jeffries?"

"Yes, sir?"

"I don't think you need to worry about them attacking us."

The soldier turned his head to look back at Clive and Justine. "Why not?"

"Check the elevator," Clive said. "I'm sure it's been disabled. As are, I'm certain, all our communications. They have no intention of fighting with us. Why would they? We are exactly where they want us, safely tucked away in this little prison of our own making."

Clive laughed, but it was a hollow, bitter sound. "You may as well stand down until we arrive wherever it is they are taking us, or until they initiate contact."

∞

The forward velocity increased, and the liner's vibrations lessened to normal levels as the ship finished its launch from Canada Station Three and started in on its trajectory.

What destination? Justine asked herself. "They can't be heading for any of the other space stations. Everyone will be alerted to them by then. They can't be going to Luna Station or anywhere on the Moon for that matter," she said out loud to Clive.

After the abduction of Alex Manez had revealed the extent of Chow Yin's infiltration into the station, security measures had tripled not only on every settlement on the Moon, but for all space traffic coming to and from the planetoid. Non-commercial or non-military vessels were under the highest scrutiny.

Whoever they were, the hijackers were obviously well organized and funded. Another thought came to her: were they hostages? Or were they incidental cargo? If all the hijackers wanted was the Kinemet, they didn't need her and the soldiers. It would be an easy enough task for them to shut down the life support system in the cargo bay and just wait until any threat was neutralized.

She clung tighter to Clive's arm.

Justine still had her PERSuit harness on—she would be completely lost without it—and watched as Lieutenant Jeffries and his men did a full recon of the cargo area, checking the elevators to confirm Clive's supposition. It wasn't that they didn't believe him, but Justine knew from her days in the military that redundant confirmation had proved itself time and again.

Corporal Marks, the second-in-command, tested his communications equipment, and tried to tap into the onboard computer. The result was as Clive predicted. Dead air.

After stationing his soldiers at strategic locations around the cargo area anyway, the lieutenant returned to report. "We're completely shut in and shut off. Grounded."

As if reading Justine's thoughts, he added, "Life support is still fully functional."

"So they want us alive," Justine said in conclusion.

Ever pragmatic, the lieutenant said, "Maybe."

"What do you mean?"

The officer shook his head. "There are a lot of scenarios that could be played out. Holding us as hostages is only one of them."

Justine let her thoughts follow some of the possibilities. They could hold them for ransom. They could release them at a later time as a gesture of goodwill. They could kill them later to serve as a warning, or a distraction. They could sell them into slavery—human trafficking was uncommon, but still an issue in the world.

Before her imagination took her down paths even more frightening, she said, "What now?"

"Now," Clive said in a drawl and glanced at Justine. "Now we need to figure out where we're going. Maybe that will give us a clue to the hijackers' intent."

Lieutenant Jeffries turned as Corporal Marks reported. "I tried to tap into the onboard computer, but it looks like they set up their own firewall."

"It's too bad we didn't have Alex here," Justine said, and

then when Clive gave her a curious look, she quickly added, "Because of his ability to see extraspacially. We're all blind in here without instrumentation."

Clive put his arm around her and growled. "There has to be something we can do other than just wait for them to initiate contact."

Corporal Marks had an odd look on his face as he fixed his eyes on Justine's harness. "Even if I had something more powerful than my holoslate, it could take weeks to break the firewall. But…"

"What is it, Corporal?" the lieutenant prompted.

A hint of a smile played at the young man's lips. "That's a PERSuit, isn't it?" he asked Justine.

"Yes."

He said, "I believe it has built-in gyroscopic sensors and an inertial reference platform."

For a moment, Justine had no idea what the corporal was getting at, but then she clued in. "As well as an attitude indicator, vertical and horizontal positioning. Along with visual and olfactory sensations, the suit can also provide inertial sensations to viewers. If I were at sea, or on a roller coaster, viewers who are susceptible would experience motion sickness, it's that real." She sounded like a brochure.

The lieutenant, excited, asked the corporal, "Can you access the suit and the data?"

Corporal Marks nodded. "I think so. With any luck, I should be able to track our course from the moment we launched. I have astrogation charts in my holoslate—maybe I can figure out where we're going."

He cocked his head to one side and said to Justine, "You'll have to remove the suit, though."

∞

Though she had been blind for years, there was always a part of Justine that hadn't completely accepted the fact. There was that glimmer of hope that one day she would wake up and be able to see. The universe had played a cosmic joke on her, and at any moment, it would deliver the punch line, everyone would have a good laugh, and then she would be normal again.

Sitting back in the webbed cargo seat without her PERSuit sensors or her optilink, which the corporal needed to interface with his holoslate, her world had completely plunged into darkness.

She experienced a few moments of all-too familiar despair. It wasn't a joke, it was a cruel prank and she was only fooling herself into thinking it wasn't permanent.

Then she felt a warm hand slip into hers. Clive. He gave her hand a quick squeeze of reassurance.

She leaned into him. "Thanks."

"For what?"

"Just being here."

He laughed hollowly. "All things being equal…"

"Same here." She smiled at him, though she had no idea if he was looking at her or watching as Corporal Marks rigged a connection from the PERSuit to his portable holoslate.

"Listen," he said, "we'll get through this. The hijackers haven't turned off our life support so they obviously need us alive. That gives us an opportunity."

"I know," she said. "I just wish I could do more. I feel so helpless."

In answer, Clive put an arm around her shoulders while they waited.

It was only a few minutes later that the corporal called out that he'd made the connection.

Clive stood up from the seats to approach, and Justine went with him.

"What have you got?" Lieutenant Jeffries said.

"It's compiling the data at the moment. We should have a readout in less than a minute."

There was a hushed silence as everyone circled around the corporal and his computer. Justine felt a deep frustration that she couldn't see the screen and had to wait for someone to feed her the information secondhand.

"Here comes the trajectory now," the corporal said.

A moment later, Lieutenant Jeffries spoke, and his voice took on a caustic tone. "That can't be right."

"What?" Justine asked.

Jeffries said, "Are you sure you have the correct information? Maybe the computer reversed the coordinates or something."

"What coordinates?" Justine asked again.

Corporal Marks tapped repeatedly on his computer again. "No, it's right."

Justine grew frustrated. "What's right?"

She heard Lieutenant Jeffries take a deep breath and let it out in a hiss. "Well, according to our current trajectory, the hijackers are pointing the *Diana* directly at the Sun."

17

Lunar Lines Vessel, *Diana*:
Solar Trajectory:

It had been a frightening and crazy week for Terry. At first, when he and Jose had confiscated the alien scroll—along with Terry's grandfather—he had felt empowered.

He was finally taking control of things and able shape future events. With like-minded people on his side, Terry had taken the first steps toward returning the Mayan people to their rightful place in the world. If he had anything to say about it, his people would not suffer and die needlessly like Itzel.

As with any revolution, there were bound to be casualties. Deep down, Terry knew this; he wasn't so naïve as to think all they had to do was brandish their weapons and people would simply give in. Though he steeled himself for the possibility, he still wanted to avoid violence as much as possible. Jose assured him he felt the same way. He assigned Terry and another Cruzados, Carlos, to guard the shuttle's cabin, in the unlikely event one of the American soldiers managed to get out of the cargo hold and infiltrate the upper decks.

Since joining the Cruzados, Terry had been surprised at the size of their network of sympathizers in the USA, Inc. government and NASA. There was an even larger number of people who they could bribe or blackmail into doing what was needed for their principal mission.

One of those they had bribed was the ship's navigator, Lieutenant John Franks. Terry didn't know the details, but from what he had overheard, he guessed the navigator may have had a gambling problem and rising debts.

Within an hour of successfully breaking away from the station, Franks stepped out of the cabin and demanded to speak with Jose.

Pointing a meaty finger at the man, Carlos said, "He's busy. What do you want?"

Franks growled. "I want more money."

"You'll get what you agreed on."

Franks shook his head. He looked very frazzled. His hair was in disarray, his skin flushed and his pupils were dilated. Terry thought he might be on drugs.

Franks growled. "I need more. And I want to settle this now."

Carlos kept his voice even, but the lids of his eyes dropped, and his irises unfocused. "It's too late. The deed is done. When we get to our destination, you'll get paid. Now go back to the cabin and do your job."

Either Lieutenant Franks didn't recognize that he couldn't bully or cajole Carlos, or he was too far gone in his panic that he didn't care. The navigator held up his holoslate and showed them the screen.

Even from a bad angle, Terry was able to make out the message someone had sent to Franks. He had obviously received it just before the hijacking, but by then it was too late for him to do anything until they were well under way.

The message was from Lunar Lines head office. Franks had been suspended pending a criminal investigation for smuggling.

"See this?" he said. "It was just a couple lousy cases of rum. People do it all the time. Why'd they have to pick on me?"

"Sorry to hear that," Carlos said. "But it's not my problem."

"Don't you see? They're already on to me. I need to completely disappear, get a new identity. I need more money for that."

Carlos was losing his patience. "You're getting enough from us to do that."

"I need more!" Franks said.

His eyes flicking wildly back and forth, the lieutenant made a motion as if to race past Carlos and Terry. Holding out one hefty arm, Carlos clothes-lined the navigator, and the man fell back into the wall.

Carlos produced an ion pistol and pointed it at the navigator. "I said: get back to the cabin."

"You son of a bitch!" Franks screamed and rushed Carlos.

A crimson flower blossomed out of the middle of the navigator's forehead. Terry barely registered the whir of the ion pulse.

Franks' eyes widened in sudden shock for a brief moment before the life went out of him, and he sank to his knees and toppled over on his side.

"What the hell did you do?" Terry yelled at Carlos.

"He was crazed. High or something. We couldn't have him creating a panic right now. Or sabotaging the flight computer. There's no telling what people like that will do." Carlos was once again completely calm. He showed no more concern than if he had slapped a bug with a flyswatter.

"But you killed him!"

Carlos turned his full attention to Terry. "Are *we* going to have a problem now?"

Terry stammered. "N-no. It's just—"

"What?"

"I don't know. Couldn't we have just knocked him out? Tied him up or something?"

Carlos scratched his hair behind his ear. "I thought you were on board with this mission."

"Yeah. I am." Terry stared down at the blood pooling under the navigator's head. He could feel Carlos's eyes watching him. "It just caught me off guard, you know. Sorry."

Anything else they might have said to each other went unspoken as two men approached at a jog. It was Jose and one of the other Cruzados, Alberto.

Jose surveyed the scene and asked, "What happened?"

With a shrug, Carlos said, "He got out of hand."

Jose glanced at Terry for confirmation. Reluctantly, Terry gave a quick nod.

The leader of the Cruzados took a breath. "All right. Clean up the mess. We'll have to find someone to take his place and help our pilot fly the liner." He pointed at Terry. "You up to it?"

Terry, still trying to come to terms with the killing, blinked dimly at Jose. All three men were looking at him expectantly.

"Uh. Yeah," he said finally.

The Cruzados leader nodded and left with Alberto. Carlos tapped Terry on the shoulder.

"Take his legs. Help me get him into one of those freezers."

∞

Terry remained somewhat withdrawn over the next two days as he assisted the pilot—the first non-Mayan Terry had met in the Cruzado movement.

Captain Gruber was an older man who spoke English with a heavy German accent. Terry's English was not very good, so it made communication difficult at first, until Gruber ran a translator program from the ship's haptic console.

At first, Terry had been overwhelmed with the myriad

controls and banks of computers, but that quickly settled into tedium.

Captain Gruber told him that, for the most part, he could pilot the liner himself; all flight crew were trained to fly solo should the need arise.

"Basically," he said to Terry, "I just need you to babysit the console when I sleep. Someone needs to be here at all times or the sensors will shut the ship down. Don't worry, it's on autopilot, and if anything happens, the alarm will sound. Your main duty is to call me or come and get me if that happens."

They rotated in twelve-hour shifts. It gave Terry a lot of time to think about his role in hijacking the liner and whether he had made the right decision.

He had spent most of his life believing everyone in his family had made bad decisions. His parents lived in squalor, never trying to better themselves or providing a higher standard of living for their family. His grandfather had a precious artifact which he could have traded for great wealth for his community. And now, he had to admit, Terry had followed in their footsteps. In an attempt to make a difference, to better his family and community, he had fallen in with a group whose ideals were aligned with his own, but whose methods were extreme.

And Carlos! He had killed the navigator without batting an eyelid. There was no remorse or doubt afterwards. With no more thought than stepping on a bug, Carlos had ended a man's life.

Terry was certain they could have restrained the man and resolved the situation without resorting to murder.

There was a line Terry had vowed not to cross. Now, upon reflection, he realized that the line had been breached the moment he agreed to kidnap his grandfather and steal the ancient scroll.

How far was too far? It was all too far, Terry knew. But the problem was that he was in too deep to back out now. They would certainly eliminate him if he made too much trouble. The Cruzados had Terry's grandfather and they had the document. They did not need Terry any more.

If he was to survive this thing, he would have to continue to play along and wait for an opportunity to escape.

Where they were going, however, there was no place to run.

∞

It was three days later that Captain Gruber, looking ruffled from a broken sleep, came in while Terry was on shift. He offered up a token smile of greeting, then motioned for Terry to move aside.

"What's happening?" Terry asked.

In a gruff tone, the captain said, "We're stopping."

"Stopping? We won't have enough fuel to build velocity again."

Glancing up at Terry in annoyance, the captain said, "We don't have more than a day's worth of fuel left anyway. What did you think, that we were just going to coast the rest of the way?"

Terry hated to admit it, but that was exactly what he had assumed.

The captain pressed his lips together. "We're going to rendezvous with another ship and unload the cargo."

"And the hostages?"

Frowning, Captain Gruber did not reply.

A dark look settled over Terry's face. "We can't just abandon them and let them drift in space. They'll run out of food and water before any rescue ship finds them."

The captain either didn't have a reply, or chose not to say

anything. Instead, he concentrated on bringing the liner to a dead stop.

Within an hour, a bright speck appeared in the distance, and Terry pointed at it. "Is that the new ship?"

"Looks like," the captain said and called up a display. "Yup. It's the *Ultio.*" He pressed the intercom button and announced the new arrival.

Moments later, Jose and Carlos entered the cabin.

"He's here?" the leader of the Cruzados asked. His face was lit up with anticipation.

Terry wondered who, but didn't ask out loud. He had the realization that he had been kept in the dark about many things. Though he hadn't spent a lot of time thinking about it earlier, he knew now that he wasn't as trusted as he had originally thought back in Honduras when the Cruzados had first brought him into their revolution.

When he looked up at Jose, he saw that the other man was watching him ponderingly, and Terry flashed a smile to show that he was still on board with the operation.

They all watched as the other ship grew larger until it completely filled the display. The *Ultio* pulled alongside the liner and an umbilical tube extended out and attached to the main door.

All four men exited the cabin and made their way back to greet the new arrival.

It was with growing anticipation that Terry waited as the cabin door unlocked with a hiss of escaping air, then slowly opened. Only one man stepped out.

"Jose, I'm glad everything went well." Tall and blond, with piercing blue eyes, the man was in his late twenties or early thirties, though he carried himself as if he were years older. He wore a black suit in a modern cut without a tie. His white shirt did not have a fold at the collar, but instead circled the man's throat in a restrictive circle. His smile held no humor.

It was at that moment that Terry detected a faint resemblance between him and Captain Gruber. His notion was confirmed when the two of them stood together and shook hands.

"Uncle," the younger man said in English. "How was the trip?"

"Uneventful."

Jose, a wide grin on his face, stepped up and shook the blond man's hand as well.

"Your plan worked perfectly," he said.

"I'm glad to hear it." The man turned his steely gaze on Terry. "And is this who we must thank for providing the opportunity?"

"Yes," Jose said. "This is Te'irjiil, who goes by the name Terry Fernandez. Terry, I would like you to meet our benefactor, Mr. Klaus Vogelsberg. His uncle is Captain Gruber. Without their support, we would still be meeting in deserted buildings and just *talking* about the movement."

A corner of Klaus's lip went up in a humorless smile, and he extended his hand to Terry. "Very pleased to finally meet you. We've been waiting years for the so-called geniuses at NASA to figure out the ancient scroll, and in the end, the secret is unlocked by a simple villager. How perfect is that?"

Terry felt very uncomfortable under the other man's penetrative gaze. He didn't know if he was being complimented or insulted, but didn't want to say the wrong thing, so he nodded and offered up a smile of his own.

Turning his attention back to Jose, Klaus asked, "I trust we didn't have any trouble with our guests down below?"

"No. They are completely secure. All entrances are magnetically sealed. They already had enough food and water for the journey down there, and aside from one of them attempting to blow open the elevator door with some small explosive—which failed of course—we haven't heard a peep."

"That's good."

Terry found his voice. "They aren't going to be harmed, are they?"

Letting out a sudden barking laugh, Klaus said, "Going to be harmed?" He shared an amused look with his uncle, then continued: "If we wanted them harmed, we wouldn't have taken them hostage."

The relief Terry felt was quickly replaced by a measure of embarrassment. These people must think him some kind of country rube. He vowed not to open his mouth again until he had something intelligent to say.

Klaus turned to Jose. "Speaking of which, you may transfer them and the cargo to my ship. Use knockout gas; filter it through their air system." He glanced at Terry and gave a wink. "No conflict, no fighting, no harm. You see, we've thought of everything."

Terry flushed red.

Jose, a pleased smile on his lips, motioned to Carlos and the other men. "Let's go secure the prisoners." As he left with them, he called back over his shoulder to Terry. "You can stay with Captain Gruber and help him."

Gruber gave Terry a level look. It was obvious what the pilot was thinking: Terry's status in the movement was on a downward slide.

When Jose and the other Cruzados were gone, Klaus took a step closer to Captain Gruber.

"Once we have everything aboard, I need you to set the autopilot to point the liner back at the Sun. With any luck, the authorities will waste time trying to save a ghost ship. By then, we'll be very far away. We have a lot of work to do, and we don't want to be interrupted."

Terry started to say, "But, I thought…" And once again, he felt the heat rise in his neck and cheeks as Klaus looked at him with an amused smile.

"What," Klaus said, "did you think the governments of Earth were just going to give in to our demands if we turned over the cargo and hostages? Restore you to your rightful place as ambassadors to the stars? Ha!" This time, his laughter had the sound of a threat in it. He was obviously growing tired of entertaining Terry's ignorance.

Terry knew he was pushing the limit of Klaus's tolerance, but he had to ask one last question:

"If we aren't holding the Kinemet for ransom, what are we going to do with it?"

There was a chill moment when Terry thought Klaus was going to order his uncle to shoot him where he stood, but then the younger man's face broke into a wide grin.

"I'm glad you asked," he said to Terry. "Because I need you to work with me to complete the translation of the scroll, and uncover its secret. For that, we need the Kinemet, and a few test subjects."

With that, Klaus gave his uncle a nod, and then headed in the same direction as Jose and the others.

Captain Gruber gave Terry a tap on the arm with the back of his fingers. "Let's get moving."

∞

Trying not to be too obvious about it, Terry took a careful look at the unconscious hostages as they were loaded on gurneys and transported one by one from the liner to the *Ultio*. Aside from a few bruises here and there, and an overall pallor of gauntness from lack of nutrition, they all seemed to be healthy.

He did notice the one woman among them, a civilian, and recognized her from the news. It was the captain from the missions to Pluto. Terry was quite surprised to see her, but made sure to keep his expression neutral around the other Cruzados.

Within an hour, the hostages and the Kinemet were transferred to a safe hold on the *Ultio*, and Captain Gruber asked Terry to help him fire up the *Diana's* engines and set its course for oblivion.

For the most part, Terry had no idea what he was doing, but whenever the captain said to press this button or that, he did. Soon, the liner was fully prepped and ready for its final voyage into the Sun.

"If we aren't going to return to Earth or Luna," Terry asked after screwing up his courage, "where are we going?"

"You know, you ask a lot of questions," Captain Gruber said in German. Though the translation came across in a pleasant programmed voice, the captain's original tone had been acerbic. He switched to English. "Curiosity could get you in trouble. If Jose wanted you to know, he would have told you."

Terry forced himself to keep his voice light and casual. "Maybe it slipped his mind. He's quite busy." When the captain didn't immediately reply, Terry asked, "What's the big secret, anyway? I'm going to find out soon enough. So what's the surprise?"

Eyeing the young Mayan, Captain Gruber took a minute out from his final preparations and flicked on a backup navigation holoscreen. He tapped in a few commands on the haptic console and the image of a familiar planet came into view.

Terry's lips fell open as if to make an exclamation, but no sound came out. He finally found his voice. "I would never have guessed."

"Precisely why Klaus chose it," Captain Gruber said. "Not only is it right there in plain view, but who would think to look for us in a ball of poisonous gas and sulfuric acid?"

The captain finished programming the computer and got up to leave. "My boy, if there is such a thing as hell, where we're going is the closest thing to it in this universe."

NASA NewsFlash :
May 2102 :

Nearly one hundred and forty years after Venus became the object of the first successful interplanetary mission, the Lucis Observatory orbiting Earth's sister planet is now vacant and abandoned.

Citing budgetary constraints and lack of public support for the research station, NASA's board of directors voted early last year to cease manned operations to Venus. The final crew disembarked this morning after finalizing the automation of the remaining sensor equipment. They should be arriving home by the end of the month.

For more details, please follow our MeshSite…

Canada Station Three :
Lagrange Point 4 :
Earth Orbit :

The one thing Kenny insisted on was to record the experiments on holo.

Since they wanted to keep the administration of Quantum Resources out of the procedures until they could come up with some solid conclusions, both Alex and the physicist decided to conduct their tests in Alex's apartment after official hours.

For the most part, Alex's involvement in the core research at the lab had become minimal—there were only so many experiments they could do without any Kinemet. It had only been on Kenny's original insistence that Alex had been there on a more regular basis the past few weeks. Now that Kenny's official reports did not show any progress, Alex was allowed to spend his time as he saw fit, so long as he remained on call should the need arise.

Since recharging himself with the Kinemetic radiation on the liner before it was hijacked, Alex was completely restored. He had not, however, reported his recovery to the administration, and wouldn't until he and Kenny had a chance to do some of their own research.

His complexion was hale, his legs were strong, and he had more energy than he'd had for years.

He had not gone to see Doctor Amma for his regularly

scheduled checkup, but sent her a message that everything was going well for him. Although the doctor had the best of intentions, Alex knew any diagnosis she reached would not provide him with any great insight into his condition. It would, however, raise some serious flags back on Earth if they reported he had gone into complete remission. For the time being, he could not afford that kind of attention.

Alex wanted time to investigate other aspects of the Kinemetic ability without the hindrance of the scientists who had spent most of the last ten years getting him to perform the same useless tasks and scratching their heads when they couldn't figure out what it all meant.

In Kenny, Alex saw the spark of someone who wanted to know the answers without using the knowledge for their own political or professional gain. Although Kenny had come on strong—trying to prove himself—once he had a glimpse of what Alex was, and what he could become, Kenny's primary instincts kicked in.

Most scientists initially entered their fields in the pursuit of knowledge, to be the first one to solve the puzzle. After years of the politics and squabbling inherent in the scientific community, many lost sight of their purpose. Right under the surface, Kenny was still motivated by his original passion, and Alex recognized it.

But while NASA and Quantum Resources *wanted* to know the extent of Alex's condition, Alex *needed* to know. And if it meant going behind the backs of the administration to find those answers, so be it.

At first, when he no longer needed the hydraulic braces, Alex was certain someone would notice him walking around Canada Station Three under his own power, but after years of dismissing his presence, no one seemed to be able to tell the difference. Still, Alex kept mostly to himself in his rooms, except to go to the mess hall, or to the labs when he was called.

He didn't need to go to any physical location; once again his clairvoyant ability allowed him to visit any area on the station without leaving his room. All he had to do was close his eyes and concentrate. It was a simple matter of will for him to push his senses outward. Like a ghost or an astral walker, he could frequent every corner of Canada Station Three.

Alex was able to see Kenny with his ability long before the physicist arrived at the apartment for their nightly experiments.

A moment before Kenny pressed the buzzer, Alex extended his thoughts to the door panel. While it was just as easy to walk over and press the release, or even use voice control to allow the door to open, Alex preferred to exercise his electropathic ability to trip the switch. It was good practice.

"Hello, Alex," Kenny said as he stepped inside.

Without any additional preamble, Kenny pushed a cart filled with equipment toward Alex's computer station and began to connect the sensor leads to the bus ports.

"You had an idea, Kenny?"

The physicist nodded. "Yesterday I noticed that there was a fluctuation in the ambient temperature when you used your *sight*." He glanced over at Alex. "I hate using the word 'clairvoyance.' Sounds like something a fortune-teller would say."

Alex shrugged.

Kenny continued explaining: "I'd like to run a series of tests to measure the temperature change around you in relation to the distance that you extend your *sight*. It could be important; if you require more energy to see farther, it could make a difference to how much Kinemet someone would need to pilot a ship to different locations."

"I keep telling you, piloting a ship in that manner is not what was intended. That's just incidental."

Kenny looked up from the computer and nodded. "Yeah, I know. But if we're going to get the government corporations on board with this—and get you more of the Kinemet—we need to give them some tangible purpose. They want to see black on their profit and loss statements, not red. They need results. Things they can get behind; like cheap space travel."

"All right. But tonight I'm going to try to push my *sight* farther than I ever have before," he said, adopting Kenny's word for the ability.

"What do you mean?"

Alex lay back on the sofa while Kenny trucked the cart over and placed the sensors around and on Alex.

"The very first time I experienced the *sight,* I saw the entire solar system laid out for me. It happened over a four-hour period, but in my memory, it was more like an afterimage from a bright flash. There was no controlling it. It was almost like something in my mind was calibrating my senses, getting my location.

"After that, my range was considerably less. I could only see about a hundred and fifty kilometers away. Before I went to Centauri, I used that ability to help the group who was sheltering me, by warning them of incoming ships. When they went on salvage missions, I would scout for them. I had plenty of time to practice and push my ability."

Kenny asked, "You worked for the pirates who kidnapped you, right?"

"We came to an understanding." Alex closed his eyes and tried to relax. "I've never been able to go farther than about a hundred and fifty kilometres, and when I try, it's been an enormous strain." He looked at Kenny. "I can sense there's something out there, beyond the limit of my clairvoyance—my *sight.* Maybe there's something out there I can only see if I'm quantized."

"You mean, when you shift out of our reality?" Kenny paused to look at Alex.

"Yeah. But when I enter a quantized state, I don't have any senses at all. It's like I'm in some kind of stasis. I know that's not the way it's supposed to be, but… It's like I'm a baby bird that has ventured out of its nest for the first time and sees the limitless sky. It can tell it's supposed to be able to fly, but hasn't figured out how to use its wings yet. Until I can complete my transformation, I won't know what I'm capable of when I become quantized."

"So what is it that you are proposing tonight?"

Alex breathed deeply, and paused to collect his thoughts. "When I spent those few hours on the *Diana* recharging myself with the Kinemet, there were others there who were also exposed to the Kinemetic radiation."

"Yes?" Kenny's interest was piqued.

"Perhaps if I focus on them, since they've been marginally irradiated, I'll be able to bridge the gap between us."

"And," Kenny added, a knowing smile on his lips, "perhaps get a location on your kidnapped friends?"

Alex nodded. "That's the plan."

"I'm on board with that. Let me just finish hooking you up."

It only took Kenny a few more minutes to complete the set up. As he tested the sensors and got an initial reading before they started their experiment, Kenny looked as if there was something he wanted to say.

"What's wrong?" Alex asked.

"It's only been three days since you were restored," Kenny said. "I know you've used your abilities far more than what I've seen."

Alex admitted, "Yeah. So?"

"So, the Kinemetic radiation in you is not unlimited. You're going to run out of juice at some point, and we have no idea when we'll get more for you."

Alex leaned back into the sofa and smiled dismissively. "I know, but I'm good for a while longer. Let's get on with this, Dr. Frankenstein."

Once Kenny finished attaching the sensors to Alex, measuring his vital stats as well as brain waves and electromagnetic emanations, he flipped on the spectrograph and gave Alex a thumbs up gesture.

Shutting his eyes, Alex willed himself back into that transcendent state. Over the past few days he had become quite adept at the technique.

This time, instead of visualizing the station and allowing his senses to float through the corridors and rooms, he pushed his senses outward. Trying to ignore anything tangible within the scope of his *sight,* he focused on any Kinemetic energy signatures in the area. There was a link between him and that element, and if he could simply train his extra-spatial senses to detect it, he was certain he could send his incorporeal form out to find Justine and the others.

As he scouted in a sweeping pattern outside the station, he felt an extrasensory tug, accompanied by a note or two of the haunting melody that always seemed to be in the periphery of his senses when he was using his Kinemetic abilities. Without being conscious of what he was doing, he gathered all his will and pushed himself in that direction.

At first, his spectral senses soared at an alarming speed, but it was as if he were on the end of a giant elastic. Once Alex reached approximately a hundred and fifty kilometres distance from the station, the effort to move himself even a meter more became exponentially more difficult. Like a marathon runner who reaches their glycogen limit, Alex felt a sudden burning fatigue and lost focus.

Disoriented, he suddenly could not determine which way to return to his body. He was lost, adrift in space, and he didn't have enough energy to sever the link and snap back to reality.

Alex panicked, and he felt his consciousness fade away into a nothingness as dark as the farthest regions of space.

20

Unknown Plantation :
Honduras :
Central American Conglomeration :

For what seemed like an eternity, Michael and George lay on the floor of the van as the Cruzados transported them to an unknown location.

Trussed up like a hog around his ankles and wrists, Michael was unable to find a position where every pothole they hit in the road didn't send him bouncing and jostling against the steel floor. Twice he banged his head against a metal tool box; the second time he nearly blacked out and almost vomited from the sudden nausea. He wasn't sure his kidneys would survive the ride.

Like George, Michael was gagged, and could only glare back at the rebel soldier who watched over him with callous eyes. Unlike George, Michael was still conscious.

The first time George had tried to protest his capture, struggling against his bonds, the solider guarding them kicked him in the side and barked, *"Silencio!"*

After a particularly jarring bump, George once again growled through his makeshift muzzle. The soldier struck him in the side of the head with his rifle butt, and then gave Michael a challenging look when he tried to wriggle over to check on his friend.

A small trickle of blood ran down George's face. He was knocked out, but breathing. Still alive, though he didn't regain consciousness during the remainder of the journey.

It was hard to judge how much time had elapsed, but it seemed like hours before the van slowed, turned a sharp corner, and then rolled up to its final destination.

Michael heard shouts in Spanish as orders were given, acknowledged and carried out. He estimated from the voices that there were more than a dozen men in the vicinity.

When the back doors of the van opened, and he and George were pulled out into a moonlit compound, Michael saw that his assumption was correct.

A number of armed men approached to assist in unloading the prisoners. While two of the soldiers grabbed Michael by the arms, a third cut the rope around his ankles. They escorted him from the van to a large storage shed. Four other men lifted the prone figure of George out and carried him.

In addition to the shed where they were heading, there were three other outbuildings—barns converted to barracks, Michael guessed as he spied more men milling around in front of them. The buildings had been erected on either side of a packed dirt road which led up to a main house. It was dark except for one room on the second floor. A silhouetted figure stood in the window, as if overseeing the activity below.

One of the soldiers yanked on Michael's arm, getting his attention and dragging him roughly to the storage shed.

Stepping inside first, the soldier pulled a thin string attached to a bare light bulb hanging from a rafter, and harsh yellow light bathed the inside of the shed. Wooden barrels were stacked in one corner. Against the other wall was a dilapidated gas generator that looked as if it hadn't worked for a decade. The floor was of packed earth, but there was a dirty straw mattress near the back of the shed. The soldiers carrying

George dropped him on it without exercising any amount of care.

In heavily accented English, one soldier said, "Sleep now. No trouble."

Turning off the light, the Cruzado exited the building. Michael heard the snap of a padlock and the soldier ordering a man to stay posted out front.

There was one small dirt-stained window beside the door, but it was large enough to let in some light from the moon, and Michael's eyes soon became accustomed to the night.

With his hands still bound behind his back, he moved over to check on his friend again. He got down on his knees and leaned in for a closer look. George was still unconscious, but his breathing was evening out.

Michael spoke in low tones, "It'll be all right George. We'll get through this."

He looked around the shed again, his mind racing. First things first, Michael wasn't going to be able to do much with his hands tied together.

Awkwardly struggling to his feet, he approached the generator and turned his back to it. Reaching out with his fingers, he felt a sharp length of broken metal jutting out just far enough that he might be able to cut the rope at his wrists. He worked the rope over the edge repeatedly.

Soon enough, the rope fell free from him, and Michael brought his hands out front to examine them in the dim moonlight for damage. Several tiny cuts marred his skin and a few trickles of blood ran down his arm, but he was otherwise unscathed.

He set to work untying George's bonds and trying to arrange the man into a more comfortable position until he regained consciousness. That accomplished, Michael sat on the foot of the mattress and leaned back against the wall.

With the shed locked and guarded, and Michael unarmed, there wasn't much else he could do. They had been sending updates to John Markham every morning. When they failed to check in tomorrow, Michael hoped that John would send out an alert to the authorities and contact Calbert at Quantum Resources. However, even if they were made aware that Michael and George were missing, they would have no idea where the two were.

Michael had no idea what had become of their equipment. George's video mask had a GPS tracker in it. If the Cruzados had taken it with them, then all Michael had to do was turn the camera back on and wait for someone back home to notice. If the machine were destroyed, then Michael would have to find some other way to let their location—wherever that was—be known.

In the back of the van, Michael had been disoriented and distracted. He'd had no bearings. Had they gone north, west, east, south? And for how long? Hours for certain. But that could mean they were anywhere, even in one of Honduras's bordering countries, like El Salvador or Guatemala.

Michael sat up for another hour, worrying over their situation and speculating on what would happen the next day. After a time, exhaustion crept in and sleep took him.

∞

It was one of the most uncomfortable nights Michael had ever spent, and he woke with a sharp pain in his neck from sleeping upright against the wall.

George was already awake, and sitting on the edge of the mattress, elbows propped on his knees, one hand gingerly touching the swelling bump on his head.

"You look like I feel," he said to Michael in a grave voice.

"Thanks." Michael tried to work the kink out of his neck. "How's the head?"

"Feels like a watermelon in a microwave. But no permanent damage, I think."

"That's good."

With exaggerated care, George pushed himself to his feet and tested his balance. He looked around the shed and then stepped closer to the small window. "Where are we?"

"Not sure of the exact location, but it's obviously some kind of base camp for the Cruzados."

George glanced sharply at Michael. "Our equipment? The camera?"

"I'm not sure. They may have destroyed it."

"We can only hope!"

Michael stood up. "What?"

With a knowing smile, George winked. "I installed a backup circuit running off a lithium battery. It was in constant contact with one of the geo satellites we were using. If the link is severed, it trips an immediate alert back home. The GPS uplink would give them our last coordinates. At least that would give them a starting point from which to track us."

"What if they didn't destroy the camera?" Michael asked.

Shrugging, George said, "Well, the longer it takes Calbert to notice we're missing, the harder it will be for him to find us."

"That's what I thought," Michael said, pressing his lips together in a grimace.

They both turned when they heard the clanking of metal. Someone unlocked the shed's padlock, and the door swung open. Two Cruzados with rifles at the ready stood just outside, looking in. One of them glanced down, saw their hands unbound, and narrowed his eyes. He made a gesture with his weapon and said, *"Siga con nosotros."*

With one soldier in front, and one behind, the two prisoners were led up the packed road to the main house.

∞

Inside, they were greeted at the door by a dark haired, middle-aged man with a thin black moustache which drooped around the corners of his smiling mouth.

"Please come in," he said with a sweeping gesture of his hand. "My name is Oscar Ruiz, and this is my plantation. I apologize for the unpleasantness of your quarters last night, but we were unprepared for your arrival. We have had many guests of late, and we are not always able to accommodate everyone."

Michael blinked, unsure how to respond. He shared a look with George.

A burly man with a thick moustache appeared from another room. He was dressed in a dark grey shirt and denim overalls. At the end of a leather strap slung over his shoulder was a submachine gun. It rested between the back of his arm and his side.

Noticing the new arrival, Oscar nodded in his direction while keeping his eyes on Michael and George. "This is Humberto, who is part of my new protective detachment, and is assigned to household security. If you will follow him upstairs, he will show you where you can clean up. Breakfast will be served shortly. I cannot wait for you to try our own home-grown coffee—it's world famous, you know."

Oscar gave them a quick nod, took one step back and spun on his heel. As he disappeared into the same room Humberto had come out of, he called out some instructions in Spanish to the house staff.

In a thick accent, Humberto said, "Upstairs." When Michael didn't move right away, the soldier put his hand on the back of his arm and pushed him gently but firmly toward the staircase. "Now."

George needed no prompting, and led the way to the second floor. Humberto followed them up, and called out directions which brought them to a sparse bedroom furnished with a single mattress flat on the floor, a wooden chair in one corner, and a ratty looking sofa.

There was a four-pane window looking out over the plantation, and a quick glance showed dozens of *campesinos* tending the rows of plants. Thick iron bars covered the window, providing no means of escape. Not that it was an option at this point. Even if Michael and George were able to get away from their captors, they were both unequipped to survive in the open on their own for any length of time; at least for however long it would take them to make their way to a populated area where they could call someone for help.

Humberto took a few steps to the wall opposite the sofa and pushed back a slatted door.

"Wash here," he instructed them.

Without another word, he left the bedroom, closing the door behind him and locking it.

Michael looked at George. "What the hell is going on? Are we prisoners or guests?"

"Yes," was George's answer. He smiled. "If I were to make a guess, I would say Mr. Ruiz is a supporter of the Cruzados movement, but he might not be a willing supporter. I wouldn't count on him knowing much more than whatever rhetoric they feed him."

"How's that?"

"Look at it from his perspective," George said. "He's a wealthy landowner with a profitable business, at least by local standards. Central America has been rife with civil war of some sort for centuries, and someone who wants to maintain their status needs to work within that reality. I'd say he's just hedging his bets. Obviously the Cruzados are a larger organization than we suspected. If they manage to attain their objectives, then he'll be remembered for his contribution. If their revolution gets put down, he can always point to his 'guests' to prove how hospitable he was; he could maybe even go so far as to claim the Cruzados forced his cooperation."

George was the first to enter the water closet and he grunted in disapproval. "Well, at least it's indoor plumbing," he said when he turned on the tap and watched rusty water pour into the cracked porcelain sink. He did his best to wash the sweat and dirt from his face and neck while Michael sat on the chair and waited his turn.

"So how do we play this?" Michael asked.

George stepped out of the washing room, dabbing at his face with a towel. "We don't have a lot of options. We don't know where we are; the authorities don't know where we are and we don't have any means of contacting them. They're not going to kill us, and I don't think they'll hold us for ransom— at the most we'll be used as hostages. In the meantime, we should act as guests, ingratiate ourselves with Oscar, and pump him for as much information as we can get. Even if he's not directly involved in the Cruzados' politics, I'm sure he knows more than we've been able to guess so far. Your turn."

Michael barely had enough time to wash up before there was a knock on the door for them to head back downstairs.

∞

Michael smelled the fresh-brewed coffee well before Humberto led them into a large dining area. The table in the center of the room was filled with breads, fruits, sausages and fried potatoes. Eyeing the breakfast hungrily, Michael almost didn't notice there were two people sitting at the table.

As Michael and George entered the room, Oscar stood up and motioned to two empty chairs. "Please, sit. Join us. I implore you to tell me what you think of my coffee; the beans were freshly roasted and ground only a few minutes ago."

But Michael didn't reply. Both he and George stopped short when the second man turned and directed his toothy smile at them.

In Spanish, Yaxche said, "George. Hello. Where is your funny hat?"

21

Lucis Observatory :
Venus Orbit :

Justine was the first to regain consciousness, and a knife of panic sliced through her awareness when she couldn't hear or sense anyone else in her vicinity. She began to hyperventilate.

Without her PERSuit harness or optilink, she had no idea where she was or who was with her, if anyone. The after-effects of the sleep agent made her feel like her head was filled with cotton, and there was a persistent ringing in her ears.

She thrust her hands out to try to grasp something—anything—familiar and orient herself. Her fingers brushed against fabric, and then with both hands she tentatively felt along its length. It was the sleeve of someone's jacket. Only one person in their group wore a suit.

Gently shaking his arm, she whispered, "Clive? Are you all right?"

A moan escaped his lips as he came to. "Oh, my head," he growled. "Did a planet land on me or something? How are you?"

"I'm all right." Now that she wasn't alone in the darkness. "Can you see?" Justine asked. "Where are we?" Absently, she scratched at the inside of her elbow.

She heard him groan as he sat up. "We're in a large room of some sort," he told her. "Maybe a conference room or a lab.

All the furniture has been removed. There's one door; it's barred, but it has a small window. There's light coming in from it."

Clive made some rustling sounds as he struggled to his feet. "The others are here, too, but they're still unconscious."

Justine experienced a moment of unreasoning panic when Clive stepped away from her, and her fingers reached out for him of their own accord. If Clive was aware of her momentary desperation, he did not acknowledge it. She took a deep breath to center herself. She was stronger than this; succumbing to her fears wouldn't help the situation.

Justine heard Clive rouse Lieutenant Jeffries, and after a moment, the squad leader groaned and coughed as he awoke.

"That was one hell of a Mickey Finn," he said, his voice rough as sandpaper. A moment later, he asked, "You two all right?"

"Aside from the mother of all hangovers, yeah," Justine said. "Do either of you have any idea where we are?"

"Obviously we didn't crash into the Sun," the lieutenant said, his voice sardonic. "Though it feels like it. My skin is on fire." A moment later he said, "It looks as if they've taken all of our weapons and equipment. They even took my boots and belt."

Before they had been rendered unconscious, when they were in the hold of the liner, the soldiers had their ion rifles and supplies. Of course, they were completely ineffectual, but it had provided Justine with a psychological cushion. Now, it sunk home that they were completely at the mercy of their captors.

Justine heard the lieutenant go from man to man and shake them awake. Most of them woke in a symphony of moans and complaints, and Corporal Marks made a remark that he felt a tingling sensation in his legs, as if they were still asleep. When one soldier woke, Justine heard him roll over and vomit.

"Do you see anything out there?" Lieutenant Jeffries asked, his question directed to Corporal Marks, who answered from a distance away.

"An empty hall. I see a few other doors. We're in some kind of lab complex, I would say. None of the other windows are lit."

"Any markings?" the lieutenant asked.

"Just room numbers. Wait—" There was a moment of silence, and then Corporal Marks said, "Huh."

"What?" Justine asked.

"I know where we are," he said, his voice rising in surprise.

"Well?" she prompted.

Clearing his throat, Marks said, "At the end of the hall is a little trolley. There's a symbol etched into the front of it. A circle with a small cross hanging from the bottom."

Lieutenant Jeffries asked, "The symbol for a female?"

"No," said Corporal Marks. "Venus."

"Venus?" the lieutenant asked. "I thought Venus was a ball of hot acid."

The answer popped into Justine's head. "Lucis Observatory."

"Right," said Clive, back beside her. "In Venus's shadow. It's the perfect hiding place. The orbital has been abandoned for years, but the computer still collects data and transmits it home on a regular basis. As long as the computers keep spitting out periodic data to Earth, no one would ever suspect anyone was here."

Using a wall to stabilize herself, Justine stood up. "We're missing something."

"What?" Clive asked.

"Right before we were knocked out, the liner slowed."

Corporal Marks said, "Docking here?"

"No, I think we were docking with another ship, and we were transferred over."

Clive took a step closer to her. "What makes you say that?"

Justine reached out and took his hand, and lifted it up. "Two reasons. First, the liner wouldn't have had enough fuel to make the trip here." She pushed up his sleeve and ran her fingers along the skin at his elbow. There was a tiny bump there. She pressed it.

"Hey, that hurts," he said.

"Second, we weren't merely unconscious, we were given a dose of thiopental or some other barbiturate. If you check, we all have a puncture where they had us on intravenous."

Clive whistled. "Induced coma? How long were we out?"

Corporal Marks spoke up. "Rough calculation, based on how far the liner had traveled, and the remaining distance to Venus, I would say at least two or three days in transit. There's no way to know how long we've been here, but judging by the scab on my arm, we've been off the IV for the better part of a day."

Justine nodded, not knowing if anyone saw the movement, and said, "So if you add those two facts together, that would mean they want to keep us alive, but they want to keep our— and their—existence a secret."

She had continued to keep her grip on Clive's arm, but now she squeezed it hard. "I don't think we're being kept here as hostages."

Lieutenant Jeffries asked, "Then what do they need us for?"

His question was interrupted when the soldier who had vomited earlier cried out, "What the hell?"

"What is it, Private Jackson?" asked the lieutenant.

"Sir, my apologies, sir. I couldn't help it. I—I voided myself. But, sir, it hurts."

Justine heard some of the others hurry over to investigate,

and she let Clive lead her towards the group.

Clive said, "Oh my."

"What?" asked Justine.

"That's not shite," Clive said.

Corporal Marks' voice was tight. "It's blood."

And that's when the pieces of the puzzle fell into place for Justine.

22

Ruiz Plantation :
Honduras :
Central American Conglomeration :

It took Michael a moment to regain his thoughts. The last person he had expected to be there was Yaxche. The old man looked healthy and hale.

George was the first to speak. *"¡Hola! Ha sido un largo tiempo."* He stepped around the table to shake Yaxche's hand, and continued speaking in Spanish: "Unfortunately, I don't know where my funny hat is, but I wish I had it right now."

Without the benefit of a translation program in his portable computer, Michael struggled to keep up with the conversation. His Spanish was very rusty, but he knew Yaxche didn't speak English, so he let George do most of the talking. Whenever he could, he translated for Michael.

"We came down to Honduras to find you," George said to Yaxche. He took a seat at the table when Oscar, with a gracious smile, motioned to two chairs and then snapped his finger for a servant to pour two cups of coffee.

"I am right here," Yaxche said, as if that had been an obvious fact all along. There was a slight crack in his smiling façade that Michael noticed. The old man was just as much a prisoner as they were.

"Are you all right?" Michael asked. One thing he realized

quickly was that Yaxche's grandson was not present. Was he someplace else? Was he ill? Dead?

"Yes." Yaxche nodded. "Oscar has been very kind."

"The only thing that separates us from the beasts is manners," Oscar said. "Please, fill your plates. Eat."

They didn't need any more prompting. Michael's stomach rumbled as he loaded his dish with half a dozen strips of bacon, two hardboiled eggs, and spread jam on a hot piece of toast. He dug into his breakfast with gusto. It was a feast fit for a king, as far as Michael was concerned, especially after having had nothing to eat since the previous morning.

He wanted to grill Yaxche, but without knowing more about the situation and getting all the facts, Michael decided to hold off on his questions for the time being.

Between mouthfuls of food, George nodded to Señor Ruiz. "Perhaps we can impose on your generosity with a question?"

"Of course," Oscar said, with a flourish of his hand.

"What is to become of us?"

"For now, the three of you will remain here as guests, so long as I have your word that you will not abuse my hospitality." He looked into Michael's eyes for a moment, and then George's to ensure both men understood and agreed to the condition. "As for the future, I cannot say; though it is my understanding that you will not be ransomed."

So they were to be held as hostages, Michael concluded. A second thought occurred to him. If they didn't need to ransom them, then the Cruzados already had enough money to fund their operation. It was a little scary to think this organization had grown so quickly without the notice of the international security agencies.

There was still the question about where Oscar's loyalties lay, but Michael had to assume their host would report every word of their conversation to whoever gave him orders. The entire *hacienda* could be bugged, for all he knew.

Although his mind screamed for answers about the events surrounding Yaxche's kidnapping—and their own—Michael instead took a long drink of his coffee. "You are right. This is the best cup of coffee I've ever tasted."

Oscar beamed with pride. "Thank you. It is from my personal stock. Only the best for my guests."

George, picking up on Michael's lead, asked, "Perhaps you could give us a tour of your operation sometime."

"Of course," their host said. He looked up as a younger man dressed in a light grey suit appeared in a doorway and nodded to him. Absently, Oscar said to George, "It would be my pleasure, but we will have to do this at some other time. Right now, I have some business matters to attend." He stood up and bowed to his guests. "Please, finish your breakfast. Help yourselves to as much as you want. You may, if you wish, stretch your legs with a walk around our grounds. I'm sure Humberto, as always, will escort you."

With that, Oscar took one last sip of his coffee and left the room.

Michael was chomping at the bit to grill Yaxche, but he wanted to find a place where they could have at least some semblance of privacy. Waiting until George had cleared his second helping of breakfast, he looked back and forth between his friend and Yaxche, and said, "Perhaps we could take our coffee outside, and sit for a while?"

One of the servants, picking up on Michael's suggestion, immediately loaded a serving cart with the coffee urn, a dish of sugar and a small pitcher of cream, and led them outside to a veranda.

Half a dozen palm tree saplings had been planted in large ceramic pots and placed strategically around the veranda to provide as much shade as possible. It was still early morning, but the tropical sun was already beating down. A few dribbles of sweat began to form on Michael's forehead and neck.

They sat in wicker chairs around a patio table, the base of which was made of carved wood, and the round top was a mosaic of various pieces of hand-cut stone.

Humberto took up a position at the edge of a set of stairs, putting himself between the hostages and the field—and possible escape. He was far enough away that, if the three of them talked in low voices, they wouldn't be overheard. There was no way to guarantee there wasn't a hidden microphone in their vicinity, but Michael had to assume they had enough privacy to discuss the events that had led the three of them to their present circumstances.

As they conversed in Spanish, Michael interrupted only occasionally when he didn't understand a word or phrase. Again, he let George do most of the talking.

George started off by telling Yaxche what they knew; which wasn't very much.

"When we arrived at your village, we were told your grandson was also abducted. Did they take him someplace else? Is he all right?"

Yaxche's face fell at the mention of his grandson. "He was not taken," he said. "It is my great shame to say he was the one who took me."

Michael and George shared a surprised look. "What do you mean by that?"

"He is not the boy he used to be. He has changed. His heart, I believe, has seen too much pain."

Concern in his voice, Michael said, "We spoke to your daughter. She told us about his fiancée."

"Itzel," Yaxche said in a whisper. "She was an angel, but her time was short. Te'irjiil could not forgive himself, or us."

"You?"

"He blamed all of us—me, the village council, even our country—for not saving her. He always thought we should have sold the ancient scroll to NASA for medicine and machines."

"But," George said slowly, casting his eyes back and forth between Michael and Yaxche, "your daughter said he came back from a long trip with medicine and technology. If he blamed the people from your village, why would he help them?"

Yaxche stared out into the field. "It may be darkened, but I believe it is still a good heart that beats in his chest."

Michael asked in broken Spanish, "I understand he told everyone he made the money gambling. Do you think he may have sold the scroll instead?"

"Not the scroll," Yaxche said. "Its secret."

Michael immediately glanced up to see if Humberto was listening in. The Cruzado was busy looking bored and chewing a dirty fingernail.

"We've had hundreds of cryptologists, translators and decoding computers working on that document for over a dozen years," Michael said. "NASA has all but given up on it providing them with any significant meaning, and I believe Quantum Resources has mothballed the project." Michael gave George a glance for confirmation of that last point. "And all this time, Alex was right; you had the secret?"

Yaxche looked down at his hands, folded on his lap. "No. I do not know the secret. I have failed my ancestors. I was entrusted with the story, but I now realize I have never understood its true meaning. I had hoped to pass the scroll on to my grandson, that he might protect it through the next generation, but his eagerness to learn the story was a trick. I saw in his eye that he discovered the truth that been hidden from me all along." The old man fell silent while Michael's mind raced.

What was the secret that had eluded so many scientists and educated minds? How had a simple villager figured it out? Was it something so obvious and plain that seasoned professionals had dismissed it? Or was it a genetic puzzle that only a descendant of the first transcribers could comprehend?

George lightly touched Yaxche's wrist with his fingers. "No one blames you. But perhaps if you could tell us exactly what happened, what sparked the Cruzados to kidnap you, we might be able to help you understand."

Yaxche said, "For a year, Te'irjiil had sat with me every evening, reading the story with me. Talking about its meaning. He would hold up a small box—one of your computer machines—and tell me it agreed with some of the story, but not with other parts. At times he would get angry and say the scroll told nothing more than a bedtime story, and there was no meaning. That we wasted our time.

"I thought, the last night I saw him, he would once again leave our village and not return. But he asked me to tell him the story again. I do not know how he came to understand the secret of the scroll, but I saw it in his eyes. And then came his betrayal."

Once again, Yaxche fell silent, and Michael could tell it was difficult for him to tell the tale. It was obviously very personal and very painful.

Over the past decade, Michael had read and re-read the translation of the scroll, telling the story of how the Mayan people—one of the most advanced civilizations of the pre-Columbian world—had come to the brink of extinction over a thousand years before, after a failed civil war caused their gods to abandon them. Like Yaxche's grandson, Michael had always thought it more of a parable than fact.

Yaxche had always claimed that the story had been

transcribed from the words of their ancient gods before they left Earth to return to the stars. The scrolls themselves were of human manufacture, and of biological origin, as was the ink with which the story was written. The only fact that lent credence to the scroll's ancient link was the Mayan inscription on *Dis Pater*.

Goozal Kinich Ahua; Inti ba Rahn; Goozal Kukulcan.

"Beware the Mighty Door of Kinich Ahua; Eternity is now Before You; Beware the Power of Kukulcan."

Both the scroll and the inscription on the monument on Pluto mentioned Kinich Ahua—the Mayan god of the sun— and Kukulcan—the feathered god of war who could affect the elements and cause earthquakes.

Historians had struggled to comprehend the symbology behind these ancient deities and what the scroll was trying to tell the descendants of the Mayan people. At one point, a group of physicists from Arizona had assigned each of the gods mentioned to various elements from the periodic table. They tried combining these elements with Kinemet in various formulations to no discernible results. For years, the 'secret' of how to effectively use Kinemet for effective interstellar travel had eluded the best minds on the planet.

But for some unknown reason, Te'irjiil—the son of a plantation worker without the benefit of a formal education— had solved the puzzle.

"Yaxche," George said, "I hope you know that we are here to help you. Do you remember Alex Manez?"

"Yes, Colop is always in my thoughts, though I have not spoken with him in many years."

Uncertain that what he had to say would come across correctly in Spanish, Michael asked George to translate: "Alex sent us a message from one of our space stations to find you. He said that you have the secret, even if you don't know it. He couldn't tell me anything more, because he fell into a fugue state."

"Ahyah. He has had a vision, then."

Michael understood the reply, but continued speaking in English: "I don't know that. I haven't had the opportunity to talk to him since then, though I received word that he had recovered. But before he went unconscious, he said I needed to hear the story. Wait—"

Eyes widening, Michael glanced up at George and said, "You know, after all this time, I just realized: I've read the translations and interpretations, and I listened to the recording you made when you first interviewed Yaxche, but I've never actually *heard* the story itself."

"What do you mean? You heard Yaxche telling us the story on my recording."

"In Spanish. And then translated into English. I haven't actually heard it in Mayan."

George blinked at Michael. "I'm sure we have the Mayan version on record somewhere. We had a few linguists on retainer who could interpret the Mayan glyphs, and I recall several of them reading the scroll out loud. Are you sure you didn't access one of those recordings?"

"I don't think so, but I also don't think it matters. Alex said, specifically, 'You have to hear *him* tell you the story.' Not one of our linguists, but Yaxche himself."

Shaking his head, George said, "What good will that do? Without a computer to translate, it will all just sound like jumbled words to us."

Michael opened his hands. "At this point, what harm can it do?"

George shrugged and turned to Yaxche. "Are you able to tell us the story on the ancient scroll from memory?"

"Ahyah," the old man said, as if the question had stung his

pride. And then he closed his eyes and began to recount the tale of the end of the Fourth World in his native language.

At first, Michael strained to listen to the words and phrases, trying to find anything familiar in the lyrical sound of the story. He hoped his brain could make any kind of connection, that some kind of revelation was forthcoming.

Soon, however, he realized George was correct. It was just a big jumble of incomprehensible sounds. Out of politeness, he waited until Yaxche finished reciting the complete tale, and then turned to George to acknowledge the researcher had been right all along.

But when he looked at George, he saw in his eyes what Yaxche must have seen in his grandson's eyes. A quick glance at Yaxche confirmed it.

Somehow, George had figured it out, too.

"What?" Michael demanded. His voice was a little too loud, and Humberto jerked his head and took a step toward them.

Raising his hands in a pacifying gesture, Michael said to the Cruzado, "Sorry. Everything is all right. We're just debating something. A scientific point."

With a grunt, Humberto eased himself back into his post, but he kept suspicious eyes fixed on the three of them.

Yaxche took a deep breath in anticipation of what George would say next. There was a pained look in the old man's expression, and Michael guessed that having not one, but two people understand something he did not, something that he was entrusted with, was difficult to accept.

"What is it?" Michael pressed.

"I wish I had a computer right now," George replied in a growl. He licked his lips. "I can't be a hundred percent, but I think I know the key to the secret, at least."

His eyes moved back and forth, as if scanning his own memory. "You know how, in grade school, when you wanted to remember something for a test, there were a number of mnemonic techniques you could use?"

"You mean like acronyms or acrostics?"

"Or rhymes or songs," George said. "In this case, I think the tale itself is a way to get the teller to remember the song itself."

Michael made a connection. "When Yaxche was telling us the tale, it did have a lyrical quality to it." He tried to quell his excitement, in case it drew Humberto to investigate. "You think we need to analyse the story as if it were a song?"

"Not for the lyrics, but for the melody. I think the story is just that: a story. It could probably be of any subject. It's simply there to help the keepers of the scroll remember the *melody*. There were certain parts of the tale where Yaxche's voice hit a certain note and used a particular inflection. I think that's important."

George turned to Yaxche and spoke very quickly in Spanish, summarizing his theory.

"Yes," Yaxche said in Spanish. "That is how I was taught the Song of the Stars. It is very important to sing those parts in the correct manner; to honor the gods."

"The Song of the Stars?" Michael asked. "That's the title of the story? I've never heard mention of this in any of the translations. It's not written on the scroll. Is it?"

"No," George said, "but then again, no one ever asked what the name of the story was." He let out a breathless laugh. "It's more than a lack of translation, it's about a lack of a common frame of reference."

"What do you mean?" Michael felt his face flush as he couldn't put the pieces together in his own mind.

"From Yaxche's cultural point of view, he must have assumed we would already know that the tale was in the form of a song. After all, that's how stories have been passed down from generation to generation. We have ballads that date back centuries.

"On the flip side, from our scientific point of view, we were so busy looking for measureable evidence in this document that we didn't take into account the one fact that was obvious from the start."

Michael still didn't make the connection. "And that is?"

"The song itself is a translation from another language. Not in the literal sense of the words on a page, but as a means of passing down the melody itself."

"Sonics," Michael said in a gasp. "When Macklin's Rock first reacted, the *Dis Pater* gave off cyclic wave emissions which corresponded with the changes in its light spectrum."

"Different notes on the musical scale can be charted by their compression waves," George said. "And although the difference between the wave-particles of light and the frequency in sound would be in the factor of, I don't know, a billion hertz or so, I think there is a solid correlation, and I think this is something a suitably advanced civilization—one that used computers—could program and calculate."

"We need to get you to a computer," Michael said in conclusion.

"And we need to record Yaxche's song in a sound room."

All the while the two of them talked, Yaxche looked back and forth between them. The look on his face was a mix of consternation and panic. He had no idea what they were talking about.

George, flicking his eyes up to make sure Humberto wasn't listening, said to the old Mayan, "We need to get you out of here and to safety."

"I am not concerned for my well-being," Yaxche said, making no effort to lower his voice. "But if you wish, I can show you a way out."

Michael cocked his head. "You know a way to escape this place?"

"Ahyah," Yaxche said. "My friend Humberto told me of it."

23

Lucis Observatory :
Venus Orbit :

The Mayan culture had always placed great significance in Venus, which they referred to as both the morning star and the evening star because it could be seen at either time.

As some of the most sophisticated astronomers of the time—and being a calendar-conscious and mathematical civilization—the Mayans had charted Venus's yearly cycles and discovered that five of Venus's years correlate almost exactly with eight Earth years. To them, this was an obvious sign of its link with Earth and proof that Venus itself was a deity. The Mayan people would time any of their great events, such as a war or the coronation of their leader, with the cycles of *Noh ek'*, their name for the sky god.

And so, when Terry first realized Klaus had set up his main base of operations on Venus, a part of him felt it was more than coincidence; it had to be some kind of divine influence.

From the moment Terry had joined the Cruzados, he had imagined that he had been chosen to spearhead a holy revolution, that he would singlehandedly restore the Mayan culture to the frontlines in the quest for interstellar progress. In his naive fantasy, the world would honour him as an ambassador for Earth once mankind had overcome the limitations of travel between the stars, and made first contact with the thousands of alien races who were waiting out there.

Terry had been taken in by the romantic notion of a holy crusade, with an army of Cruzados at his back.

Terry, however, had no idea how he was going to accomplish that, and after two days on the orbiting observatory, he began to give in to despair. Gradually, he realized that once he had handed the Song of the Stars to Jose and Klaus, his dream had begun to unravel bit by bit, and it looked more like a nightmare with each passing hour.

The Cruzados were not an honorable group. They did not have the ancient Mayan spirit in them. He was coming to understand that they were just another gang of disgruntled peasants and greedy opportunists who, in turn, had thrown in their lot with someone Terry could only describe as a madman—granted, one who certainly knew more about computers, Kinemet and astrophysics than most.

In one of the Lucis Observatory's workshops, Klaus Vogelsberg sat hunched over a haptic console. There were seven holoslates set up in a half-circle around him. Periodically, he would adjust an input or type in a series of commands.

Terry stood half a dozen steps to the side and waited. He had been relegated to the role of Klaus's personal servant, and though it grated on his pride, he knew he only had himself to blame.

There was one other person in the workshop. Jose watched as his partner in crime tended his programs. There was a look of dark concern on his face as he stared at the monitors, clearly unable to decipher what he saw.

"You've been at this for days. Are we any closer to the solution," Jose asked.

"Every minute that passes brings us closer," Klaus said sardonically.

"You know what I mean." Jose pointed across the room.

"He's the third, so far. At this pace, we will soon run out of lab rats. And every day we spend here increases our risk of being discovered."

Terry grimaced at the words, and couldn't help but look past the two men where Jose had pointed. Adjacent to the workshop was a lab, shielded with titanium and electromagnetically sealed. A wide pane of tinted glass—created with particles of titanium—allowed them to see inside the experiment area.

Strapped on a medical gurney, one of the captured American soldiers lay unconscious and naked. Dozens of sensors and leads were attached to his arms, chest and head.

Beside him was a tray on which rested one milligram of unshielded Kinemet—which Klaus had shaved with what had looked like an invisible saw. He had told Terry the beam was simply a non-reactive laser coupled with a chemical coolant, and that he required complete concentration to get the cut just right, "so kindly keep your mouth shut from now on, unless I ask you a question," he had said through gritted teeth at one point.

When Klaus didn't reply to his last statement, Jose said, "You promised us you could unlock the secret and give me complete control of space travel. That was the only reason we agreed to your terms. I wonder if you maybe overestimated your capabilities."

"There is always a measure of trial and error when conducting scientific experiments," Klaus replied evenly, speaking with much more patience to Jose than he had to Terry. "I assure you, I will have the proper sequence locked down very soon."

A moment later, however, he matched Jose's harsh tone. "And don't forget, the power will be ours together. You may have contributed men and the ancient scroll itself, but without my money and knowledge, you would still be sitting in a darkened warehouse making empty plans. We are *partners* in this."

A ripple of irritation passed over Jose's features, but he quickly reined in his emotions. "Very well, *partner*. If we are equals, then we should both know exactly what you are doing now."

"I'm not sure you would understand the scientific terminology."

Jose narrowed his eyes. "I have taken a few physics courses at university. I'm certain I can follow."

Klaus shrugged and turned back to his computer. He took a deep breath and seemed to debate his next words. "All right," he said finally. "We have a little time before we can measure our subject's reaction, anyway."

He called up a file and played one of the many animated presentations of the Kinemetic reaction which had peppered the EarthMesh newsfeeds over the past decade.

"Back when Quantum Resources was in its heyday, they used a bombardment of hydrogen photons to create a reaction in Kinemet; it caused the metal to convert into a quantum kinetic force. As a raw fuel, this works, but there's no control once it quantizes. Whatever is in proximity to its sphere of influence at the time of reaction gets quantized—turned into light. Any electrical impulse is neutralized. When the Kinemet stops reacting with the photons, and returns to solid state, all the electrical systems are disabled. Someone, or something, needs to kick start them, or you're adrift in space without light, heat … air."

"Yes," said Jose. "I know this much."

"Just making sure."

Klaus called up another animation. This one was watermarked with the NASA logo on the bottom right, the

Quantum Resources stamp on the bottom left, and the word 'Confidential' along the top. It was a conceptual recreation of Alex Manez's voyage to Centauri.

"Now," Klaus continued, "that problem is compounded. After rematerialization, there is a secondary reaction in the Kinemet, a nuclear fission, which causes the Kinemet to release its photons in an exothermic reaction—something like an atomic bomb. Why? Well, when you drop a rock in water, and it causes a temporary void, when the surrounding water rushes back in to fill that void, there's a splash. Energy is released. The splash is enough to cause the Kinemet to start reacting to itself. Instead of quantizing, it fissions, and this happens quite quickly.

"The 'pilot' is there to give the electrical generators a kick start, so the dampers can prevent the fission from occurring. In the case of the *Quanta,* the pilot was too slow to rematerialize, and that is why the ship exploded, and that's the problem they've been struggling with for the past few years. How to stop the bomb from exploding once the fuse is lit." He chuckled at the concept.

Jose asked, "So how does the ancient scroll fix that?"

"The problem is not with the Kinemet. The problem is with the pilot, or more specifically, the irradiation process to create a Kinemetic pilot. It's something far beyond the quantizing process, which in and of itself is biologically harmless.

"Alex Manez was exposed to the reacting Kinemet under unknown and uncontrolled circumstances, and was irradiated during that process. Among other things, he became electropathic—and gained the ability to manipulate those electronic dampers needed to stop the 'splash'—but there is something in him that failed to complete the change. He was unable to materialize in time, and the Kinemet exploded. The incomplete Kinemetic process also resulted in his deteriorating health and will be the cause of his inevitable demise.

"Unfortunately, no one has been able to reproduce the exact conditions that created Alex's new physiology. They tried photons from other elements like helium and the other noble gases, but that had no effect. The closest they came was to try to prime the Kinemet with a burst of ultraviolet rays. They were on the right path working in the electromagnetic spectrum, but their methodology was wrong—they didn't have the proper sequence to prime the Kinemet, and so the *Quanta* experiments continued to fail.

"Some pilots died moments after initial exposure in the lab environment. Two lived for a month before radiation poisoning killed them. Those were the earliest experiments. Five survived the process, but in the field they—like Alex— were unable to rematerialize quickly enough to engage the Kinemet dampers. Boom. Even though Alex somehow managed to survive the explosion on the *Quanta*, he is also considered a failed conversion.

"So now, the question remains: what is the correct process to create a Kinemetic pilot?"

Klaus pointed to the ancient scroll, which was resting at an angle on a nearby worktable. "You see, the Mayan document contains a key code, a sequence of sound waves which the computer can map to their particle-wave counterparts. We then bombard the Kinemet with that frequency before the quantizing process. Different frequencies—and combinations of frequencies—elicit disparate reactions in the element, conditioning it to give off a subtly different form of radiation." He shook his head. "It's an amazing element, and I'm certain it will take decades to chart every aspect."

Klaus turned in his chair to face Jose and drew in a deep breath. "So you see, I'm reproducing some of Quantum Resources failed experiments, but using the correct frequencies

I recorded from Terry's vocal rendition of the story to prime the Kinemet first. Of course, this is all assuming Terry recited the story exactly as his grandfather taught him—" Klaus glanced over at Terry, who stiffened at the implication that he had made any mistakes.

Klaus continued, "I've mapped the notes where he used particular inflections, and I'm hoping they provide the proper combination to unlock the puzzle."

"Hoping?"

"Well, it's been a millennium since the scroll was first written. Even if Terry recited the song exactly as he'd been taught, how can we know that every generation passed down the sequence without a single mistake? There are a few other dynamics to consider."

Jose took a few measured paces towards the window, as if he could see the internal changes in the soldier in the other room. "What are you telling me? How many uncontrolled factors are there?"

"I don't have complete records from Quantum Resources, so I have had to repeat some of their failures."

Jose ground his teeth. "How many more failures?"

There was a hint of a smile playing across Klaus's lips; it seemed he enjoyed tormenting Jose. "Quantum Resources underwent more than a dozen full trials, and established a number of constants. For the purposes of my trial, I've been using those confirmed results. There are still some variables in their tests, however, and once we get past candidate number three, here, I only have two more factors to account for, and then we will know whether Terry's rendition of the Song survived unchanged over the centuries."

Jose inhaled, then let his breath out in a slow hiss, as if to release the tension that had built up inside him. "Good. Then by all means, proceed." He turned back to the window to watch.

Klaus wrinkled his forehead in annoyance, but Terry was the only one to see the movement. There was obvious friction between the two partners, but Terry didn't know if he had the wit to use that against them.

He knew any action he took that made him look more disloyal at this point would most likely earn him a bullet. Now that he had given them what they wanted, the scroll and the song, they had no use for him outside of being Klaus's personal attendant. After Terry's behavior on the liner, Jose didn't trust him anymore and wouldn't allow him to even carry a gun.

For now, Terry would bite his lip, endure the heartache brought on by witnessing the inhuman experiments, and bide his time until he saw an opportunity to repair the wrongs for which he was responsible.

∞

They did not have to wait long until one of Klaus's monitoring programs let out a short alarm.

"Ah," Klaus said. "The sequence is now programmed into the computer. We can proceed with trial number three."

"How long will this take?" Jose asked. "When will we know if it worked?"

Without answering the question, Klaus punched in a command to his console. "Here we go. Now I'm bombarding the Kinemet with the thirty-two ultraviolet frequencies of photons in the prescribed order, and the sensors indicate the Kinemet is undergoing the transformation. All right, now for the main attraction: hitting it with hydrogen to start the quantization."

All three men looked up into the shielded room to see the Kinemet suddenly light up in a fashion similar to a magnesium flare. A moment later everything in the room turned into the same light. If not for the Kinemetic dampers in the other room, the Kinemetic radiation from a milligram of the element could conceivably quantize most of the Observatory, as Klaus had informed Terry earlier.

The entire lab room was filled with a brightness so sharp Terry had to put his hand up to protect his eyes. The sensors that had been attached to the soldier stopped transmitting data to Klaus's computers, since they were also affected.

"They've quantized," Klaus said by way of commentary. "During the Macklin's Rock incident, Alex Manez was exposed for approximately four hours. The actual length of time required could very well be four seconds, for all we know. Quantum Resources used the four hour marker as a constant, so I've been doing the same."

Jose, who also had his hand up between his eyes and the lab, asked, "So that's when we'll know?"

"We'll know if he is altered or not. Once the Kinemet has completed its process, everything in the room will return to a solid state, and then we can go in and take some readings on the subject. After that we'll perform a simple quantization procedure and see how quickly he rematerializes. Anything more than nine seconds is a failure; the pilot wouldn't have enough time to get his bearings and initiate the dampers."

Giving a nervous cough, Jose asked, "What about the 'splash' effect you mentioned?"

"There won't be any Kinemet left for a secondary reaction," Klaus said. "If they had only packed enough Kinemet for a one-way trip to Centauri, there would never have been any fission and the *Quanta* would never have exploded."

"So we're safe?"

"Yeah." Klaus typed a few more commands into the computer, and then spun around on his chair. "The lab is electromagnetically sealed. No one can get in or out. Meanwhile, I'm hungry. Time for something to eat."

∞

Before leaving, Klaus punched a key on one computer, and the window between the main workshop and the lab room grew darker, enough so that it was no longer physically uncomfortable to look directly at it. Of course, there was nothing to see beyond the glass other than a bright blur.

Following Klaus out the door, Jose ordered Terry, "You stay here. Make sure no one enters except us. Anyone else tries to get in here, send me an alert on the comlink." Almost as an afterthought, he added, "I'll bring you back a sandwich or something."

∞

Terry, who had remained stoic while the co-leaders were in his presence, let out a curse and punched his open hand with his fist in frustration once he was alone.

His anger was directed not only at Klaus, Jose and the Cruzados, but at himself for being such a sucker.

Everything he had done had been to honour Itzel, and to ensure what happened to her never happened to his people again.

And he was right at the center of it; he was the catalyst. If he hadn't run away from home like a petulant child; if he hadn't naively taken up with the Cruzados; and if he hadn't betrayed his grandfather by stealing the ancient scroll, none of this would have happened. How many people—innocent or not— had died because of Terry's actions? How many more would die?

In the past two days, Terry had been helpless to do anything but stand by as Klaus experimented on the American soldiers. Once he had determined the first subject had failed to change completely, Klaus ordered the victim taken out of his sight, and never followed up on his progress. Terry had never seen anyone with such a lack of remorse or conscience. Klaus was completely absorbed in his task, and didn't exhibit any signs that he cared who lived and who died in the pursuit of his goal.

One day, while eating lunch by himself, Terry had overheard some of the other Cruzados a table over talk about Klaus, and how he and his uncle had been the ones who had kidnapped Alex Manez a decade ago, and had been somehow betrayed by him.

Terry hadn't seen much of Captain Gruber. The man spent most of his time teaching the Cruzados combat techniques for ship-to-ship battles and how to fight inside space stations.

That last bit of information drove home the reality that Terry was part of an insurrection, rather than the liberation and rebirth of the Mayan culture he had dreamed of.

And it had only been possible because of him.

There had to be something he could do to stop them. But he knew he wasn't clever enough by far. He didn't know how to fight, and he was too transparent to become a politician and sway the Cruzados to his views.

He took a few measured paces towards the window of the lab, and he felt a pang of guilt knowing that the soldier inside would most likely endure hours, days, or weeks of agony before dying of Kinemetic exposure. He hadn't even found out what the soldier's name was.

His grandfather was most likely completely ashamed of Terry. He hoped the old man was all right. Jose had promised to keep him safe and secluded in case anyone from Quantum Resources or NASA tried to use him to figure out where the

Cruzados were and what they were doing. Terry realized now that they were, in effect, holding Yaxche hostage against Terry's continued cooperation.

It was a complete disaster. He probably couldn't have screwed things up any worse if he had planned it that way.

He pulled up a chair near the window and sat down to wait out the rest of his vigil. Although he wasn't the kind of person to give in to despair, he half-hoped the Kinemetic radiation might leak through the window somehow and permanently turn him into a being of light.

∞

A few hours later, Terry looked up when he heard footsteps out in the hall.

The workshop door opened and Jose entered the room.

"How is it going," Jose asked, and Terry shrugged.

"All right, I guess." Terry looked, but he didn't see a plate of food or even a bottle of water in Jose's hands. The Cruzados leader must have forgotten. Stomach rumbling, he said, "You mind if I take a break?"

Jose, stepping toward the window as if he could see what transpired within, waved his hand dismissively to Terry. "Sure. Be back in an hour, would you? That's when the experiment should be over. We'll find out if the price we paid is worth it."

∞

Before heading down to the mess hall, Terry stopped at the lavatory. Inside, he entered one of the stalls and sat down on a chrome toilet lid. He had no need to relieve himself, but just needed a few moments to pull himself together before facing any of the Cruzados.

They were all very rough men, raised in some of the most poverty-stricken regions of Mexico, Guatemala, El Salvador and Honduras. If Terry didn't act as tough as them, they would see it as an act of weakness. He had already lowered himself in their eyes by his protests on the liner. If he had any chance of getting out of his situation alive, at the very least he had to maintain whatever status he had left in the eyes of the Cruzados.

While gathering up his courage, Terry heard the washroom door open and two men entered. He recognized them by their voices. It was Klaus and his uncle, Captain Gruber. Making himself as still as could be, Terry waited for them to go about their business and leave.

The two men spoke in German, so Terry had no idea what they said, but their tones were full of menace.

Klaus said, *"Achten Sie darauf, Ihre Männer sind bereit. Ich werde Signal, wenn der Vorgang abgeschlossen ist. Sie wirst sie töten Jose und Terry."*

When Terry heard his name, the hairs on the back of his neck stood straight up, and he cursed himself for not being able to understand what was said.

In English, Captain Gruber asked, "What about the rest of the Cruzados?"

"I have enough evidence to convince them Jose was just using them for his own benefit; he was never a true believer. Don't worry about them; without a leader, those sheep will soon flock to my banner. —Oh, and if you can, make sure it looks as if it was Jose who killed Terry. Fuel for the fire."

After a moment, Gruber said, "Shouldn't be too hard."

"Soon, Uncle, we will finally take what Alex Manez promised but failed to deliver. I won't rest until that little brat is dead, too."

"You're late," Jose said in a reprimanding voice when Terry returned to the workshop. "The Kinemet has almost burnt out."

Klaus didn't look up from his computer. Captain Gruber stood off to the side, but the older man didn't look directly at Terry. His eyes, however, took everything in, and a chill ran down Terry's spine.

"Uh, sorry," Terry said and shrugged as Jose shot him a scathing look.

He tried to make sure none of the three other men in the room saw how his hands shook, how his breathing was ragged, or how hard his heart thumped in his chest. Almost, he had decided to run and find a hiding place somewhere in the observatory. He knew, however, that if he had, it would have only been a matter of time before they discovered him.

He was a dead man anyway. He knew it deep in his heart. Even if he returned to the lab, once the experiment was proved a success, Captain Gruber would murder him. After all that Terry had done, he felt he deserved it, and decided to face his destiny. If he was to die, at least he would die brave, instead of running like a coward.

"Not a moment to spare," Klaus said and motioned toward the other room.

The light inside the lab flared and suddenly extinguished, and Klaus retracted the window tinting.

Soon, everyone could see the soldier slowly rematerialize as thousands of tiny flashes of light coalesced and went out.

The entire transformation took less than six seconds, according to a timer display on one of the monitors, and Klaus stood up, obviously excited.

"Did it work?" Jose asked.

"I don't know," Klaus said, never taking his eyes off the soldier. "I need to revive him and run some tests. If he shows all the signs of a successful metamorphosis, then we can run him through a simulation and measure his reactions." He tapped a command, and an intravenous tube in the lab turned blue as some kind of stimulant was introduced into the subject's system.

Within moments, the solider stirred. His legs jerked as sensation and consciousness returned to him.

Through a microphone, Klaus called out, "Private Teegs, can you hear me?"

"Whass," the soldier said, his speech clearly not at full capacity. He licked his lips, forced his eyes opened and tried again. "What's going on? What happened?"

"How do you feel?" Klaus asked. "Can you describe the sensation?"

"I heard it," the young man said, voice filled with wonder. "It was a song. Haunting. It filled my head. It—"

Just then, his entire body shook with a convulsion. A look of panic spread across his face and his eyes bulged out. Veins popped up on his forehead and neck.

"What's happening to me?" he cried out.

Klaus spoke in a hard voice into the microphone. "Calm down. It's just an after-effect of the procedure. I assure you, you'll be fine."

But the man was anything but. Both Terry and Jose ran forward to look as another spasm took the soldier and he fell off the gurney to the floor.

Like a fish out of water, he writhed and twitched, all the while howling in agony. The imaging machine and medical monitors sparked as they were overloaded with electricity. Most fizzled and went dead, but one caught fire and popped with a couple of tiny explosions until the overhead sprinklers shot CO^2 into the room to smother the flames.

"You have to help him!" Terry shouted, looking over his shoulder.

There was no concern or empathy evident in Klaus's eyes; merely a look of disgust and frustration. "It's over."

"But he's dying."

Without replying to Terry, Klaus turned to his uncle and shook his head. Captain Gruber, who had looked as tense as a tiger ready to spring, relaxed visibly.

Jose, watching the soldier's final death throes, asked, "What now?"

"We'll have to clean up the lab, reset everything and try again tomorrow. Only one variable left; at least we'll have a fifty-fifty shot." With that, Klaus walked out of the workshop, his uncle following a few steps behind.

Terry turned to Jose. "We can't just stand here and do nothing. He's dying."

"He's already dead," the leader of the Cruzados said, his voice hard and steady. "Nothing we can do at this point."

Trying not to let Jose see the tears streaking down his face, Terry turned away from the window. His hands continued to shake.

If the soldier had lived, Terry would now be dead at the hands of Captain Gruber. Which was the more just outcome?

Terry remained alive, but now he had more death on his conscience.

"Sometimes," Jose said quietly, "I wonder if you are fully committed to our cause."

24

Unofficial Transcript :
Alex Manez Interview Part One :
Dated August 2103 :

Edgar: "Good morning, Alex. My name is Edgar Janz. I'm the assistant to the science advisor for USA, Inc.'s Board of Directors' oversight committee for Quantum Resources."

Alex: "Morning."

Edgar: "Did you have any questions before we begin? I've cleared the entire day, so there's no rush."

Alex: "I had hoped to be debriefed by Michael Sanderson."

Edgar: "I'm sorry, he's retired from Quantum Resources. I'm afraid his security clearance has been downgraded since then. Anything you speak to him about must be of a personal nature only."

Alex: "What about Captain Turner?"

Edgar: "*Major* Justine Turner is attached to the training facility at Kennedy Space Center. I'm sure you can arrange to speak to her after your debriefing. Are there any other questions I can answer for you?"

Alex: "I guess not."

Edgar: "Well rested after your trip to Honduras?"

Alex: "Yes, thank you. I'm sorry if that delayed your report."

Edgar: "I won't lie. There are a lot of people waiting to hear your story. It wasn't easy putting them off. But that isn't a big problem. I have a preliminary report I already submitted, but we need to verify some facts. Are you ready?"

Alex: "Yes."

Edgar: "Excellent. All right, let's do this. *Ahem.* This is the official debriefing of Captain Alex Manez, first human to travel to another solar system. It has been five days since his return to Earth. All medical and psychological tests have come back, and aside from the difference in his biological and chronological ages, Alex Manez has been given a clean bill of health. —Yes, Alex?"

Alex: "I've been a little achy since yesterday."

Edgar: "Uh. I'm sure that's just an after-effect of all the traveling. The doctors cleared you."

Alex: "All right."

Edgar: "Good. Now, can we start at the beginning? Can you describe your experience traveling in a quantized state?"

Alex: "For me it was instantaneous. I didn't experience anything. One moment I was here; the next moment I was there."

Edgar: "I'm going to ask you a series of questions. They might seem repetitive or obvious, but this is for the benefit of the oversight committee. I would like to start with the events leading up to the explosion of the *Quanta*."

Alex: "Of course."

Edgar: "Was there power in the ship when you first materialized in Centauri System?"

Alex: "No there wasn't."

Edgar: "According to pre-flight experiments this was expected. Just for the record, can you explain why?"

Alex: "Of course. There were two separate quantities of Kinemet on the ship. One for each leg of the trip. As I understand it, the Kinemet that had been primed with photons would burn out just as I arrived in Centauri. The second load, which had not been primed, was merely quantized as was every other substance on the ship. The astrophysicists determined that once the non-charged Kinemet rematerialized, it would re-react with its own photons and cause a secondary reaction. Without applying a coolant, it would reach critical mass and undergo a nuclear fission."

Edgar: "And this is why there is a need for a human pilot at this point, correct?"

Alex: "Yes. Assuming I would be rematerialized as well, my only task was to restart the onboard electrical systems. I merely had to turn on a generator, which would return electrical power to the ship. The onboard computer would then initiate the Kinemetic dampers and interrupt the second load of Kinemet before it reacted."

Edgar: "And was there a problem preventing you from sparking the generator?"

Alex: "Yes. The ship had turned solid, but I remained in a semi-quantized state and was unable to physically grab the pull ring to charge the generator."

Edgar: "Do we know why you didn't fully return to a physical form?"

Alex: "One of the analysts surmised the longer a biological entity was in a quantized state, the longer the transition to a normal corporeal form."

Edgar: "Do you agree with this theory?"

Alex: "No."

Edgar: "Uh … Alex. I don't have anything in my notes about your disagreeing with that assumption."

Alex: "I know."

Edgar: "Well, what do you think is the reason?"

Alex: "I believe I have not been fully transformed into a Kinemat. I am an aberration. I didn't know this before the trip, but I do now. We need to stop thinking about using Kinemet for light-speed travel and start examining its other properties before more people end up like me."

Edgar: "Will you excuse me a moment, Alex?"

Alex: "Of course."

Edgar: "I just need to make a call."

∞

Edgar: "Hello, Alex. Sorry that took so long. I hope you're comfortable."

Alex: "They served me an early lunch."

Edgar: "Good. I've been instructed to strike your last comment from the official record and concentrate on the actual verifiable events only. Please restrict your answers to facts rather than conjecture."

Alex: "All right."

Edgar: "Where were we? Right. There was a delay between when the *Quanta* rematerialized and when you returned to physical form."

Alex: "Yes. But during that short time, I was conscious and aware of where I was. I was halfway between light and matter."

Edgar: "And how long, exactly, were you in this transitional phase?"

Alex: "It was about eight or ten seconds before I brought myself back to material form. It's hard to judge."

Edgar: " 'Brought yourself?' Alex. I have nothing in my records stating that you brought yourself back."

Alex: "I know."

Edgar: "Did you tell anyone this before?"

Alex: "Of course, but they think it was just my imagination, or my memory playing tricks. Did you need to leave the room again?"

Edgar: "No. Let's just skip that last part for now."

Alex: "All right."

Edgar: "So you rematerialized. How long did you have before the ship exploded?"

Alex: "Just a few seconds. I wasn't thinking straight, and tried to pull the kick starter ring."

Edgar: "But … I thought that's what you were supposed to do."

Alex: "It didn't have any effect. I tried to tell them before we left. The generator needed more of a boost to get started than a simple pull cord—being quantized for that amount of time, the electrical system was weakened. I had to use my electropathic ability to start the generator."

Edgar: "Electropathic ability? What is that? Alex, I'm not sure I can report any of this. My record and your story doesn't match up. I have nothing here that says anything about this."

Alex: "I'm sure they'll edit the parts they don't want to hear."

Edgar: (coughing sound)

Alex: "Okay … the generator started, but it was too late to start the dampers."

Edgar: "It was too late?"

Alex: "There was only about a second or so left before the Kinemet reached critical mass, and the coolant required at least four seconds."

Edgar: "How did you survive the blast?"

Alex: "Well, the automatic capsule ejector launched the cockpit just as the *Quanta* silently burst into fragments of light."

Edgar: "All right. That's what I have in my report as well. What happened next?"

Alex: "I was a little stunned by the escape, and I was dazed. After a few minutes, I realized I was stranded more than forty-trillion kilometers from home with no way back, and I started to panic."

Edgar: "That's understandable."

Alex: "All traces of the *Quanta* were gone. The capsule only had about a week's supply of oxygen and food. I … felt completely alone."

Edgar: "What happened next?"

Alex: "I instructed the shipboard sensors to scan the vicinity for trace electromagnetic vibrations. The ship's spectrographic analyzer picked up a signal."

Edgar: "The signals were similar to those emitted by the artifact in our solar system, the *Dis Pater?*"

Alex: "Yes. The computer calculated it was a little over twenty-thousand kilometers away."

Edgar: "Then what?"

Alex: "I programmed the navigation system to fly to it."

Edgar: "Based on the calculations you provided, at the capsule's top speed, it would take a little over a month to get there."

Alex: "Correct."

Edgar: "You only had a week's worth of oxygen and food. So how did you survive the trip?"

Alex: "I put myself back into a quantized state."

Edgar: "You put—? Alex, there are significant discrepancies between my reports and what you are telling me. I'm not sure we can continue until I get this straightened out."

Alex: "I tried to tell the analysts, but no one believed me."

Edgar: "We'll continue this debriefing tomorrow. Right now I need to get to the bottom of this."

25

Lucis Observatory :
Venus Orbit :

Justine had never been more frightened in all her life. She had never fully experienced the acute isolation and helplessness of being blind like she did now.

When she had first lost her sight on Pluto, she had run the full gamut of emotions on the six-month voyage home: anger and frustration, denial and false hope, depression and finally acceptance.

During the trip home, however, she had never once feared for her life. The entire ship's crew had been as supportive and accommodating as anyone could be. NASA had kept in constant communication with her and made arrangements for her optilink surgery upon her arrival back on Earth.

For those first six months, she had begun to compensate for her blindness in a natural way, relying more on her other senses: hearing, touch and smell. After the surgery, even though she had adjusted to life as a blind person, her visual prosthetics had been a huge crutch for her. The only time she was without technological aid was in the comfort and safety of her apartment. The sensory skills she had begun to cultivate over that first half a year had never fully developed.

Now, she had no time to expand her natural abilities and compensate for her loss of sight. Her current situation was indeed dire, and her life was in very real danger.

The Cruzados had shown their complete disregard for life by experimenting on the captured members of the security squadron, and Justine was more than helpless; she was an added burden on the remaining soldiers, and on Clive.

She was relieved and more than grateful to have him with her. As if she were a toddler, he hovered over her day and night. From helping her navigate to the lavatory, to ensuring she was able to eat the tray dinners their captors brought in, to holding her hand whenever there was a sharp unexpected sound; Clive never left her side. Justine knew he had to be going through his own emotional journey, and the shame of putting the burden of her wellbeing on him filled her with guilt and despair.

…And anger.

She had been a commissioned officer of the United States Air Force, the decorated captain of a NASA space vessel. She had traveled to Pluto and been on the team that discovered evidence of alien cultures in the galaxy. And here she was, hiding in a darkened room, barely able to care for herself, and fearing for her life.

There were others in her group who were far worse off.

When she had realized Private Jackson was the Cruzados' first attempt at creating a Kinemetic pilot, she was outraged.

That outrage quickly turned to horror when the young man went into spasms and cried out in agony as his body began to die from radiation poisoning.

Over the next three hours, he developed an angry rash that turned first red, then black, as Clive described to her in a very low and somber tone. The private's skin bubbled with melanomas, and he continuously secreted bloody pus from all of his orifices. At the end, he could barely summon the strength to moan before he finally died. Justine could still recall the wretched sounds the poor man made; they haunted her.

Dormant Kinemet carried extremely little risk to humans. The minimal radioactivity it gave off was considerably less than getting a medical X-ray.

Kinemet reacted differently to other forms of radiation. Once it was bombarded with hydrogen photons, it quantized and became an extremely powerful fuel source.

Justine knew, from reading some of the briefing reports, that Quantum Resources had experimented with ultraviolet radiation and Kinemet. When exposed to this combination, humans exhibited symptoms similar to Alex Manez's: a few of the subjects who had volunteered for the experiment reported a heightened sensitivity to any electronic field in their area; they seemed to experience a kind of heightened perception, as if they were dislocated from their corporeal bodies; and they described a high-pitched sound that permeated their hearing. It was like a ringing in the ears, if the ringing changed pitch on a random basis.

They also exhibited classical symptoms of radiation poisoning, and died of rapid mutagenic melanoma. The same melanoma that the private exhibited.

The remaining members of the security detail kept a silent vigil while Private Jackson died a painful death. Over the next thirty-six hours, two more soldiers were taken.

Private Anderson was the next subject; he was gone for ten hours, and when they brought him back, he seemed physically unaltered, except that he was completely catatonic, and had to be force-fed by one of his fellow servicemen. His condition worsened, and though he displayed no physical symptoms, he was dead for an hour before they realized it.

Private Teegs was missing from the room before Justine had woken up that morning.

The soldiers had largely grown silent with despair.

Lieutenant Jeffries made his best effort to boost their morale, but no one laughed when he cracked jokes, no one responded when he tried to make idle conversation, and he had no takers when he attempted to start a few parlor and word games. He gave up trying after a few hours, and the entire group settled into a general atmosphere of malaise.

The injustice of it all made Justine simultaneously want to rage against her circumstances, and curl into a little ball in the corner and cry until she ran out of tears.

Justine did neither, however. She was determined to put on a brave face, despite her handicap, and try to think her way out of this situation. A kernel of thought had gestated in her mind over the past few days, and if she could only concentrate hard enough, she might come up with a solution.

The only comfort Justine found, as they passed the anxious hours, was being as close as possible to Clive. The two of them found a spot a little way off from the others to get some semblance of privacy. Backs against a wall, they both sat with their legs touching. Justine folded her hands in Clive's and leaned her head against his shoulder.

"I'm so sorry to get you involved in all this," he said to her quietly.

"Nonsense." She clucked her tongue. "It's not your fault."

"Maybe, but I feel responsible just the same." Clive reached an arm around her and pulled her close, tucking her safely to his side. "We all feel like there should be something we could have done differently. Second-guessing is part of being human."

"And so is speculation," Justine said.

"How's that?"

"I've been so scared over the past few days my brain feels like it's been dipped in molasses."

"Not to mention lack of proper sleep," Clive said. "I would

kill for a mattress or even a blanket. I think my hip bone is going to come right through my skin."

Justine patted his hand. "Do you get the sense that there's something we're missing in all this?"

"Like what?"

She thought about it for a moment. "Well, up until a week ago, I had never heard of the Cruzados movement. No one was forewarned about this uprising until they stole the old Mayan scroll. Since then, somehow, they've managed to infiltrate Canada Station Three, hijack the *Diana* and bring us to Venus. I mean, they've obviously been here at the observatory for some time, setting things up. From the briefing I received in Houston, the authorities didn't really think the Cruzados were a serious threat."

"And what do you make of that?" he asked.

"First of all, if they didn't think the Kinemet was at risk, why move it to Luna? Why not just put it on a military base?"

She felt Clive shift. He said, "Perhaps they thought moving the Kinemet was a preemptive measure. Remove temptation and all that. Like you said, no one thought the Cruzados had spread beyond Central America."

"Then why on a commercial liner? Why not on a military transport?"

"That was the first plan," he said. "However, a few hours before take-off, the rocket developed some kind of computer glitch. It would have been days before it was repaired."

"Still," Justine said with an edge to her voice, "there's something more going on here than we've seen."

"How so?" he asked.

"I don't think the Cruzados are the only threat here."

"Uhm—" Clive started to interject.

"No, listen," she said, holding up a finger to illustrate her point. "Honduras doesn't have a space program at all. Even the nearest spaceport is Mexico City. There has to be someone else behind the Cruzados. It can't just be a grassroots historical preservation movement. Someone has supplied them with arms and training. Someone got them to Canada Station Three. Someone set things up here on Venus. This whole thing had to have been planned for months, or even years. And—"

Justine fell silent as the missing piece of information came to her. A hundred thoughts bombarded her, and she struggled to make sense of it. She stood up suddenly, as if the motion would clear her head.

A moment later, Clive got to his feet. "What?"

"They had to have inside information and help." Justine tapped a finger against her lower lip.

Clive scoffed. "How would that be possible?"

"Someone has to be using the Cruzados as a cat's paw," Justine said. "They can't have the resources or information to pull this off."

She had spoken loud enough that Lieutenant Jeffries and the others heard.

Corporal Marks, sitting across the room, asked, "Then who would have the resources?"

With a quick tilt of her head, Justine said, "At this point, it could be any of the major country corporations. USA, Inc. and Canada Corp. haven't been keen on sharing the tech, hedging against the future. World resources are strained; one of the country corporations might be getting desperate enough to make a play. They might think they can do a better job, or they might have been doing their own research all along and thought they'd made a breakthrough which we overlooked."

Lieutenant Jeffries said, "If that's the case, they've been playing it pretty close to the vest. I haven't heard anything through military channels."

"I'm on the mesh all the time," Corporal Marks added. "If

an entire country corp. were making this kind of move, no one's made a peep about it."

"Then who?" Justine wondered out loud. "They had to have someone who could pilot the liner. Someone who knew the Kinemet would be on the flight, and according to Clive that was a last-minute decision."

With one hand lightly touching a wall, she stood up and began to pace. "Maybe if we work backwards," she said. "I know it's a wild shot, but if we can figure out who might have pulled the strings, maybe we can make the connection."

Corporal Marks asked, "Do you think it might be someone in Lunar Lines?"

Shaking her head, Justine said, "I found out about the shipment the morning of the flight from Director Mathers. He's been with the company for almost twenty years. He's a family man, a decent guy. I can't believe he had any part in this. What about you?" she asked the soldiers. "When did you find out about the mission?"

Lieutenant Jeffries said, "I was called in for a briefing by Colonel Gagne the day before. He told us he'd received the request for a security squad from NASA that morning. The decision to move the Kinemet had been made only moments after we found out about the theft of the Mayan scroll. The way everyone was scrambling, it was all news to the military. I wasn't even aware there had been another ship involved."

"Well," said Justine, "none of this explains anything. It's obvious someone higher up is involved. Someone with access to both the military and NASA."

"I have a question," said Corporal Marks. "And I really hope this isn't out of line, ma'am."

"Go ahead, Corporal."

"Why you?"

For a moment, the question caught Justine off guard. "What

do you mean, why me?"

"Well, pardon me for saying so, but the only factor that doesn't make sense is why they chose you to accompany us. I've been on two missions in conjunction with Lunar Lines in the past year; we've never had an attendant assigned to us before. We've always sent a private up to get food. And, no offense, ma'am, but why would the military request someone with a handicap as part of an important operation like this?"

Lieutenant Jeffries cleared his throat. "That'll be enough, Corporal."

Justine fought to control the flush of heat that rose to her cheeks. "I certainly hope you don't think I had any part in this? I'll have you know I have dedicated my life to NASA. I've—"

"That's not what I'm saying." Corporal Marks sounded clearly uncomfortable. "But if you remember, Lieutenant, even Colonel Gagne sounded bewildered that we were assigned an attendant at all. The request must have come from NASA itself."

Justine barked out a hollow laugh. "It's nothing so nefarious as that. Clive is the NASA liaison. He just thought it was an opportunity for us to spend some time together. Right?" she asked Clive, turning her head in the direction she thought he would be.

But he didn't reply to her question. Justine, unable to see, felt a sharp needle of panic at his lack of response.

"Clive?"

"That'll be quite enough of this," he said finally, but his voice came from the far side of the room. "Everyone stay where you are."

Justine shook her head. "What's going on?" she demanded.

It was in a low, steady voice that Lieutenant Jeffries said, "He has an ion pistol."

"A gun? —Clive, what's going on?"

But then, the pieces of the puzzle fell into place. Her mind screamed that she was wrong; that she'd leapt to the wrong conclusion. She didn't want it to be true. How could it?

"You arranged everything?" she said in a gasp. "No, you can't be part of this. It's a mistake. It has to be."

She took a step in the direction of his voice, but Lieutenant Jeffries' firm hand held her back.

"Clive, tell them they're wrong."

She heard a vigorous knock from the inside of the lab door. "You weren't supposed to know until it was all over, and we had the power," Clive said, his voice harsh and angry.

"The hijacking … the experiments!" Justine could not fathom any reason why Clive would be involved in such a heinous conspiracy. A man she had begun to love. She had opened her heart to him. "No, I can't believe you had a hand in this. It's treason. It's murder!"

"It was necessary," he said, and Justine heard him knock on the door again, this time harder. "NASA is filled with bureaucrats and politicians, more worried about their funding than about progress."

Lieutenant Jeffries growled. "How long have you been working against us?"

"Since the beginning," he said. "Every time the news announces massive layoffs, or higher taxes, or government corruption, it makes it easier to see what needs to be done. People are tired of having their lives run by faceless corporations who don't care about them."

"Clive!" Justine still couldn't wrap her mind around it. "You've been lying to me all this time?"

"Not about us," he said. "It's not too late, Justine. You can come with me. You were there at the beginning. The world needs to unite under one banner, one power. You can be part of that."

"You're insane!" Justine screamed, and Lieutenant Jeffries could not hold her back as she lunged towards Clive's voice.

She heard Clive yell, "Get back, all of you!" and then the electric whir of the ion pistol.

Someone beside her screamed, and she barely registered it as she collided with Clive. Not thinking about what she was doing, she lashed out at him in an attempt to knock the gun out of his hand. He was stronger than she was, and he was not blind. It was all too easy for him to disable her, grabbing her arms and pushing her to the ground.

Another heavy body crashed into the two of them, and they all fell in a tangle, Justine pinned beneath them. She heard someone grunt as a punch connected.

With her feet, she tried to push herself out from under them, all the while flailing about with her hand, trying to locate the ion pistol.

Just as she felt the metal of the nozzle, and tried to grab for the handle, the gun was pulled from her grip.

There was another whirring sound, and then the two fighters were no longer in motion.

Justine heard the sounds of the three other soldiers rushing over to help their lieutenant.

Justine, her head ringing from the fight, reached out and, in a ragged voice, demanded of anyone, "What's happening?"

A voice, thick and deliberate, answered, "Justine."

"Clive?" Her fingers touched the fabric of his jacket, and she squeezed her hands around his arms.

"It was supposed to be you and me until the end. I made a place for us in the new regime. I'm so sorry," he said, and let out a wet cough. And then he spoke no more.

She moved her hands up to his chest and felt the warm spread of blood running from a gaping wound. A sob came out of her, and her eyes stung from the sudden tears that flowed down her cheeks.

Corporal Marks spoke from just off to the side. "Someone help me get Lieutenant Jeffries up. He'll be fine. Just knocked out."

Her mind threatened to close in on itself. There was too much happening in too little time. It was as if she could hear the sound of her heart breaking.

"Clive," she gasped out, calling to the memory of the man she thought he was; not the man he turned out to be.

"You," Corporal Marks ordered to one of the soldiers, "see if Miss Turner's all right."

The soldier—Justine couldn't tell who—gently drew her away from Clive's dead body and pulled her to her feet.

"It's over now," he said in a soft, consoling voice.

Grief, fresh and raw, swelled inside her, and Justine let out another cry, and buried her head in the unknown soldier's shoulder.

Before anyone had time to catch their breath, though, a new voice permeated the room.

"That will be quite enough of that. Put the gun down, Corporal, or my men will open fire."

Justine heard the sound of boots on the floor as a number of men entered the room.

"Thank you. Now if you would all be so kind as to move back to the other wall, we can sort this out."

The newcomer had a slight, somewhat familiar accent. Justine's mind, hit by too many revelations and too much emotional pain at once, was muddy and slow to respond. She didn't move from where she stood.

"What's going on? Who are you?" she asked meekly.

"Major Justine Turner," the man said. A moment later, she could smell his hot breath as he stepped in close to her. "Do you not remember me?" he asked. "We never met, but I'm sure if you think about it, you'll figure it out."

"Klaus Vogelsberg!" she gasped. "You? You were behind this? Why?"

"Your golden boy promised me something, and I mean to collect it. Now that we no longer need you to keep Clive happy, you can help us next."

"What do you mean by that?"

To the Cruzados, he said, "Bring her."

She heard the American soldiers protest, but the sound of rebel guns raised into position stopped them.

Rough hands grabbed her shoulders and pulled her out of room.

26

Ruiz Plantation :
Copan Departmental, Honduras :
Central American Conglomeration :

It was all Michael could do not to choke on his coffee. "Humberto?"

George swatted him on the arm. "Not so loud."

But it was loud enough for the large Cruzado to hear. Shooting the three guests a dark frown, Humberto quickly shortened the distance between them.

He kept his voice low and spoke in English, but it was edged with warning. "It is important you continue to act the gracious guests of Señor Ruiz. Do nothing suspicious. I will tell you when it is safe to move. Perhaps tomorrow; perhaps not." It was the most Humberto had ever spoken to them at once.

Michael opened his mouth to ask a question, but Humberto silenced him with another look of warning. He then moved back to his post at the patio steps, narrowed eyes scanning the fields of the plantation dutifully.

Clearing his throat in an obvious way, George lifted his coffee cup. "I think I'll have one more, and then maybe we can have a look around the house. I thought I spotted an art gallery of sorts at the other end of the main hall."

When he got Michael's attention, George pulled on one ear lobe and flicked his eyes at the manservant who was hovering just inside the house—the servant glanced over at them, and then quickly looked away. Michael got the message.

He nodded and moved his own coffee cup closer. George poured for both of them. He then motioned to Yaxche's cup.

Giving a small shake of his head, Yaxche stood and excused himself. "It is almost time for my morning game of checkers with Alondo, the cook," he said in Spanish. "He can only play one game before he must go back to the kitchen. Either of you are more than welcome to come and play a game after, if you have nothing better to do today."

Michael answered Yaxche. "Thank you. That sounds good. I look forward to it."

With a pleasant smile and an unconcerned gait, the old man ambled off to find the cook.

Michael watched him go, his thoughts racing in every direction, but he schooled himself to remain outwardly calm. Pouring a small amount of cream into his coffee and adding a teaspoon of sugar, he sipped his drink slowly.

Trying to be as casual as possible, he scanned the area around them. There were three patrols of two Cruzados roaming the grounds outside the house. Inside the big windows, he saw several servants cleaning up the breakfast dishes. Everywhere he looked, there was someone who could overhear anything he said. Most likely, their conversation with Yaxche had already been reported.

"We need somewhere to talk."

George grimaced. "Yeah. Harder to do than to say, though. As gracious as our host has been, I don't think giving his hostages any level of privacy is high on his list of priorities."

Michael continued to look around, but he couldn't think of anything they could do that wouldn't raise suspicion. Humberto, while maintaining his proximity, pointedly looked away from them. Obviously, he was one of those people who would not say anything until he was good and ready to do so.

George leaned in slightly. "Let's just bide our time. We can't do anything about it without more data anyway. And I don't think Señor Ruiz would be so accommodating as to give me access to a computer with an uplink to Quantum Resources." He barked out a dry laugh at the thought. "Meanwhile, it might make it easier if we pretended we were on vacation."

Raising one eyebrow, Michael said, "Vacation? This is the weirdest vacation I've ever been on. I don't think I'm going to recommend it to any of my friends."

∞

Michael almost went crazy from the waiting.

As a man who had spent the majority of his life in a position of authority, he was used to getting constant updates and progress reports from those who worked under him. He was also accustomed to having people answer him when he asked questions.

The few times Michael tried to extract information from Humberto, the most he could get out of the Cruzado was a monosyllabic response and a dark look of warning.

Michael was not used to subterfuge. A straightforward man, biding his time wore on his nerves. He had trouble sleeping, and the next morning he was slow to wake, and was very groggy.

There was only so much they could do to pass the time. They wandered around the house and admired Oscar Ruiz' collection of art and handcrafted furniture. Careful of the hot sun, they sat out on the patio and lost innumerable games of checkers to Yaxche.

They didn't see Oscar the rest of the day. When questioned, one of the servants said he had several plantations and could be at any one of them.

All the while, they were under the watchful eyes of half a dozen Cruzados who were posted in and around the household. Though Humberto was one of them, he rarely spoke to any of the rebels.

The day took forever to pass, and that night, despite being overwhelmingly tired, it took Michael hours to finally nod off to sleep.

His mind was whirling in a hundred different directions. How would the discovery of the Song of the Stars change Kinemet? Of course, he would ensure Quantum Resources was involved at every stage of development; but with the world economy so tight, and public interest in space programs at an all time low, would NASA and the CSA re-open their *Quanta* programs? Would this discovery help to heal Alex?

∞

"Wake up!" a voice whispered very close to his ear. At first, Michael flicked his hand at the disturbance, as if one of the many flies buzzing around the room had found a way under the mosquito netting hanging over his bed.

There was a gentle nudge on his shoulder, and Michael snapped awake. It was the black of night, and only a vague light from the crescent moon outside illuminated the room to any degree. A shape loomed near him, and he quickly identified George as the person who had roused him.

"What?" he asked, his mouth still dry from sleep.

"It's Humberto. He said we need to move now."

Swinging his legs over the side of the bed, Michael untangled himself from the netting and slipped on his shirt. "I'm ready. Let's go."

In the hall, Humberto and Yaxche were waiting. The old

man rubbed one eye and smiled a greeting.

Humberto spoke in English, and George translated for Yaxche.

"Make no sound," the Cruzado said. "Señor Ruiz is still away, and half the guards are sleeping, as are the household servants. The entire perimeter of the plantation is wired with an electric fence. I have arranged for my cousin to 'accidentally' drive his jeep into one section. Several of the guards have gone to investigate. You will make your way through the rows of coffee plants to the other side of the property—I showed Yaxche the trail. I left an unregistered truck behind a large group of trees off the road, hidden from view. It has a full tank of gas, enough to get you to Santa Rosa de Copán; it is a little over one hundred kilometers from here. I left a map."

"Wait," Michael said. "You're not coming with us?"

"No. They will find me downstairs in the main hall. I will be unconscious from a blow to the head by one of Señor Ruiz's very heavy and priceless vases."

"How will that happen?" George asked.

"You will have to do it," Humberto said, and turned to lead them toward the stairs.

Michael grabbed him by the shirt. "Why are you helping us?"

Clenching his jaw, he answered, "Because I believe in our cause; I just do not think our leaders believe in our cause. They believe in money and power. Once they are removed, the Cruzados will once more stand for what is right and just."

George whispered. "Come with us. With your inside knowledge, you could assist the authorities directly."

Humberto leaned closer to them. "I will not betray the movement; only correct it. Taking hostages was wrong. There are many of us who feel the same, and soon we will act."

Michael said, "Our liaison in the capital is John Markham;

he's with the Canadian Embassy. You can trust him. If you can get information to him, he may be able to help you overthrow your leaders."

Humberto paused, as if considering. He nodded, finally, and then turned to Yaxche. Putting his hand on the old man's shoulder, he said, "Do not be too disappointed in your grandson. His heart was blinded by memory of a loved one. He, too, can be saved."

∞

George was reluctant to hit Humberto over the head with the vase, and when he passed the artifact to Yaxche, the old man scrunched up his shoulders and shook his head.

Sighing with resignation, Michael took the vase from George and eyed Humberto. "Are you sure about this?"

"Yes. You only need to swing hard enough to break the vase, not my skull. When I hear them approach, I will pretend to regain consciousness."

Lining up his shot, Michael swung the ceramic at Humberto, who braced for the impact. As it turned out, he didn't hit hard enough, and the vase remained intact. Humberto, however, stumbled forward a step and rubbed at the back of his head, wincing. He shot a perturbed look at Michael, but instead of bracing for a second blow, he yanked the vase out of Michael's hands and threw it on the tile floor.

It smashed spectacularly.

Still touching the tender part of his head, Humberto said, "At least I'll have a nice bump there to show them. Good enough." Looking back and forth between Michael and George, he slowly got down on his knees. "They'll be back soon. You had better be off. I've cleared the path, so you shouldn't need to use any more light than what the moon gives off."

With a final look at the three of them, Humberto sank to his belly and lay down.

"Good luck," Michael said to him, and the three men hurried out the back way and into the coffee fields.

∞

As if he had walked the path a thousand times, Yaxche marched at an even pace down through the rows of flowering coffee shrubs in Oscar's plantation.

Although Michael wanted to hurry the old man, he appreciated the surefootedness of their guide, and made his best effort to follow Yaxche's footsteps exactly.

They were most of the way to the tree line when they heard a distant shout coming from the main house.

Michael's first reaction was to run, but he caught himself when he almost ran over Yaxche, who had come to a complete stop.

"What is it?" he asked. "They've figured out we're gone. They'll be after us."

Yaxche turned around slowly. After listening to George repeat Michael's words in Spanish, he replied in a very quiet voice. "Ahyah. We must wait here."

Michael opened his mouth to ask what for, but Yaxche raised his arm and pointed to one of the trees near him. At first, he couldn't see what Yaxche was pointing at, but then he saw a brief silhouette of some kind of small animal jumping from one branch to another directly over their path.

As if it spotted something amiss, it paused and scanned the surrounding forest for signs of danger.

"Monkey," George said in a breathless whisper. "If we spook him, he'll howl like a banshee."

Michael couldn't make out what kind of monkey it was, and he didn't want to get any closer to find out. Silently, he prayed the little primate would go on its merry way.

More lights flicked on from the main house, and the shouts grew louder. The monkey stood up straighter, hearing the sounds, alert for danger.

Holding his breath, Michael waited an eternity before the monkey decided to get as far away from the disturbance as possible. Letting out a short chittering sound, it leapt into the branches of the next tree and scooted off.

George, who was also holding his breath, let it out with a whoosh. "That was close," he said.

His words startled a second monkey they had not spotted.

It screeched in alarm, shook a tree branch, and then raced after the first monkey.

Several flashlights from the main house turned in their direction, and before Michael could duck, the beam passed over him. One of the Cruzados hollered a command in Spanish, and the entire group broke towards them.

"Go!" Michael barked out. "Run!"

Yaxche looked to be a man in his late seventies or early eighties, Michael was in his late sixties, and George was well into his fifties. The men who chased them were much younger, and would soon catch up.

Even though they had a head start, the road where Humberto had stowed the truck was at least a kilometer away. By the time the three men stumbled through the copse of trees, the Cruzados were almost on top of them.

Making painful sounds as he tried to catch his breath, George took a quick look over his shoulder to check the distance between them and their pursuers. He promptly lost his balance and tumbled to the ground, crying out in pain as he twisted his knee.

The lead Cruzado yelled, *"¡Alto!"*

Michael reached down to help pull his friend back up. Gasping for air, George shook his head. "I'm done!"

"Bullshit!" Michael said. "Get up!"

With a grimace that showed he was in excruciating pain, George tried to get to his feet.

There was a loud snapping sound, and George abruptly looked up at Michael in surprise. At first, Michael thought he might have broken his leg, but then he saw a shadow spreading out from George's white shirt. It looked black in the darkness of the woods, but the metallic smell of blood wafted up.

"My wife…" was all George managed to say before he fell back to the forest floor.

"George!" Michael said, and tried in vain to pull his dead body back up.

A firm hand grabbed his arm. *"¡Vamos!"* Yaxche said.

Michael couldn't think. He was frozen by the shockingly sudden killing. George had been his friend for over a decade, both when they had worked together, and when Michael had retired.

There had been no reluctance or second thoughts when he'd agreed to join Michael's expedition to Honduras. George, ever-curious, ever-helpful, was dead.

When the two of them had been captured by the Cruzados, it had been a frightening few days, but at the back of his mind, Michael never really thought their lives were in imminent peril.

It was Michael's fault. He had dragged George halfway around the world only for him to be murdered in a jungle.

Before his grief could consume him, Michael heard a sharp whistling sound as a bullet sped past his head and splintered a tree branch.

Yaxche grabbed his arm with both hands and shook him. *"Prisa,"* he said, and Michael's paralysis broke.

They were only a few dozen meters from the road. Though he hated himself for leaving George's body behind, Michael knew he and Yaxche would most likely join him in death if they tarried.

Trying to block out thoughts of his friend, Michael hurried down the makeshift trail after Yaxche. Another shot rang out, and Michael ducked. He felt a tug at his shirtsleeve as the bullet narrowly missed him.

There were angry shouts behind him, but Michael couldn't make out any of what they were yelling.

Quelling the blinding panic that tried to seize him, Michael scrambled up the embankment at the main road and quickly scanned for the copse of trees Humberto had mentioned.

He pointed. "There!" Pulling Yaxche alongside him, he raced across the dirt road.

By the time they got to the patch of trees, the Cruzados had crested the road. There was another brace of shouts as the men spotted them.

One of the men chasing them dropped to his knee and raised his rifle to take careful aim. Michael pushed Yaxche out of the way as the man fired.

Letting out a curse in Spanish that Michael couldn't identify, the Cruzado started shooting wildly in their direction.

For a brief moment, as Michael and Yaxche reached the other side of the copse of trees, he thought either they had run to the wrong area, Humberto had set them up, or someone had stolen the truck before they got there.

Michael let out an expletive of his own and threw his hands up in frustration; but then Yaxche tapped him on the arm and pointed. In the shadow of a jicaro tree, under a hasty covering of leafy branches, was a beat up gasoline-powered truck similar to the one he and George had rented, though this one was a light blue color and had a canopy over the short bed.

They both sprinted toward the vehicle and jumped in. The keys were in the ignition, and when Michael pumped the gas and turned the switch, the engine fired up immediately.

Slamming it into gear, Michael drove the pickup as fast as he could through the field, directly away from the Cruzados.

The rear windshield suddenly spider-webbed as a shot ricocheted off it, but by the time Michael got the truck back up on the main road, they had left the Cruzados too far behind for them to have any hope of hitting their fleeing quarry with another bullet.

Michael hit the steering wheel with the heel of his hand in anger.

Yaxche spoke in an assured voice. *"Tu amigo vela por nosotros desde el cielo."*

'Your friend watches over us from heaven now,' Michael figured out after a moment.

Setting his jaw, Michael fixed his eyes on the road ahead and concentrated on finding his way to Santa Rosa de Copán.

27

Lucis Observatory :
Venus Orbit :

Terry saw himself as a young boy at the height of the Mayan civilization. Dressed in traditional costume, he stood on a raised platform with four others his age.

In the field, throngs of Mayans were gathered together as the astrological advisor to the king spoke about the coming of the fourth world, and that it would be signified by a great omen: the sky would turn to fire and the heavens would burn. Lightning would strike the earth and destroy their temples, and the gods themselves would fall from the sky and smash into the world. Conquerors from a distant shore would arrive in the aftermath and rebuild the world according to their own design.

In order to save themselves from the wrath of Hanub Kú and survive in the fourth world, they must build a monument in his honor; a staircase to the heavens where they could rise above the coming disasters and ride out the chaos.

The king, his priests and his most trusted astronomers had chosen that spot where Terry and the other four boys stood to begin construction.

To commemorate the undertaking, they had chosen the five boys as a special sacrifice to gain Hanub Kú's favor.

Two large men grabbed Terry by his arms and bent him backwards over a sacrificial altar.

The priest approached him with a long knife—

∞

Terry shot straight up from his cot and gasped in panic. His eyes scanned the darkness of the small room he'd been sleeping in, and he clutched one hand to his chest where his heart thumped like a hammer. Slowly, his breathing returned to normal when he realized he'd been having a nightmare.

Swinging his legs over the side of the cot, he found his shoes and slid his feet into them. He closed his eyes, held his head in his hands, and thought about what he had just dreamed.

Terry's grandfather always stressed the importance of dreams, and the need for remembering nightmares. The Mayans of old believed dreams were a way of communicating with the gods, and with other people both living and dead, revealing knowledge that could not be shared during their waking hours.

Always regarding this as mysticism, Terry had never paid too much attention to his grandfather's interpretations. Now, however, with the realization that there was far more substance to the legends his grandfather had recounted, Terry had become a believer.

Calming himself by sitting up straight and regulating his breathing, he tried to remember his nightmare before the threads of his memory evaporated like smoke in the wind.

He had no idea what it meant, or why he had dreamed it. Although he'd had more frequent dreams of the ancient Mayans since Itzel's death, none of them had ever dealt with human sacrifice or portents of the remaking of the world before; nor had any seemed so much like a vision.

Before he could sort out the reasons for his nightmare, and

whether it had been one of the special dreams his grandfather had talked about, the chime on his nightstand sounded and a familiar voice issued out of it.

Jose said, "Terry, we're heading up to the lab to begin with the next subject. Klaus wants you there standing by in case he needs something during the experiment."

Like coffee or a sandwich, Terry thought to himself. Out loud, he said, "All right. I'll be there in a few minutes." And then he clicked the communicator to shut it off.

He rubbed his head as if the action would clear his thoughts from the nightmare. Padding over to the washroom, he splashed cold water on his face to wake himself up. Finally, he went out to fulfil his role as servant to a madman.

∞

Terry arrived at the lab just moments before Klaus and Jose. Both men bore determined looks. Behind them, several large Cruzados escorted the fourth subject for the Kinemet radiation trials.

It was the woman. Major Turner.

Terry had completely forgotten about her. He had been preoccupied with the recitation of the Song of the Stars for Klaus and performing menial tasks for him. At no time had he gone to check on her or any of the prisoners, but even if he had wanted to look in on them, he couldn't have. The section of the observatory where they kept the prisoners was under heavy guard, and no one was permitted entry without express orders from Klaus, Jose, or Captain Gruber.

As they dragged the woman past him, he got his first good look at her. Her eyes did not focus, and he recalled that she was blind.

Her long hair was disheveled and her cheeks were streaked

with tears. Major Turner looked like she had been through a tough few days, but she held her head high and set her jaw defiantly as her escorts steered her past Terry and toward the lab.

"Jose," Terry said, finding his voice. "She is a woman, and she is disabled. We can't do this."

Jose glanced up at Terry, but it was Klaus who raised his hand sharply to cut him off. "On the contrary, boy, we can and we will. If it makes you feel any better, I really have only one more variable to test for. She's got a fifty-fifty shot of becoming the first fully transformed Kinemetic human. Of course," he added with a wry smile, "she still might die from radiation poisoning. We're really just stumbling around in the dark hoping for the best here."

It was too much for Terry. He knew there wasn't anything he could do against six men who were much larger and more prone to violence than him. He could feel himself shaking from frustration and anger.

Although he had undertaken combat training at the monthly camps the Cruzados held, Terry had never really taken it as seriously as the others, and never committed himself to the instruction. He had believed from the beginning that his destined part in the movement was geared more towards a leadership role than as a fighter. But he wasn't even a figurehead in the Cruzados revolution; once he had unlocked the door to the Song of the Stars, they had relegated him to being nothing more than Klaus's servant.

All he could do was stand there while the brutish Cruzados herded the woman into the lab.

Inside, one of the men reached over to unbutton Major Turner's shirt at the collar. She swore at him, and Terry couldn't make out her exact words. Her meaning, however, was very clear. She punctuated her words with a slap to the

Cruzado's face.

The man immediately belted her across the cheek with the back of his hand, knocking her into the examination bed.

Terry instinctively stepped forward to help, but a strong hand grabbed his shoulder. Klaus's fingers dug into his skin.

Reaching up, Terry ripped the hand away from him with as much strength as he could summon, and glared at Klaus, who was smirking back.

Terry pointed toward the other room. "Is that really necessary?"

"We can't risk the possibility of contamination from her outfit," Klaus answered, mistaking the cause of Terry's protest. He weighed Terry with a critical eye, and his voice carried a heavy undercurrent of disdain when he spoke again.

"You really aren't cut out for this, are you? You're a dreamer, and dreamers never survive in the real world."

There was a scream from the lab, and Terry turned to see the four Cruzados forcibly strip the clothes from Major Turner. Naked, she fought wildly, but another slap disoriented her long enough for them to haul her up on top of the table and strap her down. One of them inserted a needle in her arm from an intravenous drip. When Justine tried to pull her arm away, the man punched her in the face.

Blinded by outrage, Terry pushed Klaus out of the way and raced over to the door of the lab.

One of the Cruzados, a big man named Esteban, saw the movement and hurried over to block the entrance. He was far too large for Terry to handle, and by the time Terry could figure out how to get past the big man, both Jose and Klaus grabbed him.

Klaus spat out his words. "I thought you said you could control him, Jose."

Instead of answering Klaus, Jose barked an order out to his

man. "Esteban, take him to his quarters and seal the door."

To Terry, he said, "I'm very disappointed in you, *niño.*"

As he was dragged out of the lab, Terry saw behind him that Major Turner was already unconscious, and Klaus had returned to his computer station to begin the Kinemetic transformation trial.

Once again, Terry had completely failed in his efforts, and the cost would be another life.

∞

Terry only had three meters of floor on which to pace, and he made the round-trip at least a hundred times. All the while, he fumed at Klaus and Jose, damning himself for his role in the entire affair.

When history wrote his story, they would not hail him as a hero, or visionary, or savior of the Mayan culture. No, he would go down in the books as a traitor to humanity. A thief, kidnapper, and accomplice to murder.

There had to be a way to redeem himself.

But what could he do? He was just one small man against dozens of Cruzados.

By now, Major Turner would be well into the experiment. She would be nothing more than a series of photons swirling around the room. In less than three hours, the speck of Kinemet Klaus used to kick-start the reaction would expend itself, and then she would either be transformed into a quantum navigator, or she would die a horrible and painful death, as had the previous subjects.

Terry had to do something.

As he paced, the seed of an idea formed in his head. Maybe he could play Jose and Klaus off against each other?

He held his breath, as if the plan might escape with his next exhalation.

Could he do it? Was he capable of following through? Or was his mind leading him into yet another foolish act?

Forcing himself to calm down, he closed his eyes and tried to even out his breathing. When his heart returned to a normal rhythm, he slowly opened his eyes once more, and then began to work out a plan of action.

He returned to the door and checked the peephole once more, but didn't see anyone in his limited range of vision.

The doors of the residential quarters only had locks on the inside. Carefully, Terry slid the latch open and gently pulled the door back a crack, and then peeked out.

Esteban was half a dozen meters down the hall, sitting in a chair and leaning back.

Keeping the door as close to the jamb as he could while still giving him enough of a gap to see through, Terry watched him. The man had to be bored out of his mind with the mundane guard duty. He already looked as if he were ready to doze off. Terry just had to be patient. With slow movement, Terry removed his boots and then approached the door once again, this time in his stocking feet.

Like a jaguar stalking its prey before an ambush, Terry peered through the gap and watched and waited. He kept his eyes fixed on Esteban and stood still.

When the big man's head dropped a notch fifteen minutes later, Terry still did not move.

Even when he heard the first light snore come from the Cruzado, Terry remained motionless.

He waited an additional five minutes after he thought Esteban was asleep, and then delicately opened the door wide enough to slide out into the hall.

The layout of the observatory's residential area was such that there were two ways Terry could have gone. The first was out toward the cafeteria and common area, but there would assuredly be any number of Jose's men loitering there. The only other way was in the direction of the laboratories. That was where Terry wanted to go anyway, but in order to do so, he would have to creep by Esteban without waking him.

He raised one foot and put it softly down in front of the other as he picked his way past his guard.

He was directly in front of Esteban when a loud clanging sound echoed down from the opposite end of the hall in the direction of the kitchen. Terry heard someone curse lightly, as if they had dropped a pan, and he froze, staring intently at Esteban.

For a brief moment, he thought the guard had woken with the sound and was staring back at him. But it was a trick of the shadow and light in the hall; Esteban continued to snore.

Terry resumed his deliberate pace until he rounded a corner two sections down, and then he quickened his steps.

At the lab area, he turned toward a flight of stairs and followed them down to the lowest level.

He would need help if his plan were to have any chance of succeeding; and there was a distinct lack of friendly faces in the observatory.

∞

The hallway to the empty lab where they kept the American soldiers was unguarded. The lock on the main door to the room had been reconfigured to lock from the outside, and there was no way the prisoners could get through the electromagnetic latches. No one expected any of the Cruzados or any of Klaus's men to open the door and let the soldiers out.

The locks were keyed with an infrared scanner. When Terry

had first come aboard the Lucis Observatory, Captain Gruber had sprayed the back of his wrist with a laser. It left no visible mark, but the old smuggler had assured him it was a kind of sub-dermal tattoo that would last for at least a few weeks. It would give him access to all the labs and common rooms with a mere wave of his hand.

There was a moment of doubt when Terry reached the door. If Klaus had updated the security databanks and removed Terry's clearances, this trip—and his plan—would be cut short. But the door opened into a darkened room. The smell of unwashed humans wafted up and he had to force himself not to gag.

He had some expectation that once he opened the door, the Americans would rush him and knock him down before he could talk to them, but when he flicked the overhead lights on, he saw that the soldiers looked weak and defeated.

One of them looked up as Terry stepped into the room, and said, "Who are you?" in English.

The others spotted Terry. Their eyes narrowed and their jaws clenched.

Terry had spent the better part of the past year learning their language, and though he still had trouble with aspects—especially slang—he felt confident enough to relay his idea to them.

"My name is Terry Fernandez. My grandfather is the guardian of the Song of the Stars scroll. I am as much a prisoner here as you. Our captors are experimenting on your *compañera,* Major Turner, and if you don't help me, they will most assuredly kill her."

∞

Klaus was hunched over a computer monitor, tapping one

long finger against his lips as he scanned the diagnostics.

A few meters to the side, Jose was looking at the brightened window between the lab and the workshop, as if mesmerized by the display. He had his hands folded over one another behind his back, and every few seconds he would make a rocking motion, lifting himself up on the balls of his feet, and then settling himself back down.

Sitting on a tall stool at a lab table, Captain Gruber held half a deck of cards in one hand. The rest of the cards were arrayed on the surface of the table in a game of solitaire. At his hip was an ion pistol in its holster.

On the other side of the room, two of Jose's Cruzados were looking bored. One of them leaned against a computer server rack and rested his elbow on the top. The other was chewing his fingernails with his teeth. Both of them had ion pulse rifles, but they were propped barrel-up in the corner a few paces away.

"How much longer, do you think?" Jose asked. His voice sounded casual, but there was a note of anticipation in it.

Klaus popped his head up from the display. "Any minute now, I—"

Then he blinked, noticing that Terry had entered the lab without anyone knowing.

A moment later, everyone else turned their heads, sensing something wrong in Klaus's voice.

Terry willed his breathing to remain steady, and his heart to beat normally and not jump right out of his chest as every person in the room glared at him, first in surprise, then with alarm.

The two Cruzados stumbled into each other as they both went for their pulse rifles, but Captain Gruber already had his ion pistol out and pointed at Terry.

"What the hell are you doing here?" Jose demanded.

"Where's Esteban? That idiot!"

Terry kept his eyes fixed on Jose. He didn't want to rush anything at this point. Unless he kept his voice level, the leader of the Cruzados would not take him seriously.

"I have something to tell you, Jose," Terry said after he was sure he had everyone's attention. He was impressed with how calm he sounded.

"Oh?" Jose blinked and shot a quick glance at his two men, making sure they had found their pulse rifles and were ready to handle any kind of trouble.

"Your life is in danger." Terry didn't make any threatening gestures, but he could immediately see the fear and uncertainty in Jose's eyes as he looked up and down to see if Terry had a weapon.

"Really?" The sarcasm in his voice was tinged with doubt. "I understand if you are upset," Jose said, stalling for time, "but I'm sure we can talk it out."

With a slight shake of his head, Terry said, "The danger is not from me."

Jose narrowed his eyes.

"When I was in the washroom earlier, I overheard Klaus and his uncle say they were going to kill both of us and take over your men once the experiment was successful."

Whipping his head first to the left at his men, who looked as confused as him, then back to the right at Klaus, Jose said, "Is this some kind of joke—?"

But he went silent when Captain Gruber swung his ion pistol away from Terry and pointed it at Jose.

Klaus, who had been watching the exchange with a half grin, said, "No joke, Jose. The little man has it right. You see, I thought it over, and even though the entire galaxy is really big, I've decided I really don't need a co-commander. But I'd like to thank you for your contribution to the cause—my cause, that is."

Jose, wild-eyed, threw a look at the two Cruzados. "Don't just stand there! Shoot him."

The men raised their pulse rifles, but they didn't point them at Klaus or Captain Gruber.

"Oh," Klaus said in a smug tone, "and I'd like to thank you for your men. As it turns out, most of them really weren't interested in your silly crusade, or in following your incompetent leadership."

Jose opened and closed his mouth in shock.

No one was paying attention to Terry all the while, and he slowly backed away from the conflict, heading toward the lab door. He unlocked it with a swipe of his wrist, and a moment before he opened it wide, he shouted:

"Jose! Run for your life!"

Seeing the open door, Jose took one step toward safety.

Captain Gruber fired the first shot, and that pulled everyone's attention back to the center of the room.

The ion stream hit Jose high in the arm, and he spun around, but did not fall. Screaming from the pain, he dove behind a table.

Just then, five American soldiers burst into the room and rushed Gruber and the two Cruzados, who fired blindly at the men without hitting anyone. Trent Gruber, however, did not panic under fire, and shot an ion stream directly into the head of the first man to reach him.

In the confusion, Terry lost track of Klaus, who must have dived for cover. He quickly skipped to the side, looking for the man, and saw two sets of legs kicking wildly from behind a metal table.

Dashing around, Terry saw Jose, bleeding from his arm, sitting on top of Klaus, his hands around the other man's throat, trying to choke the life out of him.

An ion stream from one of the rifles hit the tiled drop ceiling, and a small section broke free and crashed down on Terry. He threw a hand up to protect his head and glanced over to see two of the Americans tackle the two Cruzados on the other side of the room. Malnourished and weak, they were barely able to pull the pulse rifles out of their opponents hands. In hand-to-hand combat, the Cruzados were getting the better of them.

Captain Gruber wasn't able to get off another shot before the two other Americans, Lieutenant Jeffries and Corporal Marks, collided with him. They fought for control of the gun.

In front of Terry, Klaus and Jose rolled around on the floor, each trying to squeeze the life out of the other. Terry was all for letting them finish each other off, but he knew he couldn't chance either of them getting away.

He threw himself at the two men who had been the engineers of his downward moral spiral. The sudden anger he had for them surprised him, and he found himself punching them indiscriminately.

They had lied to him, tricked him, led him to betray himself and the people he loved, and then planned to kill him. The injustice of it all filled him with such a rage, he didn't even notice that one of them had stabbed him in the stomach with a screwdriver. It was only when Klaus, with a curse in German, kicked him off and onto his back, that Terry felt the shooting pain in his abdomen.

He couldn't breathe, and it took everything in him to get to his feet.

Klaus was bleeding from his nose and a few other cuts on his face. He spat blood as he used the metal table to haul himself up.

Jose remained on the ground, still and glassy eyed.

With his vision tunnelling, Terry saw that the Americans

had managed to subdue the two Cruzados and were keeping them pressed to the ground.

On the other side of the room, Lieutenant Jeffries was on his knees, holding his hand over his face. Corporal Marks and Captain Gruber had both hands on the captain's gun.

With a vicious kick, Captain Gruber knocked the wind out of Corporal Marks, and the American released his grip on the ion gun. Captain Gruber shot him in the chest, point blank.

Klaus, seeing this, ran to help his uncle.

Like a predator, Terry let out a war cry and charged after Klaus. He had to prevent the two from escaping. If they got out of the room and sounded the alarm, the rest of the Cruzados would easily overcome Terry and the surviving Americans.

Captain Gruber swivelled at Terry's cry, and fired a charge at him without a moment's hesitation.

Two things happened at the same time.

First, there was the feeling of a sledgehammer pounding Terry square in the chest. His forward momentum kept him from falling back to the ground, but he couldn't breathe, no matter how much he tried to force his lungs to inhale.

Secondly, a fraction of a moment later, an ear-shattering explosion sounded from behind him and the entire room filled with light as the ion stream passed clean through him and into the window of the lab.

With the window blown out, the particles of light that Major Turner had become were now free from any barrier, and spilled out into the lab.

Above the ringing in his ears, Terry heard Klaus scream, "No!" as the photons swirled and escaped out into the hall.

Terry saw Lieutenant Jeffries spring up, face bleeding, to collide with Captain Gruber, and he sensed the other soldiers race past him to help bring Klaus and his uncle down.

But the last thought that went through Terry's mind was not that he had managed to defeat Jose and Klaus, but that he finally figured out what his dream meant.

The gods of old had spoken to him. In order to save his people, Terry had to be sacrificed.

And as he sank to his knees, and the final darkness enveloped his consciousness, Terry decided he was all right with that.

His grandfather would be proud.

28

Unofficial Transcript :
Alex Manez Interview Part Two :
Dated August 2103 :

Frank: "Good morning, Alex. My name is Frank Galloway; I'm the senior advisor for USA, Inc.'s Board of Directors' oversight committee for Quantum Resources. I'll be taking over the debriefing from my assistant."

Alex: "Where's Edgar?"

Frank: "I wouldn't worry about him. He's been reassigned."

Alex: "I'm not worried. But I still want to know why he isn't here."

Frank: "If you must know, this conversation is outside the scope of his security clearance."

Alex: "And you have enough clearance?"

Frank: "To be honest, I don't think anyone has enough clearance. But at the very least I'll be able to determine whether the information you provide can be disseminated, and if so, through which channels."

Alex: "But your scientists need to know what I know, or we'll never be able to use Kinemet the way it was intended."

Frank: "I've spoken with the department heads at Quantum Resources. They've all assured me that they can make Kinemet a viable fuel for space travel."

Alex: "Maybe, but the way they are using it is dangerous and very inefficient."

Frank: "And how does it need to be used?"

Alex: "I don't know, exactly. But you need to stop them from repeating the *Quanta* mission. People will die. They need to start over from scratch."

Frank: "Alex, you strike me as a highly intelligent young man, but this is the real world. There are other factors that need to be taken into consideration."

Alex: "Such as?"

Frank: "...All right... For one thing, the space program is extremely unpopular at the moment: we are spending billions every year, and so far we haven't been able to recoup those expenses. Alex, we were hoping for a different result from your mission; something we could use in our PR campaign to bolster support, something that would fire the imaginations of the population. Heck, we'd have settled for a little green man in a flying saucer.

"In the eyes of the media and the public, the *Quanta* mission was a failure. The ship was destroyed, there was no contact with an alien race, and the viability of Kinemet as a fuel is still years—if not decades—from refinement. We need a success, and soon. The USA, Inc. Board of Directors are generally not scientifically inclined; they're motivated by opinions and polls, and if they enact policies and expenditures that go against the shareholder majority, they may lose their seats in the administration."

Alex: "Politics, you mean."

Frank: "Yes. Exactly. And so, you must also understand that any information you reveal today that goes against the *Quanta* missions may never go beyond this room."

Alex: "So you would let Quantum Resources continue down a path doomed to failure rather than set them straight? All for politics?"

Frank: "I'm afraid that's not my call, but if that's the final decision, it will come from the CEO's offices."

Alex: "It will cost lives."

Frank: "That's why I'm here. I want to know everything you know so that we can prevent future accidents."

Alex: "Nothing I say at this point will help you."

Frank: "Now, Alex, please be reasonable."

Alex: "…Do you believe that I was able to put myself into a quantized state when I was in the Centauri system?"

Frank: "The consensus with the department heads indicated that what you think happened may be a result of disorientation or fatigue."

Alex: "But what do *you* think?"

Frank: "I'm not certain there is any way to verify your story. I mean, it would go a long way if you could quantize yourself again and allow our scientists to observe the effects."

Alex: "I used up all the Kinemetic radiation in my system in Centauri. And it's also not something I can do here on Earth—there's too much geomagnetism on a planetary body. If I was recharged, and back in space, I think I might be able to do it again."

Frank: "That might be a difficult request to fulfill, Alex. There are many people in key roles who cautioned against letting you go on the first mission. They are using the failure as leverage to forward their own agendas and to ensure your removal from the program."

Alex: "What you are saying is everyone has already made up their minds."

Frank: "Not everybody, but enough of them to make your request difficult to grant."

Alex: "So what does this mean for me?"

Frank: "I'm sorry, Alex. I've been instructed to tell you that if you cooperate, and reconfirm your non-disclosure agreement, we can offer you a generous compensation package. You'll never have to worry about money again for the rest of your life."

Alex: "What if I refuse?"

Frank: "Well, as far as the world knows, Alex Manez is a seasoned pilot for the Canadian Space Force on loan to NASA, and who is of a considerably more mature age. We even have a digital composite image of a few actors made up for the press release and any future interviews. There's no possible way we can reveal to the world that we let a teenager lead the *Quanta* mission. That would be a public relations nightmare."

Alex: "I don't like to be threatened."

Frank: "I don't like to make threats. So what will it be?"

Alex: "I want the agreement all in writing, then I'll tell you the rest of what happened out there."

Unknown :

The Music of the Spheres fills her mind and soul.
Raw and exposed, all Sol System lies before her.
The energy of the Sun floods her senses.
Like children, the planets dance in orbit.
Come and play, they call out.
Each have their own laugh.
Their voices are songs.
They are alive.
Another song…
Alex?
So small.
He is lost.
There, but not there.
She pushes her thoughts out.
His song is faint and distant.
He needs her help to come home.
A new being of light, she lacks control.
Her essence explodes outward; the galaxy is wide open.
The Song of the Stars fills her mind and soul.

Quantum Resources :
Toronto :
Canada Corp. :

It was as if he had been an entire world away.

When the skybus circled the Toronto Pearson International Airport to line up with the runway for final approach, Michael looked out the window at the buildings and streets whipping past in a blur; and for the first time in over a week, he breathed a sigh of relief. It was like seeing an old friend after a long separation.

In a way, arriving back in Canada was very surreal. Michael had been through so much in Honduras it almost seemed as if he had lived two different lives.

Yaxche sat in the aisle seat, his fingers wrapped around the armrest in a stranglehold, his eyelids pressed closed tightly. He had never been on an aircraft before. At first, he'd been excited by the experience, but his enthusiasm had dimmed at the sudden pressure put on the passengers upon takeoff, and turned completely to fear with the first bout of turbulence that shook the skybus like a baby's rattle.

The old man wouldn't listen to Michael's explanations about aerodynamics or the safety of modern air travel. The only thing he spoke in reply was a prayer to the sky gods.

Even when the plane had stopped, Yaxche still would not relax his grip on the armrests. It was only once they disembarked the plane that he regained some of his normal color.

In the terminal, Michael spied Raymond McGrath in the large hallway, waving to get his attention.

"Over here," Michael said to Yaxche in English—he had purchased a clip-on translator for him at the Tegucigalpa airport—and crossed the distance to Raymond. "I'd like you to meet an old friend of mine."

After Michael introduced the two of them, Raymond said, "It's a pleasure to finally meet you, sir. We're all very excited to have you join us in the labs. Calbert and I have been speculating like a couple of old gossips."

Raymond turned to Michael. "We'll grab your luggage and head over to the hotel. We booked you two a suite. You can get cleaned up, rest."

Michael shook his head. "I'd rather head straight over to QR—if that's all right with you," he said to Yaxche, who nodded. To Raymond, he said, "Maybe we can get some fast food on the way." They started down the hall to the baggage area.

"I miss fast food."

∞

They all slid into an autotaxi after loading their bags in the trunk, and the vehicle engaged its forward drive the moment the doors sealed.

With his thought-link implant, Raymond was connected with the EarthMesh, and was able to instantly communicate with any linked computer. While the autotaxi had a manual interface for the majority of people—like Michael—who didn't have one of the implants, Raymond was able to send the vehicle their destination with a simple thought.

While Michael always considered himself an adopter of new technology, thought-link was one advance that did not appeal to him, though he understood why a certain segment of the population jumped at the chance to be connected to the mesh twenty-four-seven.

In his life as an administrator, Michael had spent most of his workday being constantly interrupted. It took extreme organization to juggle the hundreds of daily requests from staff, review info bulletins from the scientific community, process directives from his governmental superiors, and find time in his day to tend to personal needs. To have access to the millions of meshposts, blogs, forums, and newsvids around the clock would only be another distraction.

The downside was that, unless Michael was physically in front of a computer, he had to get his news secondhand.

So when Raymond's eyes widened as he received an alert that was obviously important, and he said, "You'll want to see this," Michael had to flick on the holoslate built into the autotaxi's dash to find out what was going on.

He quickly logged into this favorite news channel and selected the headline.

∞

Honduran Rebel Movement Crushed.

In a concerted effort, the Honduran Military and the Honduran Public Police Force raided several holdouts across the Central American country corp. at dawn this morning following reports of rebel activity.

A spokesman for the Honduran Minister of the Interior reported that the armed force sustained zero casualties, though a number of rebels were killed in the process. Over two hundred arrests have been made, including several prominent land owners and government officials who are suspected of involvement.

Calling themselves the Cruzados, the movement's political mandate was to assume leadership over Earth through a monopoly of space travel. According to one source, the rebels believe their actions are destined by ancient Mayan doctrine. The Cruzados are also suspected in the hijacking of the Lunar Lines ship, the *Diana,* out of Canada Station Three. The whereabouts of the vessel and its passengers are still unknown.

In a joint statement, representatives of the Honduran and Guatemalan Heritage Societies condemned the Cruzado movement.

∞

Accompanying the story, there was video showing helicopters descending on a plantation—Michael couldn't tell if it was Oscar Ruiz's or not—and Honduran soldiers pouring out and taking up positions against Cruzados, whose faces were obscured by long kerchiefs. After a quick exchange of gunfire, the Cruzados, obviously overmatched, surrendered. In handcuffs, they were marched into armored vans.

Raymond said, "I just linked with Calbert. He received word from John Markham that Humberto was integral in the raid, feeding them all the information they needed on the other Cruzado encampments."

Yaxche said, "Of course; he's a friend of mine," as if that explained everything.

Raymond paused a moment and spoke in a somber tone. "And they've recovered George's body. It'll be flown back here within the next few days."

Michael's face was rigid, and his jaw clicked, but his reaction was not because of Raymond's last statement. The raid and the recovery of George's body was good news, but he'd been expecting it after Markham had let him know Humberto had made contact.

"What?" Raymond asked. "What's wrong?"

"Why didn't anyone tell me?" Michael growled his words.

"Tell you what?"

"About the *Diana* hijacking." Michael could feel his face flush in anger. He punched in a dozen search queries and brought up all the information he needed to get up to speed. He was particularly alarmed to read that they suspected the liner itself may have been pointed toward the Sun.

"Justine works for them," he said in a flat voice. "Was she on that flight?"

"I'm sorry," Raymond said, nodding in confirmation. "I know you two are friends. I thought you knew. It's been all over the news for a—" He shut his mouth with a snap, as if only just then realizing that Michael had been out of contact for all that time, and grimaced in apology.

Michael dismissed the apology with a slight headshake. "I've seen what the Cruzados are capable of. They couldn't have engineered that hijacking without some serious help. Tell Calbert to clear his day; we need to make some enquiries."

∞

When they arrived at the Quantum Resources administration offices, Calbert was in the lobby waiting for them.

"Glad to have you back," he said to Michael, clasping his hand in greeting.

Michael gave him a single firm nod. "Glad to be back. This is Yaxche."

Shaking hands with the Mayan, Calbert said, "We've been

looking forward to this since Michael contacted us about George's theory." He glanced at Michael quickly. "It's odd that we don't have a single audio recording of the Song of the Stars, just the translations and the attempts by our own linguists, who were obviously incorrect in their recitation."

Turning back to Yaxche, he said, "We have an entire team of technicians standing by to hear your story... Unless, of course, you're too tired from the trip."

His mouth splitting wide in grin, Yaxche said, "Old men never pass up an opportunity to tell a story." He barked out a laugh.

Raymond, smiling, said, "I can take him over there if you two need to debrief."

Calbert said, "Thanks, Raymond."

The two headed off to the recording lab. Raymond wasn't a very tall man, but he towered over Yaxche, and seemed to enjoy not being the shortest person in the room for a change.

Raymond started relating some of the theories floating around about the Song to Yaxche, his voice fading out the farther they got.

Michael turned to Calbert. "Can you fill me in on what happened with the *Diana?*"

Motioning toward the elevator, Calbert headed off first. "What you read in the news is pretty much it. Since Canada Corp. bought out USA, Inc.'s shares of Quantum Resources, we really haven't had any kind of pipeline into their governmental channels for years. Even most of the scientific information we get from NASA has already been screened and cleaned."

They reached the elevator, and Calbert let Michael get in first. He punched the button for his floor.

Michael said, "You have to have a few contacts who might give you some unofficial information."

"Yeah, I do. But no one I've talked to has any more idea what's going on that we do. Apparently, it's been a military operation from the get-go, and you know how hush-hush they are."

Michael jerked his head. "Military?"

"Someone got some information that the Cruzados were launching an operation to raid NASA's store of Kinemet, and they decided to move it all off planet. Since the Chow Yin incident, the American sector on Luna is the most fortified location in Sol System."

"If they moved the Kinemet off-planet, they assumed the Cruzados didn't have space capabilities," Michael said. "As it turns out, they did, and the information was obviously a plant to get the Kinemet in transit, where it was most vulnerable." Michael punched his fist into his hand. "You know damn well the Cruzados aren't working alone."

"The Canadian Space Force has offered its assistance to the Americans, but so far, no one is any closer to figuring it out."

When they reached Calbert's floor, they quickly exited the elevator and made their way to his offices. They entered a small conference room set up with several holoslates and a long work table. One of Calbert's assistants was there, dropping off a large food platter and an urn of coffee.

"I ordered up a few sandwiches for us. I figured we'd be working most of the day."

Taking off his jacket and draping it over the back of a wheeled chair, Michael sat down and reached for a coffee cup. "Thank you."

After practically guzzling down his first cup, Michael poured another and grabbed a sandwich. He bit off a piece and while he chewed, he launched a timeline app on the main haptic console. He began to fill in all the major events that had taken place over the past few weeks. Then he linked in as many mesh searches as he thought relevant to the situation.

Calbert got on his comlink and contacted John Markham to see if they had a complete list of the Cruzados arrested in Honduras.

It took them a few hours to collect and collate the data, but at the end of it all, they still couldn't figure it out.

Calbert moved over to his desk and opened a drawer. "Drink?" he asked.

"I'd kill for a Scotch, if you have it."

"Of course I do," Calbert said, and produced two tumblers. He poured a measure into one of them and handed it to Michael who nodded his thanks and took a sip.

"It's all connected," Michael said, turning around to look at the board. "And everything was sparked by the original theft. Nothing else would have even been initiated unless they knew they had the key to solving Kinemet. Everything hinged on that, and everything was set up way ahead of time: the rumors of an attempted theft on American soil; getting their people in position on CS3 to intercept the shuttle. They had to have people high up in administration, and—" He whistled at the thought. "—they had to have a lot of resources and money at their disposal."

"What do you think?" Calbert mused. "A rival government? There was a lot of drum-pounding back during the first *Quanta* mission. Quite a few country corporations were upset that we weren't sharing the Kinemet technology."

"The Chinese?" Michael raised a speculative eyebrow. Their voice of opposition to Western control had been the loudest after the failure of the first *Quanta* mission.

"I don't think so. They have their own space mining program. If they really wanted Kinemet, they could just go get it." He waved his hand spaceward. "It's out there; the only problem is getting it. No one's been officially looking for it for the past several years, and there hasn't been any scuttlebutt on unofficial operations."

Calbert stood up and paced over to his desk. "And then what do you do with it? As far as most everyone is concerned, we're decades away from being able to convert it into a stable fuel. Without the conversion technology, the expense is not worth it. Not when the world economy is in a shambles. People are more worried about putting food on the table than whether we can travel to other stars—especially when we don't have anything more than a hint on a floating ball of ice over four billion kilometers away that there's anyone out there besides us."

Michael set his drink down and sat back in his chair. He rubbed his tired eyes.

The entire world had gone through an emotional upheaval over the past couple of decades. With the failure of the first *Quanta* mission to make first contact, the initial euphoria of interstellar travel had deflated quickly. Once subsequent efforts to reproduce a Kinemetic navigator had failed, public opinion had turned to a level of cynicism he hadn't seen since he was a boy during the wheat crisis and the fall of public governments. Back then, the reorganization of governments into country corporations had sparked economic recovery.

Though now, he thought to himself, the health of country corporations rested solely on consumer confidence. And since confidence was low, the corporations were taking fiscal losses left and right. Budgets were cut. There was an increase in unemployment and a rise in civil unrest in most of the harder hit countries.

There was no better time for a revolution. Someone saw it coming and had gambled big. Whoever could offer a bright light for the future could write his own ticket. Michael could not believe any of the Cruzados he had met, even the gracious

Oscar Ruiz, had that kind of foresight or access to enough resources to have prepared for this eventuality years ahead.

"So someone was coming at the problem from a different angle," he said out loud. "Figure out how to use Kinemet first, and then source the metal—only they decided to steal the stuff instead of doing any of the heavy lifting."

"Right. So what did they know that we didn't?" Calbert asked. "We must have spent thousands of man-hours on the translation of the Mayan scroll. Of course," he added with a dry laugh, "with all our brilliant minds we never figured out that the medium *was* the message."

Rubbing his eyes with his knuckles, Michael yawned.

"Why don't we take a break for the day?" Calbert said. "I know a nice steakhouse around the corner. We can take Yaxche there to try some Canadian cuisine."

"Yeah," Michael said. "My brain is tired from over thinking everything. I'm probably missing the obvious."

On his comlink, Calbert connected with Raymond. "How's everything going down there?"

"Oh, we've been done for hours. The team is busy crunching numbers and looking for patterns. It could take them a while to come up with any possibilities. I've been showing Yaxche around the building. He seems to like the roof garden the best."

"We're going to break for the day, go out to the 'Beef and Brew'. Can you ask Yaxche if he's hungry? And you're welcome to join us, if you can."

There wasn't more than a moment's hesitation before Raymond said, "If I can? We're already halfway to the elevator." He laughed. "We'll stop at your floor and meet you."

Michael stood and stretched. He reached for his jacket. "Have you had a chance to talk to Elizabeth?" he asked. "I've tried to reach her a couple of times, but all I get is her answering service."

There was a sudden pained look in Calbert's eyes.

Michael knew he and George had become more than just colleagues since Michael's retirement. Before Michael's wife had passed away, the three couples had vacationed together every other year. It was Michael's own fault that he had fallen out of touch since her death. At the time, he didn't want the sympathy his friends had offered, instead preferring to wallow in his anger and loss. He hoped Elizabeth knew she could lean on him for support.

"Yes," Calbert said. "Once she found out about what happened, she flew down to Florida to be with family. I contacted her this morning as soon as I learned they'd recovered his body. She said she was making arrangements to bring George's parents and sister here for the funeral."

At that point, Michael was uncertain what to say. There were so many emotions roiling around inside him that he thought any words he spoke would get caught in his throat.

He was saved when Yaxche and Raymond appeared in the doorway of the conference room, both with bright smiles.

Calbert asked, "Everyone ready?"

"Uh," Yaxche said into his translator, "I would like to talk to Sky Traveler now."

"Alex?" Michael asked. "He's not here, Yaxche. He's on Canada Station Three. In space."

Yaxche gave him the same look one would give a small child. "I am aware of this. Perhaps we could use your EPS. That is how I spoke with him two years ago, when I was in Santa Rosa de Copán."

"Of course," Michael said, looking sheepish as Calbert smiled at his discomfiture.

Raymond blinked in the way only people with a thought-link blink. He was sending a command into the building's systems.

"I can patch the uplink right in here, if you like," he said. "We should probably update Kenny on the scroll anyway—he's our lead physicist on Kinemet development up there," he told Michael. "Only been with us for a few months, but he's come up with some very promising theories."

All four of them turned to the holoslate as it flashed the corporate logo along with an animation of a radio wave.

After a few seconds, the screen flicked to show a young woman with short blonde hair and a pretty smile. A small inset square in the top corner showed Raymond reflected in the frame.

"Quantum Resources, Canada Station Three," the blonde woman said. "How may I help you? Oh, hello, Raymond."

"Terra," he answered, "how are you? Is Kenny there?"

"Kenny?" There was a quick flash of uncertainty in her eyes. "Well..."

Calbert took a step forward into her view. "What's wrong? Where is he?"

Chewing her lip, Terra said, "I'm sorry, I thought you all knew."

"Knew what?" Calbert pressed.

"He's been arrested."

Raymond's voice went up in alarm. "Arrested? For what?"

Terra looked decidedly uncomfortable relating the information. "Someone should have told you this," she said, and shook her head. "They discovered Alex Manez in Kenny's apartment early this morning. He's unconscious—in a coma or something. The station police think Kenny did some kind of experiment on Alex. He claims he didn't do anything, but they're holding him anyway."

"Where's Alex?" Michael demanded, too distracted to follow EPS courtesy protocols and step into Terra's line of sight.

"He's in the medical wing under observation. They said they have no idea what's wrong with him. Dr. Amma said this was the second time he's gone into a coma, a deeper one this time, and she's worried he won't come back out of it."

Calbert and Michael shared a concerned look.

Raymond spoke to Terra. "Thank you for filling us in. I'll call back in an hour." He cut the uplink.

Before anyone could say anything, Yaxche, who was following the conversation on his translator, grabbed Michael by the arm.

"We must go to him right away," he said, his tone brooking no argument. "Alex is in a spirit walk, a dream state. I think he has lost his way. I might be able to guide him home."

Calbert said to Raymond, "You book them on the next flight to the Nova Scotia Space Port and get them on a shuttle to CS3; I'll find out what's going on up there."

31

Unofficial Transcript :
Alex Manez Interview Part Three :
Dated August 2103 :

Frank: "Is the agreement to your satisfaction, Alex?"

Alex: "Yes. Thank you."

Frank: "All right. We are recording this. Please tell me, in your own words, what happened after you set the escape pod on course for the source of the electromagnetic signals. —And leave nothing out."

Alex: "May I have a glass of water?"

Frank: "Of course. Evan, please bring in a pitcher and a glass."

Alex: "I have one more request."

Frank: "Alex, our patience is running thin."

Alex: "It's a little thing."

Frank: "All right. What is it?"

Alex: "Is there any way you can get me a small sample of Kinemet?"

Frank: "I'm sorry, I can't authorize that. It's extremely expensive to mine, and there's a limited supply on Earth. Seems like a very extravagant souvenir, Alex."

Alex: "Well, can I just see some for a little while?"

Frank: "Why?"

Alex: "I think I need to be around it."

Frank: "I'll see what I can do, Alex, but I can't make any promises. Are you ready to tell us the story now?"

Alex: "Yes."

∞

Alex: "I think I already told you that the trip to Centauri felt instantaneous to me, but I didn't mention that it left a kind of residual memory in me. It's hard to describe the feeling. It's like someone tells you about how they went skydiving, and described it so well that you can imagine it was you who jumped out of the airplane. Now, pretend that no one ever described that feeling, but you still have the sensations of the dive. It's an echo of a memory.

"The moment the ship was quantized, there was a link between me and the *Dis Pater* on Pluto. The only way to describe it is as a kind of compulsion. It drew me to it. That the *Quanta* itself was pointed directly at it is beside the point; even if it hadn't been, I would have felt drawn to the monument.

"When the ship reached Pluto, for a moment it felt to me as if the entire galaxy was laid out in a spider web of connected monuments, and all I had to do was *connect* myself to one of those strands and fly along its path. I believe, if NASA had not put the *Quanta* on a direct trajectory to Alpha Centauri, I would still have been able to course correct and travel along that thread. I couldn't, of course, because this thought didn't enter my consciousness until after the ship had arrived in the next solar system.

"When the ship arrived, I was able to sense the Centauri version of the *Dis Pater*, as if it were a homing beacon.

"This is why I believe we are not using Kinemet the way it was intended. I was only partially altered by exposure to the reacting Kinemet, and was never able to fully transform into what I should have become. Yaxche called me 'Colop u Uichkin', which we've translated as a god of the sun, or stars. A closer interpretation is 'Master of the Stars' or, as the term I've been using for myself, 'Star Traveler'.

"I did some reading on the way here from Pluto. The ancient Mayans were a very cosmic-minded and spiritual people. One of their beliefs was that a person was made of pure energy. Every object in the universe is made of that same kind of energy. Energy can be interpreted as frequencies. The Mayans believed that all things had the ability to transfer that energy—if they found a compatible frequency—to any point in the universe.

"Where do you think they developed that philosophy?

"I believe if I had been transformed the way it was intended, I would not have been unconscious during that trip to Centauri. With the powers I have developed since I was irradiated, I believe I should have been able to pilot the ship. My 'clairvoyance' would be for navigation, and my 'electropathy' would be able to control the amount of power put out by the quantized Kinemet.

"Of course, I was exposed to Kinemet by accident, so I am incomplete. If you conduct tests on others without fully understanding how the Kinemetic radiation will affect them, they could quite possibly exhibit worse symptoms than I have, even death."

∞

Frank: "When I said leave nothing out, I meant about the events you experienced. We need to leave the conjecture for the scientists."

Alex: "But this is something they need to hear."

Frank: "Again, that is yet to be determined. I'm sorry, but that's the way it has to be."

Alex: "Fine."

Frank: "Alex … you also understand that in order for us to fully honor our end of the agreement, we must have full disclosure from you … we need the truth. If all the Kinemet on board the *Quanta* exploded in the secondary reaction, how did you manage to return to our solar system?"

Alex: "While you may or may not believe what I just told you, I promise you that what I'm about to say is the complete truth…"

∞

Alex: "I could do the math. I had less than a week of oxygen and water, but the escape pod would take more than a month to reach the source of the signal. It was a pure survival instinct that I attempted to put myself back into a quantized state. I had enough Kinemetic radiation in my system to maintain my state for the duration.

"What I didn't take into account was that, without a catalyst, I had no way of reversing the process. I could float for months or years before I burned off whatever radiation I had in me. In my theory, a properly conditioned star traveler should be aware while quantized; I was not.

"If I hadn't been pulled into dock in the alien space port, I most likely would have drifted until I died."

∞

Frank: "Stop right there! Alien space port! Alex, are you saying you made contact with aliens? If so, this is a serious breach!"

Alex: "No. No aliens. I didn't lie to anyone about that."
Frank: "Okay. Continue."

∞

Alex: "I assure you, the spaceport—the source of the signal—was completely deserted. Everything on board was fully automated. I can only assume their sensors detected me and retrieved the escape pod. I was pulled inside a large hangar. There was a series of platforms that looked as if they were docks for ships of all sizes, but besides my pod, there were no other vessels. The hangar itself was very sparse. I couldn't see any windows or bay doors anywhere. The walls looked like they were made from some kind of polished stone, rather than metal.

"My first thought was to open the escape pod to step out, take a look around, but my pod's canopy was jammed. Besides, I didn't have an EVA suit, and I didn't know what kind of atmosphere the port had, so I had to remain where I was. There must have been a quantity of Kinemet there, because I began to feel rejuvenated, almost immediately.

"Automated arms extended from along the platform and attached themselves to the pod. At first this scared me, because I thought they were going to open the canopy, but the gauges on the pod indicated that they were merely refuelling me with oxygen and electricity."

"Once the pod was recharged, another set of arms affixed a large object to the underside of the pod. I couldn't tell what it was, but I have to assume it was attached with some kind of magnetic clamp. The moment the mechanical arms retracted, the pod began to move away from the dock. I had no control over the navigation systems as the pod moved towards a tube. Inside, I built up speed and was shot out from the port at what

I would imagine would be the escape pod's maximum speed."

"The entire process from the moment I regained consciousness was less than five minutes.

"As my pod left the space port, I was once again quantized. I have to assume the object they attached was some kind of temporary portable Quantum engine. The next thing I knew, I was in orbit around Pluto, and the ground crew were trying to contact me on the radio. The portable quantum drive had been completely consumed during the flight.

"The rest you know."

∞

Frank: "Alex, I'm not sure what to say. That's an incredible story. Are you leaving anything out?"

Alex: "You don't believe me?"

Frank: "Well … that's not for me to say, but, I have to warn you that, well, pretty much everyone who reads this transcript is going to dismiss your report as wild speculation at best, and juvenile fantasy at worst. The problem, unfortunately, is that we can't corroborate any of this."

Alex: "I know."

Frank: "You understand that it would be extremely difficult for people to reconcile your story with established scientific fact."

Alex: "Yes. Sometimes the most closed-minded people are scientists."

Frank: "Be that as it may, I don't think the board of directors are ready for this information. As a matter of fact, I think they will dismiss it out of hand."

Alex: "I'm sorry I don't have any evidence for you, but I'm sure it's there if someone wants to look, they just have to return to Alpha Centauri. The space dock is sitting there, empty and waiting."

Frank: "That, my boy, is easier said than done. To be honest, your account raises more questions than it answers."

Alex: "I'm sorry if I've upset you."

Frank: "I'm just not sure how to present this information to the board ... or if I should."

Alex: "The world needs to take a closer look at Kinemet, and understand its relationship with human beings."

Frank: "If your story is true, then I agree, but we need verification ... All right, well, at this point, all I can do is to submit the report and get it on record. I'll leave it to the board to decide."

Alex: "So what happens now? I mean, to me?"

Frank: "For all intents and purposes, 'Captain Alex Manez' is a commissioned member of the Canadian Space Force, and will be honorably discharged. You, on the other hand, share nothing with him other than a name. Once we release you, you will be free to do as you will. I believe the current CEO of Quantum Resources, Calbert Loche, has spoken with you about a position in the R&D department on Canada Station Three?"

Alex: "Yes."

Frank: "That sounds like a very good deal. But I want to remind you: to speak about your experiences in Centauri to anyone outside of this room will be considered a breach of contract and could be actionable in court. That would be very unpleasant for you."

Alex: "I'm not a child. I understand."

Frank: "I hope you do. Now, is there anything you would like to add before I submit the report and end the debriefing? Alex...? Alex...?"

Alex: "No. That's everything."

32

Lucis Observatory :
Venus Orbit :

It was the most unique and wonderful sensation Justine had ever experienced.

Although she was no more than a collection of photons held together by her electropathic ability, she was aware of herself and her surroundings. Alex had remarked to her that he had no recollection during the quantized state, as if he were in the midst of a deep sleep.

In her corporeal form, Justine was blind, and could only use her senses of touch, smell and sound to interact with the world; now, she had a sense of sight that was far more powerful than human vision. When she concentrated, she could zoom her consciousness in to any object—as if through a powerful microscope—and see the very particles of matter in their continuous ballet.

She could also sense the planets in their inexorable orbit around the Sun. It was as if she could feel their presence in Sol System, hear the sounds of their heavenly song.

In a more subtle manner, she could sense the alien monument on Pluto, the *Dis Pater,* like a dim beacon in the dark of space. Beyond that, if she strained to the limits of her ability, she could also sense an entire network of those monuments—thousands of them—spread throughout the galaxy.

Justine had a moment of consternation when she sensed another presence within Sol System. It was like a very faint flash in the distance, and it took her a minute to realize that it was another Kinemetic being: Alex!

She wondered if Alex would be able to sense her, now that she was irradiated with Kinemet.

When she focused on him, it came to her that he was incomplete. His physical form was in one location, but his consciousness was someplace else.

Alex's essence was adrift, lost in the depths of this ghost world they inhabited. Justine pushed her senses out to search for it, but could not detect his consciousness.

It took her a moment to work through it. Alex wasn't in a quantized state. He had spoken before about the clairvoyant ability he had, and was able to utilize when not in a quantized state. Justine assumed it was the same as what she was currently experiencing—only, when she was in the quantized state, it was an extremely powerful ability, far more than anything Alex had described. In the back of her mind, she hoped that when she returned to normal, she would retain the *sight* as Alex had. That would more than compensate for her blindness. But she would worry about that later.

Right now, there were three issues she needed to address. One was trying to figure out where Alex's consciousness was.

The more immediate problem was that, as she moved her photonic essence out of the lab, she saw that the main room had turned into a war zone. People were dying.

There were two casualties already, though she did not recognize their faces. She spotted Lieutenant Jeffries on his knees holding his hand to his bloodied face while Corporal Marks wrestled with Klaus's uncle.

Four other soldiers were busy restraining two Cruzados,

while Klaus seemed to be aware of Justine and was staring at her with a startled look on his face.

The third thing Justine realized was that she was burning through the Kinemetic radiation in her system at an alarming rate and would very quickly run out of fuel. Like someone suddenly experiencing a pang of hunger, she knew she would require more exposure to Kinemet if she was going to continue existing in a quantized state. And she guessed that she wouldn't be able to help Alex if she was corporeal, nor would she be much use in the fight.

So, last thing first, she needed to refuel.

It only took a moment for her to sense where the cache of Kinemet was kept in the observatory, and though it was difficult for her to cause her photonic particles to move in tandem through physical space, she put all her concentration into the task and exited the lab in a flash.

Klaus screamed after her as she left.

∞

She tried to devise a plan while she pushed her photonic form down the hallway. In her quantized state, she had the ability to affect electrical impulses—a quick test on a nearby light proved it—and she figured that would carry over when she returned to normal, but only if she was irradiated by enough Kinemet. When Alex had been depleted, he lost both the clairvoyant and electropathic abilities, though he had retained his eidetic memory (which, she surmised, might have been a more permanent physiological aspect of the Kinemetic transformation).

Although she had only seen a dozen or so Cruzados on her journey through the hall, she knew there had to be many more of them. Even if Lieutenant Jeffries and his men were able to overcome Klaus and his uncle, they were still outmatched by the rest of the observatory's complement of rebels.

Justine was not a trained fighter or tactician, though she had taken the basic mandatory courses in boot camp. They were outnumbered, under-equipped, and malnourished. Brute force was not the answer, but she had a thought that she might still be able to user her newfound abilities to their advantage.

She sent her vision out, tracking ethereally to where the Kinemet had been stored on the observatory's lowest level, near the docking bay.

Though she was reduced to a mass of protons, she was still unable to pass through solid matter, and she had to take the long way. In her photonic-quantized state, it was actually more difficult for her to move her essence through normal space than if she were solid matter. All of her photons, held together either by some kind of mental force or physical attraction, were in constant motion inside that intangible bubble.

When she finally reached the end of the hall, she began to wind her way down the flights of stairs near the elevator.

Two floors down, she ran out of Kinemetic radiation, and abruptly rematerialized into her human self. She was, however, a meter and a half in the air and was still in motion.

In solid form, she arched and fell sharply to the landing in a tangle of barked shins and banged elbows. The breath knocked out of her, head ringing from impacting it on the wall, Justine lay in a stunned heap for almost a full minute, naked and vulnerable until her breathing returned to normal.

Very slowly, and with great care, she gingerly gathered her arms and legs under her and pushed herself up off the floor. Resisting the urge to vomit from the combined effect of the de-quantizing and nausea from hitting her head during the fall, Justine took a moment to steady herself by leaning against the wall.

Once the feeling returned to her hands and feet, she took a deep breath and oriented herself. There was a thin dribble of blood coming from just under her hairline. She touched the wound experimentally, and winced at the sharp resulting pain.

Now that she was corporeal, she had hoped that she would retain the ability to see beyond herself, but couldn't because she didn't have any of the Kinemetic radiation left in her system. She felt a sharp pain of ethereal hunger. She *needed* Kinemet. If this is what Alex had gone through for the past few years, no wonder he had deteriorated physiologically.

Justine would have to find her way to the stash of Kinemet from memory, and she found that, as Alex's memory had improved, she now possessed a perfect image in her mind of the layout of Lucis Observatory.

Conscious of her nakedness, she drew one arm over her breasts and resumed her descent of the stairs barefoot, hoping against hope that none of the Cruzados had heard her crash and come to investigate.

∞

When she reached the bottom of the stairwell, she stopped at the door and leaned her head against it, trying to hear any sign of the rebels on the other side.

The resounding silence prompted her to pry the door open a crack. She paused, listening, then opened the door all the way and tiptoed down the hallway.

When she got near to the docking bay, she started to feel an electrical buzz. The hairs on her arms stood up and she felt a warm tingle go through her. The Kinemet was close.

As she moved farther down the hall, the sensation intensified, and once she arrived at what she assumed was a storage lockup, she knew the Kinemet was secured inside.

She tried the door, but it was locked. A sudden bout of panic hit her. She had come all this way only to be stopped by a door lock.

Mentally, she kicked herself. Although the Kinemet was in a different room, and most likely inside the titanium container, there was a trickle of radiation leaking out. That was how she was sensing it. All she had to do was stand there long enough to build up enough of a radiation level to regain her electropathic ability, and then she could easily pop the lock and gain entrance.

Pressing the entire length of her body up against the cold door, she stood there, allowing the Kinemetic radiation into her system. She was painfully aware of how vulnerable she was, and prayed that her luck would hold out a little while longer.

She worried that by the time she was in a position to help Lieutenant Jeffries and his men, it would be too late, but there was nothing more she could do until she had recharged.

After what seemed like hours, but was probably only a few minutes, she felt the flow of energy course through her veins as if she had just taken a vitamin shot. The energy level in her was akin to a drop in a bucket, but it was enough for her purpose.

A mere flicker of thought was all it took to trip the electronic lock, and she darted inside the room. The door was pneumatic, and automatically closed behind her.

A few more moments closer to the titanium container charged her with enough radiation to open the lock that stood between her and the full force of raw Kinemet.

Once it was open, the Kinemetic influence washed over her like a tidal wave. She remembered the ecstatic look on Alex's face when he was in the presence of the rare metal, and for the first time, completely understood it.

The clairvoyant vision started to return to her in stages. At first, she had a disconnected awareness of her surroundings, and then the objects closest to her slowly resolved into discernible forms.

She figured it would take at least an hour for her to be fully irradiated; but less than a minute in, she heard the sound of a footfall in the corridor outside the room.

One of the Cruzados threw open the door. He was momentarily taken aback, glancing at her bare breasts. But then, with a roar of anger, he swung his ion pulse rifle in her direction.

Just as he fired, Justine quantized herself, and the ion stream passed right through her photonic self, doing no harm.

With a look of abject surprise, the Cruzado took a few steps inside the room and let out a curse in Spanish.

Justine floated past him and out the door before it closed. The man charged the door, but before he reached it, Justine used her ability to engage the lock, and then blocked the power to the device.

The Cruzado hurled more muted curses as he tried to physically knock the door down, to no effect. He was fully locked in the room as if it were a maximum security prison cell.

This proved that Justine's plan would work. Unable to overcome the greater force of Cruzados, she would have to take them right out of the situation. The entire observatory complex was run on electronic doors and locks, and Justine was now a master of any electric current she sensed.

As she pushed her essence back down the hall toward the stairs, she hoped she could get back to the lab before it was too late, and before she once again ran out of Kinemetic radiation.

∞

Outside of the workshop's main door, Justine paused and

extended her *sight* into the room.

There were several men on the floor, and the remaining five were in a standoff. On one side of the room were Klaus and his uncle, Captain Gruber, who was holding one arm limply to his side, blood soaking his shirt sleeve. They had knocked a metal lab table over and were hiding behind it. They each held a weapon. Gruber had an ion pistol in his good hand. Klaus, holding a pulse rifle, was spitting out curses at the three soldiers who blocked his escape.

Corporal Marks was dead, Justine saw. There was a trail of blood on the tiles from where Gruber had shot him to where he now lay. It looked as if he had not been killed right away, and had been pulled out of the line of fire—in vain, as it turned out.

One of the other soldiers, Private Townsend, was face down on the floor, also dead.

Justine felt a sudden pang of loss and anger. Over the past week she had become fond of all the soldiers in Jeffries' squad.

Lieutenant Jeffries and two men—Privates Vic Genero and Tomas Hodges—were holed up behind a bank of computer servers. Between them, they only had one pulse rifle, obviously taken from one of the dead Cruzados. All three soldiers evidenced wounds and bruises, but nothing looked fatal. The situation was dire, Justine saw when Vic checked the rifle's meter and gave Jeffries a helpless look. The rifle was void of any electrical charge.

Justine tried not to let her emotions get the better of her, but the atrocities committed against her and the people she cared about stacked up.

She couldn't simply seal off the room unless she was able to get Lieutenant Jeffries and his men out first, and the only way she could communicate that plan was to rematerialize.

Scanning the area near the two holdouts, Justine looked for

anything electrical that she could use her powers on. If she could cause something to blow up near Klaus, it could possibly disable them or provide enough of a distraction to get Lieutenant Jeffries out. But there was nothing she could see that would do what she wanted.

Justine decided to go for broke and hope Lieutenant Jeffries would figure out what was going on and get himself and his men to safety.

She pushed her quantized self through the small opening in the broken window of the workshop door and into the room.

All eyes turned to her as she floated into the center of the room.

Klaus raised his rifle and fired off a single shot in her direction. The ion stream passed through her harmlessly. As if the result did not completely surprise him, Klaus scuttled toward a computer keypad.

Justine had no idea what his intention was, but Klaus had obviously figured out the ball of light in front of him was her, and by the self-confident sneer on his face he most likely had a theory on how to capture or kill her. Of course, when he started the experiments, he would have thought ahead about how to control any transformed subject.

Lieutenant Jeffries wasn't taking the opportunity, so Justine had no choice.

She transformed back to her human form, and stood in the middle of the room, stark naked.

It had the desired effect on Klaus. He paused in his search for the keypad to look at her.

Justine shouted, "Get out of the room," to Lieutenant Jeffries and, accustomed to following orders, he grabbed both of his men and complied.

When she turned back to Klaus, he had his rifle pointed directly at her, his lips curling up. In his other hand he held the keypad, and his thumb was pressed down on a key.

Justine immediately willed herself to transform into a quantized state, but nothing happened.

"Too late," Klaus said triumphantly. Lifting the keypad up, he winked at her. "Kinemetic damper. The same tech they use in a quantum drive. The whole room has been wired for it, not just the lab. Now, I'm afraid, I'm going to have to terminate your experiment."

Klaus leveled the barrel of the rifle at her head.

There was the distinctive electrical whir sound, and then a frozen moment when Justine's heart stopped.

A puzzled look on his face, Klaus slowly sank to his knees. On his chest, a small circle of blood blossomed, and he fell face down on the floor, releasing the keypad.

Behind him, one of the younger Cruzados, who Justine had thought was dead, lay on his side, a small ion pistol stretched out in front of him.

"Lo siento," he said, and then his arm dropped and he went still.

Justine didn't have time to wonder what had caused one of the Cruzados to turn on Klaus, because Captain Gruber, with a roar of outrage, jumped up from his hiding spot, aimed his own pistol at her, and fired.

But Justine, free from the damper, was able to quantize herself a split second before the first ion stream sliced through her bare skin.

Lieutenant Jeffries and his two men charged back into the room.

His ion pistol spent, Gruber threw it at them in futility. They quickly tackled him and wrestled him to the ground.

Justine, sensing she was nearing the end of her Kinemetic fuel, moved her photonic self to the wall near the door of the lab. Her uniform had been hung on a hook there. She reverted to a physical form and quickly dressed while the lieutenant secured his prisoner.

"What the hell is going on?" Lieutenant Jeffries asked in what Justine thought was a very controlled voice, considering the circumstances. "What was that ball of light? Was that you? I mean, I had a briefing on the Kinemetic effect. Is that what happened to you? That's what Klaus was doing here?"

Nodding, Justine said, "I'll explain everything to you later. Right now, I need to secure the observatory. You find a communications room and get word back to Earth about what happened here."

"Uh, yes, Major."

Justine took a step toward the door, but paused, and knelt down beside the young Cruzado who had saved her life. She felt for a pulse, but the young man was truly dead.

"And, if you could, please find out who this person was. He saved my life."

∞

It took Justine a little less than a quarter of an hour to make a full circuit of the observatory and use her electropathic ability to seal off any Cruzado she found. Taken completely off guard, they didn't stand a chance. By her count, there were at least forty of them held inside the common area, and half a dozen other stragglers she trapped in their individual rooms or work areas.

When she was finished, they returned to the room where the Kinemet was stored. She used her *sight* to look inside. The Cruzado was standing in front of the container, his face painted with anger.

She spoke in Spanish, and pitched her voice for him to hear through the door. "We've taken control of the observatory.

Your leaders are dead or captured. We have reinforcements on the way. You don't have any food or water. Put down your rifle now, lay on the floor with your hands folded on your head."

There was a brief moment when she thought he either didn't hear her, or was planning on being defiant. But then he tossed the rifle away from him and got down on the floor.

Justine unlocked the door and stepped inside, quickly grabbing the ion pulse rifle.

"All right, I want you to slowly get up and move into the other room. You'll wait there until we come for you."

Glaring at her, the Cruzado nevertheless complied, and once he was safely locked away in an adjacent room, Justine returned to the Kinemet, sat down beside it … and basked in its radiance.

∞

Once she felt her energy levels were back to normal, Justine once more tried using her clairvoyant ability. This time, she pushed herself and tried to home in on Alex's weak signal.

It was difficult to get a fix on him because he seemed to be fading in and out.

Having the ability to see at great distances without physically being there was revolutionary. Alex's ability, kept top secret and shared with only a privileged few, had all but dissipated during the years he was not infused with Kinemetic radiation. He had told Justine once that he could only push his senses so far before he became mentally exhausted, even at the height of his power.

It was possible, Justine thought, that Alex had tried to use his power to find her after the hijacking and had exceeded his capacity. If so, he might have exhausted himself and didn't have enough reserves to pull his consciousness back to his body.

Experimenting, Justine confirmed what Alex had told her. At about one hundred and fifty kilometers from the Lucis Observatory, her conscious vision stopped moving forward. It was as if she had hit a barrier, and no matter how much energy she exerted, she could not push past it.

As Justine moved her *sight* back toward the observatory, she took in the deadly beauty of Venus. Unlike Earth, whose surface detail could be seen between patches of cloud, Venus was completely covered by its sulfuric clouds. It was mesmerizing, and Justine wanted to drift out there in space forever, exploring all the celestial wonders of space.

But too many people were relying on her.

Returned to her corporeal self, Justine reflected a moment on the powers she had acquired, and being a trained astronaut, she connected most of the dots.

In order to navigate at luminal speeds, a pilot would need the ability to sense the star beacons as if they were a navigational map. She assumed the clairvoyant *sight* was a reflection of that ability. The electropathy would be twofold. Although she had no empirical data on which to base her theory, it made sense that she would be able to course-correct a quantized ship in flight using the ability. Also, it would be needed once a quantized ship was returned to normal space, in order to dampen the engines and prevent a secondary Kinemetic reaction.

Or, she thought, she might be able to stop the reaction herself without the aid of a damper. There was a lot of experimentation that needed to be done.

She wasn't certain where the enhanced visual memory would come into play. It could just be a side-effect of being a Kinemat.

She remembered that was the word Alex called himself, and

had wondered at times if he was still human.

As she processed the thoughts, she continued to bathe in the radiation of raw Kinemet.

∞

When Lieutenant Jeffries found her and gently shook her shoulder, it took everything in her not to ignore him and sink deeper into the influence of the powerful metal.

"We've secured the observatory," he said to her when she opened her eyes. "All of the Cruzados are in the common room, along with Gruber. We can keep them there indefinitely."

"What about the young man who saved my life?" she asked.

"Gruber wouldn't say a word. One of the other Cruzados said the man's name was Terry, but he wasn't really one of the rebels. You'll never believe this: he was the grandson of that Mayan who had the scroll in Honduras. I didn't get the whole story, but apparently Klaus and Jose—the leader of the Cruzados—tricked him into stealing the scroll."

More treachery, Justine thought.

The lieutenant said, "You were right, we did get transferred to another ship, the *Ultio*. It's a space yacht, with some upgrades. It's in dock."

"I assume the *Diana* is lost, then."

The lieutenant nodded, then said, "We did an inventory of the computers in the lab. Most were destroyed in the fight, and if there were any data backups, we can't find them. There's no way to retrieve Klaus's work."

"Did you find the scroll?"

The lieutenant shook his head. "No sign of it. It may have been destroyed once Klaus had what he wanted from it."

"Well," Justine said, "we'll just have to trust that our

scientists can reverse engineer … me."

He looked uncomfortable with reciting the next portion of his report, and it was only after Justine prodded him that he spoke.

"We've removed all the bodies; they're in cold storage."

"Clive?"

"Yeah. Him too. I'm so sorry about that," Lieutenant Jeffries said, gently placing a consoling hand on her shoulder.

"Never mind," Justine said, pushing her feelings deep down. She would think about it another time, when she was more capable of dealing with it. "Did you contact home?"

The lieutenant cocked his head and made an inscrutable face. "It's about a five-minute delay in EPS transmissions, so we don't have the whole story. I've got Private Genero in the communication room. So far, though, it looks like we're going to be on our own."

Justine stood up. "What?"

"Colonel Gagne said it all started with a crackdown in Honduras. Apparently, the Cruzados down there kidnapped the old Mayan and Michael Sanderson, and killed a U.S. national, George Markowitz. Mr. Sanderson managed to escape with the Mayan. The Honduran military moved in and put down the rebels. Apparently, the three of them figured out what was so important about the ancient scroll—probably that the formula for … making someone like you … was in there all along."

"My God," Justine said. "George."

Jeffries took a breath and continued: "But that information was leaked, and now most of the world country corporations know that someone has worked out the solution to Kinemet. Both the People's Republic of China and the Arabic Consortium are howling mad."

"The Arabs?" Justine said.

"I guess since most countries have stopped using oil for fuel, they're scrambling for a way to get back on top. They've issued ultimatums to share the technology under threat of hostilities. The world is in gridlock at the moment. Everyone's borders are closing. There's talk of war."

It took a moment for Justine to process that, but her thoughts returned to George Markowitz. She'd met him a few times. Another senseless death. And there would be many more if matters continued down their current path.

"So," Lieutenant Jeffries said. "What's the plan, boss? We sit here and wait?"

"Did Colonel Gagne give any specific orders?"

"Nothing other than to secure and defend the Kinemet. He's waiting on higher-ups to make a decision."

"In that case, I'd rather not sit around here waiting and doing nothing. Why don't we load this container back on the *Ultio* and head back to CS3?"

The lieutenant looked surprised. "CS3? Why there?"

"You remember that boy we brought on board before the hijacking?"

"Alex, the one you told me to forget about?"

Justine nodded. "Yeah, well, he's in trouble, and I think the only way to save him is with that Kinemet."

"There's only four of us and over forty of the rebels," Lieutenant Jeffries said. "I'm not sure we can handle all of them on a trip back."

"There's enough food and water here on the observatory for at least a few weeks or so; enough time for the U.S. Space Corp. to get up here and take care of them."

Lieutenant Jeffries raised an eyebrow, looking unsure.

Justine stood up and patted the top of the container. She smiled.

"Well, are you heading my way?" she asked. "Wanna lift?"

33

Canada Station Three :
Lagrange Point 4 :
Earth Orbit :

Although Michael wanted to work through the sixteen-hour flight from Nova Scotia to CS3, he fell into a deep exhausted sleep soon after launch and didn't wake up until the ship began to slow on approach.

While Yaxche had found the skybus trips from Honduras to Toronto and from Toronto to Yarmouth horrifying experiences, he seemed to really take to space travel. After all, there was no turbulence in space.

Michael found him in the forward observation lounge, sitting on a comfortable sofa bench, watching as the two-kilometer-wide space station slowly grew larger and larger as they got closer. There were twenty or so other people in the room, all watching in companionable silence and mesmerized appreciation.

"I could not take my eyes off the Earth as we left," Yaxche said into his translator when Michael sat down beside him. "I have seen videos from my grandson's pocket computer, but it is not the same. I am a simple man from a simple village." He pointed to the massive space station. "This is like something from a dream. It is no wonder the gods reside out here."

"It's addictive, being in space." Michael crossed one leg

over the other and leaned back, sharing in the moment. "I've only been a few times. I keep forgetting how beautiful it is."

An attendant entered the room and quickly set his eyes on Michael. He approached and leaned closer. In a soft voice he said, "You have a call from Earth, sir."

"All right, thank you," Michael said, and with a smile to Yaxche, he got up and followed the attendant to a communication booth.

∞

It was Calbert.

"I don't know if you've scanned the newsblogs yet," the CEO of Quantum Resources said, "but the survivors of the *Diana* have contacted Earth."

"Survivors!" Michael said, his voice loud enough that a few other passengers who were taking calls turned their heads at the sound. His face flushed red, not from embarrassment, but from anger and worry.

"Four of the Americans, including Major Justine Turner, managed to overpower a band of Cruzados on the abandoned Venus orbital, Lucis Observatory, and recover the stolen Kinemet."

Michael breathed a sigh of relief that Justine was alive, but a thousand questions flooded his mind. He bit his tongue until Calbert was finished with his story.

"It looks like the Cruzados were led by Klaus Vogelsberg and Trent Gruber. Klaus was killed in the firefight, but they managed to capture Gruber alive."

"Klaus?" Michael hadn't heard that name for years, and had completely dismissed him from his memory.

"Yeah. Apparently, he's been trafficking in information all this time since the *Quanta* hijacking, and over the years managed to set up a network of contacts throughout Earth and the Moon. That fits in with your theory of who was behind all this. He somehow recruited the Cruzados to his cause, as well as quite a few others. They're cleaning house on Luna Station as we speak."

It did explain things, but there was obviously much more to the story. "Are they sending a rescue mission?"

"Not right away," Calbert said. "The prisoners are secured on the observatory, and Major Turner and the American soldiers are on their way to CS3—they're using Klaus' ship, the *Ultio*. We're assuming the *Diana* has been disintegrated by the Sun."

"Did you find out what Klaus was doing there?"

Calbert shook his head. "If the Americans know, they're keeping silent about it so far. Especially since the People's Republic of China has filed an official complaint with the United Earth Corporate Council against USA, Inc."

"The Chinese? On what grounds?" Michael asked.

"Can you believe it? They're citing the Nuclear Ban Treaty of '42."

Michael blinked. "I don't see how that's relevant."

"Well, Kinemet is based on nuclear technology. They demanded that we prove we aren't using it to make weapons."

"That's ludicrous!" Michael said.

With a shrug, Calbert lifted his eyebrows. "There are a lot of country corporations who feel they've been excluded from the technology. With everything that's been happening on Earth, there's renewed interest in new developments. No one wants to get left behind. The Council is convening an emergency session. Talk from SMD is the motion might be ratified. It's a political move."

Michael didn't like the sound of that. He wasn't against sharing technology; if humankind was able to fully develop reliable interstellar travel, he believed everyone on Earth should be a part of it and benefit. However, international corporate politics was renowned for its sluggish pace. Before anyone could move forward with any more research or development, the technology could be tied up for years or decades while the some oversight committee decided whether Kinemet was a danger or not.

"You think they can get it ratified?" he asked tentatively.

"Yes. Who knows, maybe they're trying to develop interstellar travel independently and don't want the competition."

Michael asked, "You think they may have been helping Klaus?"

"I don't know. Our 'big brother' to the south isn't offering up any information to us at this point. Perhaps you can see what you can get out of Major Turner when she arrives. She should be there sometime tomorrow. The Canadian Space Forces have offered protective services for the time being. I know their commander; I'll see about getting you clearance to meet with the Americans."

"Thanks, Calbert," Michael said.

"Oh," Calbert said just before severing the connection. "I also talked to the provost officer on CS3 and got him to release Kenny. Technically, he did break Quantum Resources protocol by not registering his activities—and we'll talk to him about that later—but he swears he was only taking readings. Whatever happened to Alex, it was something completely different."

With a nod, Michael said, "We're going to be docking in an hour or so. I'll call ahead and see if Kenny will meet us at the port. I'd like to get the full story straight from the horse's mouth."

"Sounds good. I'll contact you later tomorrow when we

have more information."

"See you later." Michael closed the connection and hurried back to the lounge to watch the final approach with Yaxche.

∞

While he waited for his luggage to be unloaded and brought to him on the conveyor on CS3, Michael listened as Kenny explained what had happened that night in his apartment with Alex.

"…and then he twitched and went into a coma. Only," the physicist added after a moment, "Doctor Amma says it's more of an extreme fugue state than a coma. He responds to stimuli, and appears to be awake. His consciousness, however, is not there."

Yaxche, who was listening to the explanation through his translator, said, "He is on a spirit walk."

Kenny, looking genuinely worried, asked, "Raymond said you might be able to help him; can you?"

"I will try," Yaxche said.

As Michael grabbed the bags when they passed near him, Kenny said, "They have him hooked up to IVs and they've even tried to force-feed him. But he's fading away. The doctor's explanation is that he was in remission the last few weeks, but it was only temporary. Now, whatever deteriorating disease was afflicting him before is back.

He added, "And it's progressing."

∞

It took a lot of fast talking to convince the medical staff in the infirmary to give Yaxche the privacy he needed to see if any of his rituals (Michael called them naturalistic procedures when explaining it to Dr. Amma) would help bring Alex out of his state.

Dr. Amma wasn't buying it, and in the end, Michael had to place another call to Calbert and get him to authorize their attempt.

Michael and Kenny stood in the room, watching as Yaxche pulled a few accoutrements out of the bag he had brought with him from Honduras, including a hand-carved headdress decorated with feathers, and a shawl woven with sea shells and bone. He produced two wooden sticks that rattled when he placed them beside Alex's supine form.

Part of Yaxche's traditional rituals required the use of fire to help lift spirits to the heavens, but he said he would make do with some candles and incense.

Alex looked gaunt and aged. Though his eyes were open, they stared blankly out of darkened sockets. He seemed to breath normally, but made barely discernible moaning noises once in a while. When Michael grasped the boy's hand, it felt cold and listless.

"I must enter the spirit world of dreams," Yaxche told them once he had everything arranged. "Then I will try to commune with the Sky Traveler. It may take a long time. Please make sure we are not disturbed."

Michael regarded the old Mayan levelly for half a minute, waiting for the ritual to begin, when Kenny tapped him on the arm. "I think he means he wants us out of here, too."

Yaxche gave them a toothy grin, and waited patiently for Michael and Kenny to leave the room before turning back around.

Outside, Michael looked indecisive.

"Uh," Kenny said, clearing his throat. "Raymond said they've finished the initial analysis of the Song of the Stars and have transmitted the data to our computers. Do you mind if I go and have a look at it?"

Michael smiled and checked the time on the wall holoslate. "Sure thing. I think I'll go get a bite to eat and wait for the *Ultio* to dock."

But Kenny, ever the scientist, was already halfway down the hall before Michael finished his sentence.

∞

Michael didn't have to wait long. He was in the waiting area of the docking port for less than a half an hour before the overhead monitors flicked on to announce the arrival of the *Ultio.*

It took a few minutes for them to complete docking procedures, and when the gates opened to allow the passengers to disembark, Michael stepped up to greet the survivors.

Before he took two steps, however, a small fireteam of Canadian Space Force soldiers, armed with ion pulse rifles, came marching down the hall.

Before the Luna Station incident with Chow Yin, Canada Station Three only had a small contingent of five peace officers whose primary role was to keep the seasonal space miners in order when they had come aboard for shore leave. Breaking up a bar fight was the most action many of them had ever seen.

Since then, however, the military had sent up a thirty-six-man platoon of soldiers to bolster internal defense and to provide added security for any international visitors to the station.

Michael didn't recognize any of the soldiers, but they obviously knew who he was. When they got closer, they veered toward him, and the first man lifted his right hand in a salute.

"Sir," he said. "Master Corporal Bixby."

Dully, Michael raised his hand in an attempt to return the

salute. "Michael Sanderson."

"Sir," the master corporal said in a clipped military tone, "we've been assigned to escort the American hijack survivors during their stopover on the station. The Minister of SMD informed us you would also be accompanying them."

"Oh?" Michael frowned. "Do you think they are at risk?"

The soldier gave a quick shake of his head and a cursory smile. "Just a precaution, sir."

When the main door to the docking bay opened, Michael glanced over and saw Justine and three men—all looking as if they had been through a warzone—enter and step up to the identiscan one at a time.

Once they were processed and cleared, Justine approached Michael, fighting through a weary grin with a wide smile. She gave him a hug, which he returned with as much emotion as hers.

At first, Michael hadn't noticed, but Justine did not have her optilink or her PERSuit harness on, yet she had spotted him right away and walked toward him unwaveringly.

"Justine?" Although his first instinct was to ask how she was and tell her he was glad she was safe, he found himself blurting out, "Can you *see?*"

She let out a short laugh and smiled at him. "I am still blind … but, yes, I *can* see."

"What—?" He stared into both of her eyes one after another. There was no detectible change in her irises. Her eyes were unfocused, distant.

Justine patted him on the arm. "I'll explain later. Can we go see Alex right now?"

Michael shook his head. "Soon. Yaxche's with him." He detected a sudden pained look in Justine's expression. They needed someplace private to talk; he was acutely aware of over a dozen pairs of eyes watching him.

"Um, is everyone all right?" He looked at each of the American soldiers in turn. One of them looked quite banged up; several bruises were evident on his cheek and forehead. The lieutenant was favoring his arm, and the last soldier had one eye swollen shut.

The master corporal quickly introduced himself to Justine and the others, and said, "We have an area set aside in the infirmary. If you'll all follow me, we'll get you patched up and fed a hot meal. Then you can contact home to make your debriefing. I've been told there are several USA, Inc. directors and NASA officials gathering at the capital to listen in."

"I'm fine," Justine said to him. "I don't need any medical attention. If it's all the same to you, I'd like to confer with Mr. Sanderson while you see to the others." She moved her head towards Lieutenant Jeffries, who nodded his assent.

Master Corporal Bixby called one of his men closer. "Private Ludwig, here, will escort you to our headquarters. We have a conference room set up for the debriefing if you want to use it." He regarded Michael with a calculating look. "But we also have a few smaller offices, if you prefer."

Justine and Michael followed the private while four of the Canadian soldiers took up positions around the entrance to the dock where the *Ultio* was, and the remaining men led the American soldiers to the medical section.

∞

"Are we safe to talk here?" Justine asked once Michael closed the door to a small office. Some thoughtful person had brought in a carafe of coffee and a plate of sandwiches and veggies.

Michael watched as Justine deftly reached for a carrot stick and bit into it with a snap.

"Reasonably," he said in answer. "So, you first. You can see…?"

"What I'm about to say is probably going to be classified as soon as we report back home." Justine sat down and took a deep breath. "Klaus figured out the formula to convert a human into a Kinemat. And," she added with a dramatic pause, "I am proof of it."

"What? Proof? You mean you're—?" A hundred questions all tried to pour out of his mouth at the same time. Michael found a seat and eased himself into it, all the while never taking his eyes off Justine. "Maybe you should start at the beginning."

She did, and relayed everything that had transpired from the moment they had been hijacked to arriving back on CS3, including that they hadn't been able to locate the scroll.

When she finished her story, Justine said, "Colonel Gagne was pissed when he found out we were heading here and not back to Earth. I told him we were running low on fuel. He didn't believe me, but what choice did he have but to arrange for our berthing here?"

"Why did you come here?" Michael asked.

"I knew Alex was in trouble. When I was in a quantized state, I could sense that his consciousness was separated from his physical body."

"Yes." Michael nodded. "And since he's fallen into that fugue state, his body is deteriorating. Yaxche says he's trying to communicate with Alex, to see if he can draw him back. Don't ask me to explain how. I'm not even sure I believe in that kind of mysticism, but I don't have any other ideas. You wouldn't have come here unless you did have a notion. What is it?"

"Before I tell you that, it's your turn," Justine said. "Catch me up. I've been isolated for a week."

"I know the feeling," Michael said cryptically, and then told

Justine what had happened in her absence.

Starting with the EPS from Alex when he went through his first fugue, Michael recounted the events up to their capture and escape in Honduras. When he spoke of George's death, his words caught in his throat, and he poured himself another cup of coffee.

"The political situation on Earth has been worsening over the past few days," he said in conclusion. "People aren't dumb. They've figured out there are developments in the area of Kinemet, and are demanding to be brought in. The world economy is in tatters; viable interstellar travel could be a shot in the arm—whether or not there are *others* out there. If the country corporations on Earth knew just how far those developments have gone, it could get worse. Are you going to tell your superiors that you've been transformed?"

After a moment, Justine took a deep breath. "I'm no diplomat, and I have no desire to be," she said. "I'll make my report and leave policy to them. Meanwhile, we need to help Alex, and time is running out in more than one way. As I said before, once I make my report to the USA, Inc. Board, the cat will be out of the bag. We'll all go into lockdown, and then it might well be too late for Alex."

"What do you mean?" Michael asked. "Do you know something because of ... what's happened to you?"

"I think so." She stood up and paced, gathering her thoughts. "I haven't had a lot of time to explore my new gifts, but, whenever I used any of the extranormal abilities, I could tell that I was using the Kinemetic radiation as a fuel. It worked before, and bringing Alex in proximity of Kinemet might reinvigorate him once more. I know, when I ran out of the radiation, I felt an uncontrollable hunger. I think, if I didn't charge myself with Kinemet, my health would also deteriorate like Alex's."

"So you think bringing him close to some Kinemet will snap his consciousness back?" Michael asked.

Justine shrugged. "Maybe. I think it's worth a shot."

"There's no way we can unload the Kinemet here," he said, thinking out loud. "If any of the station's security sees it, they'll report it to our government. And if we move Alex out of the infirmary, the nurses will sound an alert." Michael chewed on his bottom lip.

"It's a good thing I planned ahead," Justine said. She reached into her pocket and brought out a small control pad. "Klaus gave me the idea. He used a Kinemetic damper on me to stop me from being able to use my abilities. I figured if I was leaking any radiation at the security station, they'd notice, so I rigged up a localized damper to hide myself. And—" She reached into her other pocket and pulled out a small disc of metal attached to a gold chain. "—some Kinemet, disguised as a locket if anyone searched me. This should be enough to irradiate Alex. At least long enough to figure out our next step."

Michael stood up. "Then what are we waiting for?"

∞

On the way back to the medical area, Michael stopped at a communications kiosk and called Kenny at the QR lab. The scientist answered almost right away, but he seemed annoyed at the interruption until he recognized his caller.

"Yes, Mr. Sanderson?"

"Just call me Michael. How are you coming along on the scroll data from Raymond? And I hope you've made redundant backups of everything."

"Of course," Kenny said, pursing his lips in annoyance at the suggestion. "All data is backed up continually."

"Just checking," Michael said, putting up an apologetic hand. "What have you found?"

"We're working on the theory of pitch and frequency. Perhaps Kinemet *is* sensitive to sound vibrations."

"Try converting sound frequencies to light frequencies."

"That's not really a valid physics methodology. There's no direct correlation to—" Kenny's face froze in mid-word as it dawned on him. "It worked, didn't it?" His eyes widening, he said, "Someone solved it, didn't they? It worked on one of the Americans?"

"That's all I can tell you for now," Michael said, suppressing a grin. "We're heading down to the infirmary to see Alex. You can reach me there."

He didn't even have time to say a farewell before Kenny cut the connection, most likely off to run some computer simulations.

∞

They stopped outside the door to Alex's room, and Michael gently knocked before opening it a crack. He didn't want to break Yaxche's concentration, but his caution was not necessary. The old Mayan was sitting on a guest chair in the corner, head drooped from exhaustion. He looked up when Michael entered.

"I had a dream," he said, then noticed Justine. "Hello, Sky Traveler. I saw you in my dream."

"Uh," Michael said. "This is Justine. She was captain of the ship that rescued Alex on Pluto. Justine, this is Yaxche."

She stepped forward and clasped both of her hands around Yaxche's. "I'm so sorry to be the one to tell you this," she started to say.

"My grandson has passed from the world," the old Mayan

said, as if he already knew the fact of it. He kept a stoic face, but there was a tightening around his eyes, and he looked away as he lost the fight to hold back a tear.

Justine said, "He died saving my life." Though she did not have the ability to see out of her eyes, they nevertheless conveyed what the sacrifice meant to her.

Yaxche squeezed her hand and nodded. "I would not expect any less. Te'irjiil was a good boy."

"You'll have to tell me about him."

Yaxche nodded. "Yes. We will sit together some time and I will tell you his story."

Justine pressed her lips together and nodded. Then she turned to where Alex lay in the bed and said, "Let's see if this works, shall we?"

She withdrew the amulet of Kinemet and placed it on Alex's chest, tucking his hospital gown up over the metal.

The diagnostic machine beside the bed blipped as Alex's vitals immediately shot up. His pulse quickened, and his vital stats normalized.

Michael quickly leaned over and looked into Alex's eyes, but there was no dilation of his pupils.

"He looks better," Justine said in a soft voice. "It seems to take a few hours for us to fully charge." She shook her head and lifted one side of her mouth in a half-smile. "I say it like we're batteries or something."

But after several more minutes passed, there was no sign that Alex's consciousness had come back to reside in him. The body on the bed was still a hollow shell.

Realizing that Yaxche had not related the details of his dream to them, Michael turned to him. "Is this going to work?"

Ever patient, Yaxche had resumed his position on the chair. The translator did its best to convey the meaning of his words: "The metal of the heavens will heal the body, but not the spirit.

The Sky Traveler has always been two parts of a whole. The spirit half is frightened, and has run to the safest hiding place it knows."

Michael asked, "And where is that?"

"In my dream I saw a small station like this one, looking upon three suns."

Michael guessed, "The Centauri System."

Before he could say any more, Dr. Amma raced into the room with a nurse and two attendants. She stopped short when she saw Yaxche in his ceremonial dress.

Michael noticed Justine, who was standing next to Alex, deftly reach her hand down and grab the Kinemet disc.

"What's going on in here?" Dr. Amma demanded. "The monitors went berserk and—" She spotted Alex, looking hale and breathing steadily once more, and rushed to his side. Quickly, she took his vitals manually, and then looked between Michael, Justine and Yaxche.

"I don't understand it. All of his signs seem normal. But he's still in a fugue state. What did you do?"

Shaking his head, Michael said, "Uh, nothing. We were just standing here, talking."

The doctor motioned to the nurse. "I need to run some tests. Can you bring me the sequencer?" Then she shooed the three of them out with a wave of her hand.

∞

In the waiting room, they were on the verge of sitting down when one of the receptionists stepped into view.

"Michael Sanderson?" she asked.

"That's me."

"There's a call for you. I can transfer it to the kiosk over there."

"Thank you," he said, and quickly went over.

The call was from Calbert, and he looked harried.

Michael asked, "What's going on? Is everything all right?"

"No. The United Earth Corporate Council has granted an injunction against all Kinemet experiments until it can determine if it represents a risk to the safety of the world population."

Unable to believe what he was hearing, Michael opened his mouth, but couldn't form any words.

Calbert said, "Yeah. Happened real fast."

"And they have unanimous support?"

"Almost. The only country corporations opposed were USA, Inc., Canada Corp. and the German Federation."

"Germany?"

"The rumor mill is working overtime. Apparently, word got out who was behind the hijacking of the *Diana*, and the Federation denounced Klaus as a disavowed citizen working on his own. They're just covering their bases."

"That's one word for it."

"As soon as we receive the official notice," Calbert continued, "we are obligated to quarantine the QR Labs on CS3."

"What about our Earth-based research sites?" Michael could feel his face flush with outrage.

"They're focusing on CS3 for now. It's a smokescreen. Someone thinks we've unlocked the technology. And they're right—Raymond says Kenny thinks he has a workable theory. We could be less than a few months away from human trials."

"Not if they shut us down," Michael said in a grumble.

Calbert pitched his voice lower. "It gets worse. The Arabic Conglomerates have proposed sending a team of observers from Luna Station to ensure we're following the UECC's edict."

Michael couldn't believe his ears. "What?"

"They're already on their way. Due to arrive in about six hours."

"You have to do something to stop them. What does Ottawa say?"

Calbert tilted his head. "Cooperate. We're under scrutiny from the world court. If we balk at this point, we're admitting we've been hoarding the technology."

Grinding his teeth, Michael said, "If they start snooping around, they'll find out about Alex and everything else…"

He narrowed his eyes. "Calbert, I have to go. I have an idea, and I don't think you're going to like it. If we—"

"No," Calbert said. "Don't tell me. I can see the wheels spinning. Whatever you're going to do, I need to be able to deny knowledge of it."

That made Michael smile for the first time during the conversation. "All right. If you don't hear from me, then it worked."

"Good luck."

Michael cut the connection and quickly strode back to the waiting room where Yaxche and Justine were speaking in quiet tones. They looked up at him as he approached.

He summarized what was happening, and said, "Justine, I can't involve you in this, but I have to get Alex, Kenny and all our Kinemet research away from the Arabian observers."

It did not take her long to figure out his plan, and she put her own spin on it. "Getting us off the station is only half of it. Alex needs more Kinemet, and I know where there is a tidy little stockpile."

Michael noted her use of the word 'us' and he felt a swell of pride.

Justine said, "Turnabout is fair play. How do you feel about commandeering a pirate ship?"

Yaxche gave them that amused grin as he listened to the translation.

Canada Station Three :
Lagrange Point 4 :
Earth Orbit :

Justine knew the assembled Board of Directors for USA, Inc., as well as representatives for NASA and a few generals of the U.S. Armed Forces, would be waiting for her to report to the conference room and link back to Earth with an A/V EPS within the hour. This was only the first of several problems.

She needed to stall for time, but she needed help.

As the three of them neared the infirmary, she said, "We need to take a quick detour."

Michael turned his head to her, though he didn't break stride. "Oh?"

"Lieutenant Jeffries and the others should be in here somewhere. Let's see how they're doing."

About to say something, Michael closed his mouth and gave her a slight nod.

They found the lieutenant in one of the rooms where his men where convalescing. Private Genero had a cast on one arm, and Private Hodges had several stitches on his forehead. Only one of the Canadian soldiers stood post outside, and he saluted as the three of them passed by.

The lieutenant stood up as they entered and gave Justine a bright smile. The other two started to rise, but Justine waved them back down.

"Hello, Major," Lieutenant Jeffries said. "We're just waiting for one of the doctors to clear us, and then we're ready for the debriefing."

"That's what I'd like to talk to you about," she said. "I want you to go to the meeting, but tell them I can't make it."

"Pardon me, ma'am?"

"Just say that there are some health complications from my being held hostage, and the doctors are keeping me here overnight for observation."

The lieutenant could clearly see there was nothing wrong with Justine physically, and his eyes narrowed in suspicion.

"Something more important has come up," Justine said. "I can't tell you what it is, but unless you help me with this, everything we went through on Venus will be for nothing."

He blinked, then made a decision. "Of course I'll help."

"Thank you," she said, and then spoke to the two privates. "How about you? Are you up for the job?"

"Yes, ma'am," said Private Genero, and Private Hodges nodded as well.

"Good," she said, "because I'm going to need one of you to be a dummy."

Private Genero opened his mouth in surprise, but no words came out. Justine smiled at him.

Lieutenant Jeffries laughed. "I think you just volunteered, Vic."

"If you can spare Private Hodges," Michael said, "I might need some help in the QR Labs."

"Wouldn't Calbert or Raymond have already contacted Kenny?" Justine asked.

"Yeah." Michael gave her an odd look. "But I have a crazy notion I need to run by him."

Justine nodded. "All right," she said to them. "Here's the

plan…"

∞

Justine waited for Lieutenant Jeffries to step out of the room and speak to the Canadian soldier posted at the door.

She shifted her sight to the hall and watched.

"Private Johnson," the lieutenant said to the young man. "Can you show me the way to the conference room you set up at your headquarters?"

"Uh, just you? Sir?"

"Unfortunately, my men haven't been cleared medically yet, and I can't wait any longer."

"Yes, sir," the private said, and led Lieutenant Jeffries away.

Justine snapped herself back into the room and nodded to Michael and Private Hodges. "You're good to go."

Michael grinned and left the room with the private in tow.

To Yaxche and Private Genero, Justine said, "Let's get set up."

∞

Dr. Amma was the only member of the medical staff in Alex's room when Justine entered. She was silently tapping and swirling her fingers around the haptic control on her holoslate, updating her patient's chart.

"How is he?" Justine asked in a quiet voice.

The doctor glanced up quickly, and then resumed typing. "If I believed in that kind of thing, I would call it a miracle. It's another complete remission. Physiologically, he's in perfect condition. But it's like his mind has shut down. It's unprecedented."

She continued updating her notes, and it seemed to Justine

that she was there for the long haul.

Although she needed to be careful when using her Kinemetic talents, in case the station's sensors detected any anomalies, Justine, with a bare flicker of thought, focused her electropathy on the doctor's holoslate.

The screen went dead and Dr. Amma jerked her hand back. She shook the tablet, and when that didn't do anything, she tapped the power node a few times.

"Damn," she cursed. "If you'll pardon me. I need to find another holoslate." With an annoyed set to her face, she hurried out.

Justine watched her disappear down the hall, then signaled in the other direction. Yaxche pushed Private Genero ahead of him in a wheelchair. The private was dressed in a hospital robe and let his head, wrapped with a single bandage that covered half of his face, hang forward, as if he were sleeping.

A duty nurse glanced over as they slowly wheeled their way down the hall, and just as quickly dismissed them.

Once the two were inside Alex's room, Private Genero got out of his robe and pulled the bandage off his head. With his good arm, he helped Justine dress Alex in the costume and put him in the wheelchair. Then the private arranged himself in Alex's bed.

"You have to relax," Justine said as she reached for the diagnostic cables still suctioned to Alex's chest.

After a moment, Private Genero nodded. "All right. I'm good."

In a single deft movement, Justine transferred the sensor from Alex to Private Genero, and the diagnostic monitor blipped only once.

Yaxche once again took up duty as wheelchair navigator, and pushed Alex out into the hall.

"Thank you," Justine said to Private Genero. "And if they

try to give you any trouble, just tell them you were under orders and had no idea what was going on."

"It's the truth," Private Genero said with a smile. "Good luck, ma'am."

Justine gave him one more smile, and then followed after Yaxche.

∞

Things had been progressing according to plan, but as she and Yaxche made their way across the station to the port, their luck took a turn for the worse.

Several uniformed men where hurrying about, setting up a perimeter. Justine couldn't see any civilians in the area.

"Sorry, folks," one soldier said, spotting the trio. "We have orders to seal off the area for the rest of the day. If you had a flight, it's been postponed until tomorrow."

"No, we were just going for a walk," Justine said, and smiled benignly. She turned back around and cursed under her breath.

They went back to the main corridor. Yaxche watched her patiently as they walked.

Stepping closer to a communications kiosk, she tried to connect with QR Labs.

A harried looking receptionist answered. "Can I help you?"

"Michael Sanderson, please."

"I'm sorry. He's already left."

Justine pressed her lips together. "By himself?"

The receptionist clearly looked uncomfortable answering the question, but she said, "No, he was with Kenny and a soldier. They were—" Her head moved closer to the camera. "Are you Major Turner?"

"Yes."

"Oh, I'm sorry I didn't recognize you. Mr. Sanderson left a

message in case you called. He said…" She glanced to another screen as if to check her notes. "…'Look for me.' "

The receptionist wrinkled her nose. "I don't know what that means."

"Thank you," Justine said, and severed the connection.

Using her *sight* to find one person out of the hundreds on the station would be like looking for the proverbial needle in a haystack, so Michael wouldn't have said that unless he knew she could home in on him somehow.

She took a deep breath and expanded her senses out, and almost right away sensed the signature pattern of an object irradiated from Kinemet.

Focusing on it, she *saw* Michael, Kenny and Private Hodges pushing a large trolley down the cargo hall two floors beneath her. There was something mechanical on the trolley, but it was covered with a black plastic sheet. Whatever it was, it had come into contact with Kinemet at some point.

She quickly scanned the route to the loading area. There were scatterings of workers, but there was no sign of any soldiers.

"Come on," she said in a low voice to Yaxche. "We're going in the back door."

∞

When she reached the main loading bay doors of the port, Michael and the others were already there waiting.

"I hoped you'd figure it out," he said to her, and patted the object on the trolley.

"What is it?"

Kenny answered, "It's a prototype quantum drive. Fully functional. We just need fuel and a few hours to hook it to the ship's main systems."

"Where'd you get a quantum drive?"

Kenny smiled. "Don't forget, Quantum Resources designed the first engine. We were working on an improved version just before you Americans sold your share of Quantum Resources to Canada Corp." He said it as if he had been a part of the process. Obviously, Kenny felt that the actual date of his enrollment in the company was irrelevant to his personal investment in the organization.

Justine turned to Michael. "You're not bringing it aboard just to hide it from the UECC and the Arabs, are you?"

"No," he replied, a wild grin on his face. "We've got a ton of Kinemet, a quantum drive, and a pressing need to bring Alex's body and consciousness back together. You heard Yaxche: Alex's essence is in a world with three suns. What do you say, are you up for it?"

Justine let out a low whistle at the notion. "We have an untested ship, an untested light-speed drive and an untested pilot. Talk about flying blind." She gave a little bob of her head and a quick laugh. "Of course I'm up for it."

∞

They raised a few heads on their way across the deck to where the *Ultio* waited, but they quickly went back to work. Justine was certain they had far too much to do clearing a bay for the unexpected ship to worry about two uniformed soldiers and two scientists wheeling cargo around.

She was sure someone would ask why they had a Mayan in ceremonial garb following them while they pushed someone in a wheelchair, but they were not stopped.

They arrived at the air-locked loading bridge, which was attached to the ship like a long umbilical, traversed its length, and once they reached the end, Justine and Private Hodges turned the latch to raise the bay door. They all helped maneuver the Quantum Engine inside and back to the engine room.

Justine led the private back to the loading bridge.

"Are you up for one more task?"

"Yes, ma'am," he said.

"If we pull this off, pretty much every country corp., news agency, and police force in Sol System will call us traitors or pirates. I want you to do me a favor—and this goes for Lieutenant Jeffries and Private Genero as well."

"Anything."

"Don't defend us."

He looked startled. "Pardon me?"

"If you stick up for us, it will incriminate you. I appreciate everything you guys have done, but the last thing I want is for them to prosecute you. I told Private Genero to say he knows nothing; he was just following orders. Same for you."

"I can't do that," he protested.

"Yes you can. You could even tell them I threatened your life. Maybe you three will get lucky and get through this without a court-martial."

His voice tight with emotion, Private Hodges nodded. "Yes, ma'am. Understood."

She smiled at him. "Good. Now go find the nearest peace officer and report us to him."

∞

Canada Station Three was primarily a launching point for Canada's Space Mining Division. It's secondary function was as a scientific complex with various wings of the station leased out to interested country corporations who might not have the resources to build their own orbital.

Acting as a waypoint for flights between the Earth and the Moon was a distant third in the station's mandate.

There was usually a considerable amount of traffic to and from the station, and it was tightly monitored.

When Justine prepped the ion engines of the *Ultio,* and disengaged the electronic couplings from the loading bridge, it was less than a minute before flight control buzzed in.

"Uh, hello, *Ultio.* This is CS3 Port Control. You have *not* been cleared for disembarkation. Please identify yourself."

Yaxche, sitting in the navigator's chair, looked at Justine to see what she would do.

Instead of answering the call, Justine continued monitoring the ship systems and adjusting power levels.

Michael and Kenny were in the engine room, attempting to install the Quantum Engine. Justine had secured Alex in the captain's quarters, and had placed the disc of Kinemet back on his chest.

The port officer spoke with authority. "Please be advised: If you do not identify yourself, we will have no choice but to report your ship. You will be interdicted at any space port you attempt to reach. This is your last warning."

Yaxche motioned to the speaker. "It is not polite to ignore someone who is talking to you."

Justine made a face. "I'm sorry, Yaxche. I'm just a little too busy at the moment."

"May I?" he asked, and Justine nodded in mild surprise. She pointed to the controls on the holoslate.

Yaxche leaned forward, turned the monitor to face him, and tapped the button to turn on the two-way feed.

The port officer blinked, clearly taken aback by what he saw. Yaxche still had not changed out of his ceremonial garb.

"Ahyah," Yaxche said to the man. "Heloo."

Finding his voice, the port officer said, "Who are you?"

Yaxche gave the man a toothy grin and, remembering to speak into his translator, said, "I am Yaxche. I am on a journey to the heavens."

"Uhm. Sir? Are you the only one on board? Can you turn the ship around?"

Yaxche shrugged his shoulders. "I'm sorry, I am not able to do that. This is only the second time I have been in a space ship."

"Sir, did you press something you weren't supposed to?" the man asked. "If there is anyone else on that ship, please get them to the console. You need to turn the ship around, right now."

Yaxche said, "You look upset. Perhaps if you were to practice meditation, you would be happier. I could show you how."

Frustrated, the man opened his mouth to issue another command, but something off the visual range distracted him, and he leaned away for a moment.

When the port officer turned back, his voice took on a stern tone. "Sir. Mr. Yaxche. I don't know if you are in control of the ship or not, but I've just been informed there is an armed spacecraft on approach. Somehow they are aware of your activities and have issued a warning. Turn around and dock now, or they will pursue and open fire—"

At the last, Justine reached over and severed the communications link with CS3, and quickly ran her fingers over a number of holoslates. When the ship's diagnostics did not provide her with the information she wanted, she stepped back, closed her eyes and concentrated.

She used her *sight* to scan in the general direction of the Moon. Her body shook with the effort of straining against the limits of her power, but the oncoming ship was too far away. It was pure instinct that she changed tactic. Although she could not *see* past the hundred and fifty kilometer range, she could sense any refined Kinemet or any object that was irradiated by Kinemet at a much farther distance. Within a minute, she found what she was looking for.

And cursed.

She opened a communications link to the engine room. "Michael. How are you guys coming with the installation?"

His voice was thin, as if he were speaking at a distance away from the microphone. He would have remote activated the communications console. "Uh, we barely got started."

"I don't think it's an Arabian ship," she said, acid in her voice, "and they're not coming from Luna."

"What?"

"I don't know who they are, but they're coming from Venus."

"Venus? Gruber?" Michael asked in speculation.

"I don't know who it is, but they've got weaponized Kinemet on board. I assume it's been loaded into deep-range missiles."

"What?" Michael repeated, and stepped into the video frame. The side of his face was smeared with grease and soot. He had a laser iron in his hand. *"They're* using Kinemet as a nuclear weapon?"

"Yeah," she said. "They know we're on the run, and they know our trajectory. They're coming straight for us. If they fire their missiles and hit us, the explosion will set off a chain reaction in our Kinemet. We'll be vaporized."

"Why would they want to destroy us? Don't they want the chance to get the secret of the Kinemet from us?"

"Not if they've already figured it out and want to shut us up so they can develop the technology first."

Michael cursed. Then he said, "We're going as fast as we can, but the *Ultio* is using a proprietary operating system.

Kenny's rewriting code while I install the engine. You're going to have to give us at least a couple more hours before we can patch it in."

"Hold on to something, then," she said. "I'm going to go to maximum acceleration for two minutes—about three *g* of thrust. It'll take their ship at least an hour to course-correct. That should buy you another hour and a half before they are within missile range."

"Got it." He broke the link, and Justine's hands were a blur on the controls.

To Yaxche, she spoke while she worked. "You'll have to go back and strap Alex in; yourself, too. It's going to be a rough couple of minutes."

"Turbulence?" he asked, his face paling.

"Yeah. Something like that."

∞

Once Justine had ensured all her passengers were secured, she wiggled her fingers over the haptic console and fired the ion propulsion thrusters.

The *Ultio* was basically a reconditioned space yacht, originally designed for the comfort of its passengers. The military-class vessels used by the U.S. Space Corp used a much more powerful hydrogen engine capable of greater thrust, and Justine guessed that the enemy craft was outfitted with something similar, and could easily overtake them.

After two minutes, the *Ultio's* velocity was less than a tenth of what the *Orcus* ships had been capable of.

They were racing against time, and the worst part was, once Justine disengaged the thrusters, she was completely helpless. There was nothing for her to do but wait and hope Michael and Kenny completed their installation before they were all blasted out of space by their pursuers.

Rather than sit up alone in the cockpit and go stir crazy, she decided to head back and check up on Yaxche and Alex. The captain's cabin had a bridge monitoring station, so she could keep an eye on things.

When she got there, she found Yaxche sitting in a short legged chair he had pulled close to the captain's bed. Alex was safely bundled under a web of canvas straps, and though he was perfectly still, his eyes were wide open and unfocused. It was more than a little eerie.

"How's our patient?" she asked in a quiet tone, as if a loud noise could wake Alex. There was a small nook cut into one bulkhead where a short desk and metal bench chair were installed. She sat down on the seat and leaned forward, resting her elbows on her knees.

Yaxche spoke to her, but his eyes were on Alex.

"The spirit world is a sacred place to us. Our priests meditated all their lives in their quest to learn to walk on the path of dreams and commune with the gods. There is a story I remember my grandfather telling me, about one of our holy men who had mastered the gift of entering the spirit world through dreams. He preferred being there to being in our world, and one day he set foot on the path and never returned, though his body remained until his death."

Justine thought about that. "Are you saying that even if we are able to bring Alex to where his essence is anchored, he may not recover? May not want to come back?"

Yaxche closed his eyes and nodded. "It is my fear. The Song of the Stars is a powerful and mesmerizing thing."

He spoke the truth, Justine thought to herself. When she had been in a quantized state back on Venus, she had heard the hauntingly beautiful sound that emanated from the planets in Sol System. Each voice was distinct in a majestic symphony.

In one of Yaxche's interviews, he had called it the Music of the Spheres. She suspected this was one way the Kinemats were able to navigate in space.

For a brief moment back then, when Justine had focused her senses outside the limits of Sol System, she had become aware of the pattern of the star beacons she had sensed in the stellar distance. If she closed her eyes, she could almost hear the much more powerful and eternal composition of the Song of the Stars.

If the stars were the ethereal voices that had been calling Alex home all these years, why would he ever consider returning to normal space? It would be like having an opportunity to be in heaven. What could the mortal world ever offer in comparison?

Justine was just too new at this to come up with any conclusions, let alone viable theories on the cosmic impact of her and Alex's transformations. She was not a philosopher or a priest, nor was she a physicist who might better explain what was happening.

"Yaxche," Justine said after a time. "It occurred to me that we never asked if you wanted to come with us. Worst case scenario, we might all die; best case, if we are able to achieve light speed, it will be over four years before we arrive in Centauri. I apologize for not talking with you before."

It was the better part of a full minute before Yaxche replied. "I know my daughter loves me, but she has built a life with her husband and her two daughters. She does not have time for an old man like me. I had hoped my grandson, Te'irjiil, would follow in my footsteps and become a caretaker for the Song of the Stars, but after his poor Itzel passed, he drifted away from everyone. Now that he is gone, I have no reason to remain in this world."

He looked at Alex. "Except for the Sky Traveler. He needs

my guidance, and as long as he needs me, I will go where he goes."

They both fell into an introspective silence then, and without Justine really being aware of it, she started to nod off.

She suddenly sprang awake when the remote monitor sounded an alert.

"Here we go," she said to no one in particular, and hurried out.

∞

According to the Pulse-Doppler radar system, the enemy ship was closing in at five-thousand kilometers distance. If Justine remembered correctly, the outside range any of the U.S. Space Corp. missiles could be fired in space and still be guided with any measure of reliable control was about two-thousand kilometers. At the speed difference between the two ships, the enemy would reach optimal firing range in less than ten minutes.

Justine called down to the engine room.

"Heads up. We've got company. How are you coming along?"

After a long span, Michael answered the communication feed. "Physically, it's installed," he said, his eyes showing how exhausted he was. "We calculated how much Kinemet we would need for the trip out there and loaded it in the quantum drive."

"Perfect," she said.

"Kenny's got the initial computer systems up and working, but we're having trouble calibrating the Kinemetic dampers. There's some kind of interface issue. If we can't get it working properly, we'd have a better chance surviving the missile attack." Unnecessarily, he added, "We'd reach our destination only to blow up thirteen seconds later."

"What's the problem?" Justine asked, and endured the harried look Michael gave her.

He scratched at the stubble growing on his jaw. "There's some kind of delay—about seven seconds—between the generator and the Kinemetic damper. With the five additional seconds it takes for the generator to build up enough power to engage the dampers, that won't give you time enough to rematerialize from a quantized state and start the generator in the first place."

Justine laughed, almost too loud, in relieved surprise.

"What?" Michael said.

"There's no re-materialization on my end," she said. "That's the missing piece of the puzzle. I'm fully conscious and aware during quantization. I can start the generator instantly once we arrive. Alex—and the other test candidates—were never fully transformed into a Kinemat, and had no awareness in the quantized state. Seven seconds may not be ideal, but it is more than enough time."

Michael stood there dumbfounded for a moment, then snapped out of it. "All right, then. I'll get Kenny to map the control functions to your console. He'll have to give you a rundown, since it's a patchwork of commands—"

Justine cut him off.

"Damn," she said. "They're not even going to try to parley."

"What?"

She grimaced. "I can sense a quantity of Kinemet hurtling toward us at high velocity. They've launched a missile."

"Warning shot?" Michael said.

"Can't chance it," she said, her voice tight. "Can we engage the quantum drive now?"

Looking off screen a moment, probably at Kenny, Michael finally shook his head. "At least five minutes to finish mapping the controls."

"We'll be atoms in two."

Michael said something more to her, but Justine didn't hear it. She shut all physical awareness from her mind, and concentrated on pushing her *sight* out toward the oncoming ship.

At the speed the radar estimated the missile was traveling— a little over one-hundred kilometers per second— it would breach the distance between her outer limit of *sight* to the *Ultio* in less than two seconds.

There was a chance she could sense it the moment it came within range of her *sight*, and if her reaction time was quick enough, she might be able to detonate the warhead before the reacting Kinemet got too close and triggered their own cache of the metal.

She waited … and waited…

Like a lightning strike, the Kinemet burst into her awareness, and for a split-second, she faltered and thought she had missed her chance.

Desperately, she sent her electropathic sense on an intercept course with the missile.

The radar on her holoslate blanked as it was overloaded with feedback.

For a moment, she wondered if she had failed.

Then the *Ultio* bucked like an angry bronco, and Justine was flung hard into the bank of controls. The bulkhead screamed and the diagnostic console lit up as hundreds of sensors reported the sudden change in conditions.

"What the hell just happened?" someone screamed through the comlink.

"How's the Kinemet?" Justine called back, holding her hand to the side of her head and struggling back into the pilot's chair.

"Fine." Michael appeared on the comlink, wide-eyed. "Did you just do what I think you did?"

"Yeah," Justine said, still breathing hard. "One warhead destroyed."

"You all right?" he asked.

She nodded, though her head rang from the movement. "But as soon as they realize their missile didn't blow us to space junk, they'll launch two at a time." She shook her head, wincing. "I can't stop two."

Glancing off screen once more, Michael said, "All right. Kenny just finished the final mapping. Check your console. He's labeled all the commands for you. One to start the generator. Another to engage the damper."

"Sounds simple enough," she said, and then sent her *sight* back out.

After a minute, she *saw* what she had feared.

"They've launched two missiles. They really want us dead." She did a quick mental calculation. There was most likely less than five seconds before the missiles impacted with their ship.

...four...

"Kenny," Michael called out immediately. "Are we clear to engage the Drive?"

...three...

"Yeah," he said, his voice sounding muffled. "I labeled it 'GO.' "

...*two*...

Without further prompting, Justine reached her finger toward the haptic console and tapped the command button and—

...*ONE*...

—the universe shifted.

Partial Entry From Omnipedia :
Subject: Alpha Centauri :

Alpha Centauri is a binary star system averaging 4.37 light years from the Sun. The distance between the two stars varies during their 79.91 year orbit. A third star, Proxima Centauri, lays about .21 light years from the Alpha Centauri stars, and the three companions are sometimes referred to as a triple star system, though it is not determined whether Proxima Centauri is gravitationally bound with Alpha Centauri A and B.

Due to the significant gravitational effects of the system, no gas giant planets have formed. There is evidence that one or more minor planetoids or comets may have found their way into the system at some point, and may be orbiting at the outer rim of the system.

In 2095, the first attempt to travel to Alpha Centauri failed. Though the light speed ship *Quanta* completed the journey, a mishap upon arrival in our neighboring system resulted in the destruction of the vessel. The pilot, Captain Alex Manez, survived in an escape pod and returned to our system in mid-2103.

Tap for more…

Alien Space Port :
Alpha Centauri :
Four Years Later

—**After an eternity** of drifting in the purgatory between the material world and the unreality of the quantized state of being, Alex was abruptly ripped back to his corporeal self.

He screamed. The pain tore through his very essence. It was as if every atom in his body had exploded. He couldn't take the agony—

—and in the nanosecond before he passed out, he welcomed the oncoming blanket of oblivion.

∞

Eons later, or moments for all he knew, reality crashed back in as Alex once more regained consciousness. He could feel a bed under him. There was a musty smell wafting up, and a natural brightness permeated his eyelids. He was in his human state.

Disoriented, he tried to sit up, but gentle hands pushed him back down.

"Easy, now," a voice whispered in his ear.

Alex tried to speak, but he couldn't move the muscles in his jaw to open his mouth. He let out a groan.

"Give yourself some time," someone said. It was a woman,

and the voice was familiar. Justine. *What is she doing here?*

"You've been gone for a long time," she said.

He tried to open his eyes, but they were lidded shut. He managed to open his mouth finally, and this time was able to croak out a question. "What happened?"

A second voice, one that Alex recognized right away, spoke.

Yaxche said, "Sky Traveler, you have been on a long journey in the spirit world. We did not know if you would come back to us, so we traveled a great distance to find you. Now, you are whole once more."

Fighting against the sudden nausea that rose up as the blood pressure in his head increased, Alex forced his eyes open. It took him a moment to focus, and a few more moments to identify where he was.

He saw Michael, Justine and Yaxche, but his stomach clenched when he realized they were in a cabin on an unfamiliar space yacht.

"Where am I?"

"The *Ultio*," said Michael. He reached out and touched Alex's shoulder. "How are you, my boy? You had us worried."

"I'm fine, I think." Alex's head was clearing, and he was able to sit up without feeling dizzy. "What happened?" He needed to know.

"Well," Michael said, "it seems you fell into some kind of a fugue state, and your consciousness—Yaxche calls it your dream spirit—was anchored in Centauri System. Kenny's theory is there was an energy link between you and the alien space port. Probably from when you were here last. Naturally, your Kinemetic consciousness gravitated here."

Here? Alex's stomach flip-flopped. "Alpha Centauri?" He stared at Michael. "We're in the space port?"

"Outside of it, actually," he said. "We can't figure out how to get in. You seem very upset, Alex."

Alex gulped. "Uh ... it's ... I mean, the last thing I remember was being on CS3. Now I'm in another solar system. It's just unexpected."

Michael gave him a comforting look. "Trust me, I felt the same way. I didn't experience anything when we were quantized. It was a blink of the eye for us." He glanced at Justine when he said it.

Justine had a playful smile on her face when she asked Alex, "Are you thirsty?" and reached for a squeeze pack of orange juice beside her without looking.

Alex took it when she offered it to him, and as the liquid hit his tongue he realized he was parched. And starving.

But what had just transpired caused him to look at Justine in surprise. She did not have her optilink on, nor her harness. Yet she had passed him the juice without faltering in the least.

"How did you—?" he asked.

She smiled at him. "Use your *sight*."

He did. "You're ... a full Kinemat?" he asked in wonder.

"Yes." A contented smile on her lips, she nodded. "It was Klaus." She told him about the hijacking and the experiments.

When she finished her tale, Alex asked her, "You were aware the entire trip here?"

There was a particularly distant look on her face when she nodded.

"Yeah," she said. "It was pretty exciting at first, but after four years and however many months, well..." She fell silent for a moment, and there was a reflection of the pain of loneliness on her face.

"Are you able to sleep?" he asked her, wondering if his insomnia was a typical side-effect.

She shook her head. "No. And that took a while to get used to." Justine smiled. "We are the same in every way, except that I am aware during quantization."

Alex, like Michael and every other person who had not been irradiated by charged Kinemet, had no awareness when he was quantized. Again, that proved to him that he was not fully transformed—he was stuck somewhere between human and Kinemat. But he was overjoyed that humankind had made the next step in its chrysalis. Justine had made that transition, though it had been forced on her by Klaus.

Alex asked, "You all came here just for me?"

"Well," Justine said. "That, and we were kind of chased out of Sol System."

Alex sat up straighter. "What?"

"Are you up to hearing the rest of the story?" she asked. "We can wait until you're feeling better."

Alex shook his head. "Other than needing a sandwich or something else to eat, I'm good. Tell me everything."

They did, Justine and Michael taking turns relating everything that had happened since Alex had shifted out of consciousness, right up until they arrived in Centauri.

"About seven hours ago, we arrived in orbit around the small planetoid you described. The one with this system's star beacon," Michael said. "We scanned the area and found the spaceport you told us about. It only took us about five hours to get here. But now we're just hovering outside the structure. We hoped you knew how to get in."

Alex shook his head.

Michael said, "We've just been doing scans of the port. It looks like the hangar is only half of this structure. There's most likely some kind of working and living area on the other side, but we can't detect any signs of life. We think we found a bay door to the hangar, but can't figure out how to open it."

Sometime during the last part of the story, Kenny had arrived. When he spoke, his voice and measured and controlled.

"I managed to rig one of the spectrographic sensors up to the ship's computers. And I got a reading from the Centauri star beacon."

When everyone looked at him blankly, his jaw rippled in frustration at his inability to get his point across. "You see, when we first arrived in Alpha Centauri, the beacon went dormant right away. You know. Once we had come out of light speed."

There was an inscrutable look on his face, but then Alex connected the dots. His eyes widened.

"You were able to link to it now because it's giving off electromagnetic waves. That means—"

"—Someone's coming," Michael and Justine said in unison.

∞

In a group, the four of them rushed out of the cabin and up to the bridge where Kenny had installed the sensors. The spectrographic readout showed an ever-increasing wave signal.

Alex was a little unsteady on his feet, but the food and the hour of rest had done wonders; physically, he was recovering quickly. His heart, however, beat in his chest like a hammer.

Over the past few years, Alex had had plenty of time on his hands to research every aspect of Kinemetic science, and based on the readings he saw, he quickly calculated that whatever the new arrival to the Centauri system was, it would enter normal space in less than five minutes.

Where it would arrive in relation to Centauri's star beacon and the space dock was unknown. The first time Alex had made the trip here, he'd appeared a little over twenty-thousand kilometers away—a very short distance in astronomical terms. The *Ultio* had also arrived at the same location. The average ion drive could propel a ship that far in a couple of hours, but

Alex didn't know if it would take the newcomers that long.

He had to tell the others, but couldn't find his voice. Hope and fear both warred within him.

"Are they coming from Sol System?" Kenny asked. "Did they follow us?"

"Impossible," Michael said in answer, though the crease in his brow showed that he had a kernel of doubt.

Kenny nodded his agreement. "The only two agencies with full access to quantum drive schematics are Quantum Resources and NASA. The security checks I had to go through to get access *after* I had been hired were exhaustive. There've been informational leaks and technological espionage before, but never on this level." He glanced at Michael for agreement.

Justine speculated. "Our pursuers had weaponized Kinemet in their warheads. Maybe they've developed the tech on their own."

Kenny turned back to his monitors. "Any geek in their parents' basement can figure out how to do that. It took Quantum Resources years to develop the first functioning quantum drive. Even if these guys managed to mine their own stash of Kinemet, it would be years before they mastered the technology."

Justine countered. "Klaus was able to make a leap ahead of us, and he was just one guy."

Frowning, Kenny gave a terse shake of his head. "He had access to the scroll. I say it's a ship from *out there.*"

"Aliens?" Michael said in a breathless voice, his eyes filled with wonder.

"Well," Kenny said as the graph on the monitor spiked, and then flat-lined, "we're going to find out very soon."

∞

If the new arrival was, indeed, the mysterious warship that had chased the *Ultio* out of Sol System, and they had somehow paralleled Klaus's experiment and created another Kinemat, then Alex and his friends were in trouble.

But the other possibility was potentially worse.

Alex summoned up the courage and, as the four of them stared at the monitor, he said, "I'm so sorry that I never told you the whole truth."

At first, no one reacted. It was as if they didn't understand a word he had said. But then Michael slowly turned his head toward Alex.

"What truth?"

Taking a deep breath, Alex took a step off to the side and looked at the large holoscreen showing a panographic starfield.

He said, "Outside of you and Justine, I've never told anyone about the space port in this system, except for the oversight committee representative—and I regret telling him that much."

"You could have told me," Kenny said, looking hurt. "I had to find out about this from them."

Alex flushed. "All I told them was that when I came to this hangar on my last trip out, its automated systems attached a portable quantum drive and sent me home. I didn't want that knowledge to get out, because it would only lead to more questions that I couldn't answer."

"Couldn't, or wouldn't?" Kenny said, but there was only a hint of reproach in his words.

But it was Michael who guessed the truth. "You made contact."

Alex nodded. "Yes."

Justine and Kenny turned as one, mouths agape. "You met an alien?" Kenny asked.

"Sort of."

"What do you mean 'sort of'?" Justine asked.

"I mean I don't know who it was for sure. I didn't see anything. When I came out of quantization, I was inside the hangar, and the machines were installing the drive. The only part that I left out of my story was the voice message on my console. Once I listened to it, I had to purge it from the ship's memory."

"Which is why you blew the storage banks," Michael said.

"Yes. I panicked and pushed too hard. But I remember the message word-for-word."

"Your eidetic memory," Kenny said.

"Yes," Alex said. "And the message was in Mayan."

Kenny glanced between Alex and Yaxche. "Mayan?"

Alex nodded, and turned on the ship's translator. He spoke in Mayan, and the others listened to the English version:

∞

I offer my greetings to you, Sky Traveler. I am Ah Tabai, a Sentinel of the Collection. Our people have waited for a thousand years for humankind to walk the path of light, and journey beyond the boundaries of our home system to join with us.

It saddens me that our reunion must be delayed. I am afraid that I bring a message of despair.

Your world is in extreme danger.

Almost one thousand of your Earth years ago, the Grace vanished without a sign of where they went. They were our leaders, our mentors, our elders and caregivers. An ancient race, they were the ones who built the nexus of star beacons and infused them with their essence. The Grace existed in the galaxy eons before any culture Emerged from their systems. There has long been a legend that the Grace hid the sum of their knowledge in an unknown pre-Emerging star system.

The Kulsat, once the favored of the Grace and one-time heirs to their knowledge and wisdom, have turned aggressive and power hungry. When they've become aware of a pre-Emerged system, they've scoured them for signs of the Grace and their legacy. They have not hesitated to destroy everything in their path to find what the Grace have hidden.

I have sent instructions to the space port computer to affix a temporary light-speed engine to your ship, and it will send you back to your system. You must avoid traveling 'outside of light' at all costs, and refrain from returning to this star system, or the Kulsat may sense you.

With luck, your system will remain undetected long enough so that you may learn to fully Emerge. Only then will you be able to defend yourselves against the Kulsat.

Travel swiftly, Cousin. Go with Grace.

∞

Once Alex finished his recitation, he turned to face his friends. They were all stunned.

Kenny was the first one to break the silence. "Why wouldn't you share this with us? I mean, confirmation of alien cultures aside, the fact that one of them might invade and destroy us is information I, for one, would like to have had."

Justine answered before Alex had a chance. "If we did know, the first thing we would have done is work towards improving the quantum drives, and on weaponizing Kinemet. Eventually, someone would notice that much Kinemet being used."

"It's more important for us to 'Emerge'," Alex said. "You heard his last words. Only once we are Emerged will we be able to defend ourselves. I don't know what that entails, but I'm sure if there were any other option, Ah Tabai would have mentioned it."

Michael turned to Yaxche, "He spoke Mayan. The Song of the Stars mentions a time when a great number of your people vanished during a war."

"Ahyah," Yaxche said. "The Great War."

"Then…" Michael started to say, clearly working through the facts.

But before anyone had a chance to add to the conjecture, the ship's console lit up and an alert sounded. On the holoscreen, the faint twinkling of stars turned pitch black as they were blocked out by an enormous object.

It had taken the *Ultio* five hours to travel from the star beacon to the space port. The alien ship made the trip in five minutes.

∞

Everyone's eyes were glued to the holoscreen, watching as the outline of a ship began to coalesce several kilometers away.

"It's huge," Kenny said in a hushed voice. "At this magnification, I would say it's at least fifteen-hundred meters long."

The architecture of the vessel was unlike any craft Alex had ever seen on Earth. It was as if the metal of the hull were made of pure electricity. It glowed and swirled in continuous motion, a dance of solid energy.

The nose of the vessel extended out in a gently tapering cone. The ship's body was shaped roughly like a tube, and ended in a long taper at the back. Overall, the vessel somewhat resembled a narwhal.

As the ship neared, Alex was suddenly awash with the overwhelming sensation of Kinemet. He shivered.

"I can feel it, too," Justine said. "The ship itself is built from Kinemet!"

Once the alien vessel came within half a kilometer, it stopped and floated at that position.

"Is it the Kulsat?" Kenny asked. No one replied. "What are they doing?"

"Maybe they're scanning us. Wondering who we are," Michael said.

At the same time, Justine and Alex nodded.

"Yes," Justine said. "I can…" She gave her head a slight shake. "I don't know how to describe it. When I try to use my *sight*, I'm just overwhelmed by the Kinemet out there. It's like looking directly at the Sun. But, I feel like they are *looking* at us with the *sight*. Like they are *looking* at me—"

Her words were cut off abruptly, and when Alex glanced at her, he saw that she was transforming into quanta before his eyes. There was a look of panic on her face in the moment before she completely turned to light.

Everyone else took a step back as Justine's essence, her collection of photons, floated toward the monitors and through them. They all flickered out as she passed them, and then came back to life when she was through.

Her photons then continued to drift into the hull of the *Ultio* and finally out into space. Unconfined by any material barrier, her essence shot toward the alien ship, almost as if she were being sucked in through a vacuum tube.

"What the hell?" Kenny asked.

"It's not her," Alex said. "It's got to be *them*. They're taking her."

Michael gasped. "Why her?"

"She's the only one of us who is a full Kinemat. I'm incomplete. They probably aren't even aware of my existence."

"What are they going to—?" Kenny started to ask, but the hull of the alien ship brightened to a blinding level, and lance of pale light shot out toward the underside of the *Ultio*.

Kenny screamed, "They're targeting the engines!"

Before anyone could brace themselves, the impact knocked them all to the floor.

Michael let out a cry as he fell, and it looked as if he might have broken an arm.

The electrical systems in the bridge stuttered. One interface console exploded in a shower of sparks, and a panel on the other side of the room popped off, the wires spitting and hissing.

Yaxche, looking frightened out of his wits, had an arm wrapped around the back of the captain's chair.

The lights flickered off and on, and the artificial gravity generator failed. Alex lost contact with the floor, and floated up, smacking his head against a control panel.

There was a secondary explosion, and then the ship listed to port.

Just before the holoscreens went dark, Alex saw the alien spacecraft turn away and leave, as if confident their attack had been a fatal enough blow.

Alex held enough hope that that wasn't the case, right up until the air filters shut down, and the entire electrical system fizzled out.

They were adrift in space. Their ship was disabled, and their life support system was non-functional.

The temperature on the bridge started to drop at an alarming rate.

"Alex," Michael called out. "Can you do anything?"

He could quantize himself, but he had no awareness in that state. In doing so, he might be able to save himself, but there was no way he could navigate the ship or help the others. He pushed his senses out to see if the electrical system was repairable.

"I'm sorry, the generators and batteries are completely melted."

"What about the Kinemet?" Kenny said. "If it fissions, that's all she wrote."

Alex shook his head, then realized no one could see the

motion. "It's not there. They must have taken it when they took Justine."

After a few moments, Kenny said, "Is now a good time to panic?"

"Wait a minute," Alex said. He could feel the chill creep in to his bones. The bridge was nearing the freezing point.

The *Ultio* was only a few hundred meters from the space port, and though it was falling away, it was an agonizing thought that they were so close to salvation.

When Alex had been saved before, he was in a quantized state, and had no memory of the events, but if he made one giant assumption…

He concentrated, and pushed his *sight* out toward the space port. He had the sense that it was wrapped in something similar to the Kinemet dampers because when his consciousness reached the outer hull of the complex, he could not push his way in.

There had to be some kind of way to communicate with the space port's computer system, to let it know there was a ship ready to dock. In the case of a disabled ship, they had to have made a provision for some kind of manual override.

He searched the entire surface of the space port, but after the first pass, he had not found any way in.

Willing himself not to panic, he continued his search, and it was only at his second pass over one of the large elliptical bay doors of the hull that he spotted a slight protrusion sticking out a few centimeters. It was a tiny metal rod.

He used his electropathic ability and sent a small shot of energy into it.

Slowly, the bay door started to open, and Alex could feel a magnetic tug coming from within. He returned to his body.

Kenny was wild-eyed. "What's happening? We're drifting the other way now!"

"The space port dock has us. It's pulling us in," Alex said.

Michael cried out with joy. "You did it."

"I'm not sure it was enough," Alex said. "Maybe I only postponed the inevitable. Even if we were to manage to get one of those portable quantum drives attached to the *Ultio,* we'd be dead five minutes after arriving near Pluto."

There was a sharp jarring as the ship came to a stop, and Kenny and Michael scrambled in the dark to manually open the cabin door and lead the way to the main hatch. They opened it to reveal the inside of the alien space port.

The rush of fresh oxygen was pure heaven.

37

Alien Space Port :
Alpha Centauri :

Standing on one of the metal walkways along the pier inside the alien space port, Michael surveyed the damage to the *Ultio*. A full third of the hind section, where the quantum drive and Kinemet had been, was simply missing. The ship was as good as scuttled.

"Maybe destroying our ship was incidental," Michael said, though to no one in particular. "They wanted the Kinemet and Justine, and didn't give us a passing thought."

Kenny glanced up and frowned.

"What now?" Alex asked, sitting down near Yaxche, who had found a spot on the floor to rest.

Michael rubbed the stubble growing on his chin, and winced when he moved his arm. Not broken, but still sore.

The hangar itself was several hundred meters wide in every direction, laced with rows of berths, metal jetties, elevated piers and several walkways floating at various elevations. It looked as if the port wasn't meant for ships much larger than the *Ultio*.

All of the docking bays in the hangar were empty. The jetties were lined with large discs on the end of cylindrical beams. Michael guessed they served as dock bumpers. They gave off a steady electromagnetic hum.

When Michael and Kenny had opened the main loading

door from the *Ultio,* they'd been able to manually extend the ramp. Although the electrical systems were dead, and the few small fires had been extinguished, the structure of the *Ultio* was still unsafe. The ship groaned periodically as metal beams collapsed and the contents shifted and fell.

"I'm not sure," Michael said finally. "But we should try to go back in and get food and water. Maybe some blankets or something and make a camp out here."

"What about Justine?" Kenny asked, but the only answer Michael gave was the hard set to his jaw.

The aliens—he assumed they were the Kulsat—had abducted her, and there was nothing Michael could think of to help.

∞

They spent the next fifteen minutes making quick excursions back into the *Ultio* and gathering supplies and enough equipment to make a camp.

Kenny set up a makeshift table using a few storage containers. He brought out several holoslates for testing, and finally found one that wasn't damaged. As he worked on it, tapping, swirling and wiggling his fingers on the haptic console, Michael looked over his shoulder.

"We should conserve the battery," he said by way of suggestion.

Kenny smiled. "No need. There's a wireless electrical current running through the complex. It's powering the computer directly. I'm going to see if the space port has a network I can hook into. Maybe we can download a manual on how to get into the living quarters on the other side."

Alex had already tried to use his electropathy to open the large door at the far end of the hangar, but had reported that there wasn't any kind of switch or lever that he could find.

With Alex's help, Yaxche had used cargo netting to create a hammock between two vertical beams. When Alex went back into the ship to look for a blanket, the old Mayan sank into the netting and closed his eyes.

"Are you all right?" Michael asked, approaching tentatively.

Blinking his eyes open, Yaxche gave him that big grin. He spoke, and his clip-on translator repeated, "Ahyah. Old men get tired. I just need a nap."

Laughing, both in relief, and at the Mayan's equanimity in the face of everything that was happening, Michael said, "Quite a mess we got ourselves in."

"Ahyah," Yaxche said back. "As they say, 'Out of the pot and into the fire'." His grin widened into a full smile.

Before Michael could say anything more, Alex raced out of the wreckage of the *Ultio,* his eyes wide.

"What's wrong?" Michael asked, his heart speeding up.

Alex headed straight for Kenny and the holoslates. "There's something happening. I could feel the electromagnetics activating on one of the other docking bays." He pointed to the holoslate. "Are you able to do any scans on this?"

Kenny shook his head. "No, the external sensor on this unit is damaged."

Just then, one of the magnetic dock bumpers on the next pier over began to extend.

Kenny stood up, his face flush and his eyes bright with trepidation. "Are the Kulsat coming back to finish us off?"

A huge circular section of the hangar wall, the bay door, faded to an almost perfect blackness. The ring of the opening had a vague whitish glow to it. That was the energy barrier Kenny had theorized about earlier. While they were inside the *Ultio* being pulled into the dock, they'd been unable to see what was happening.

Michael could feel his hair tingling with the electricity as a new alien ship appeared in the opening.

It was less than a quarter of the size of the *Ultio*. As with the ship that had attacked them, the hull of the new alien ship looked to be made of Kinemet—the entire surface glowed and swirled, though the colors on this ship were a kaleidoscope of reds and yellows. Its shape was very similar to the bird-like designs of gull-wing planes from Earth. Michael guessed that this ship could serve a dual purpose as a spacecraft and an aircraft. The front of the ship resembled the coned head of a bird, with a beaked nose that came to a point.

Michael's first impression was of a phoenix.

When the vessel had fully entered the bay, the docking bumpers adjusted themselves to uniformly secure it. The hangar wall solidified once more, sealing the area against the void of space.

The four stood there with mouths agape during the entire docking procedure.

Kenny took an involuntary step back when a hatch on the side of the alien ship opened. A broad, rectangular patch of the ship's hull faded to empty space.

A platform held by two large metal arms protruded from the gap and began to descend to the hangar deck.

On the platform stood two aliens.

Both of them were bipedal. One of them was significantly taller than the other, standing almost three meters high, and it was extremely thin. The second alien was a great deal shorter, the top of its head level with the other's elbow.

When the platform stopped several centimeters above the dock, the two aliens stepped off and approached the waiting humans.

The shorter alien wore clothing that was alarmingly close to the ceremonial outfit Yaxche wore. Calf-high boots with beads and tassels were pulled over long beige pants. The alien's torso was wrapped with a tzute style cloth, intricately designed in geometric shapes and earth-tone colors. A scarf hung loosely around the neck, decorated with brightly colored baubles. The alien reached up and removed the feathered headdress, and Michael looked on the face of a being from another world for the first time.

—And it was human. The small man was dark complexioned, with black hair and a long forehead. High cheekbones framed a broad nose and wide brown eyes. He resembled a Mayan.

He gave them an easy smile.

Michael was speechless.

A moment later, the taller alien, dressed also in what Michael guessed was a ceremonial outfit—though it was one he had never seen before, made of some kind of shiny material and arranged in several folds and layers—also removed its mantle, an oblong cap with several long spines protruding from it.

Michael gaped at the tall alien.

She had the same basic features as a human girl, but the lower part of her face was drawn forward to end in a narrow jaw and tiny chin. Her thin lips framed a small mouth set also in a welcoming smile, and her eyes were overlarge and elliptical.

Instead of hair, she had what looked like the down of a bird that, as far as Michael could tell, ran from the top of her head, where it was white, to the back of her neck where it turned a light shade of yellow and extended down behind her clothes. Michael could not see her ears, if she had any, and the skin on her face and the front of her neck was bright yellow and fuzzy.

Together, the pair of aliens approached the four humans and stopped. The shorter alien genuflected.

Michael, the politician of the group, recovered from his

astonishment and bowed. He stepped forward.

Kenny reached out instinctively to stop him, but he smiled at the younger man. "It'll be fine. These are not the Kulsat."

The shorter alien spoke in Mayan, and a split-second later, Michael heard English words come from somewhere near the alien's collar.

"I offer my greetings to you. I am Ah Tabai, a Sentinel of the Collection."

The alien extended both arms and clasped Michael's hands in welcome. He glanced at Alex. "It has been a very long time since we first discovered you, Sky Traveler. I am glad you have endured."

Ah Tabai then took a step toward Yaxche, and bowed deeply.

"Grandfather," the alien said. Michael remembered from something Alex had said that it was a general term of respect for one's elders, regardless of the blood relationship. "You have traveled a great distance to be here."

"Ahyah," Yaxche said, a look of surprise on his usually calm face.

Ah Tabai motioned to the other alien, who made a quirky nod.

"My companion is—" He made a high pitched sound, for which his translator found no suitable match in English.

As if realizing this, Ah Tabai said, "You can call her Aliah. She is also a Sentinel. You would know her home star system as 'Gliese'."

With that, the tall birdlike alien woman made a chirping sound and tilted her head almost perpendicular to her shoulders. The translator in her suit said, "Pleased to meet you."

Michael said, "I'm afraid you are not finding us at our best, but on behalf of my friends here and our home world, I am glad to meet you, and extend our friendship to you."

His tone grew somber. "We were attacked by an alien ship—the Kulsat?—and they took our friend."

Ah Tabai's eyes widened. "They did?"

"Her name is Justine," Alex said. "She is the first and only one of us to become a full Kinemat—she has Emerged."

"That is why they took her," Ah Tabai said. "It has happened in the past. They will try to find out as much about your system from her as they can."

"Is there anything you can do?" Michael asked. "Can you rescue her?"

Ah Tabai dropped his eyes. "By now they have taken her back to their home system." He glanced at Aliah. "We hurried from Gliese the moment we detected the beacon in this system was active, but it is obvious we were not quick enough, else we might have been able to save her."

Kenny raised one finger. "Uh, excuse me. From 'Gliese'?" he asked.

Ah Tabai smiled, "Yes. Gliese is the closest member world of the Collection to this system."

"But—" Kenny glanced at Michael. "If you only left there when we arrived *here,* that would mean you traveled, like, twenty light-years in a little over eight hours!"

"Yes," Ah Tabai said, as if this were obvious.

"That's unbelievable," Kenny said. He looked at the alien ship with wide eyes. "You can travel at, what—" He did a rough calculation in his head. "—thirty-*thousand* times the speed of light?"

"You are mistaken in your calculation," Ah Tabai said, as if talking to a child. "It took us that amount of time to get from our planet to the beacon in our system at light speed."

"Then…?" Kenny glanced back and forth between Michael and the alien, but Michael couldn't figure it out either.

Ah Tabai said, "When we use the star beacons, we say that we travel 'outside light'. It is by the Grace that we do this. Only inside a system do we travel by light—though the beacon and the space port in this system are too close for light travel."

"So it's instantaneous between the beacons?" Kenny asked. He glanced at Alex and Michael. "It took us over four years." Stunned, he asked Ah Tabai, "What kind of engine can do that?"

Ah Tabai said patiently, "When we travel outside light, we use the Grace. All star beacons occupy the same space outside light."

Kenny stared. "The Grace. What does that mean?"

Ah Tabai put up his hand to forestall more questions. "I will answer everything as well as I am able. For now, you must listen to me."

He looked at each of them in turn to make sure they were paying attention.

"As much as I longed for the day we would meet, I had hoped you were more advanced than this. If your friend is the only one of you who has Emerged, then your world is in terrible danger.

"Now that the Kulsat are aware of you, they will gather an armada and prepare an invasion of your home system."

Michael blanched. "We thought coming here was our only hope to save Alex."

Ah Tabai nodded. "It was. We do not have much time. We must board my ship and return you to your world without delay."

His eyes reflected the gravity of his words. "You need to warn your people the Kulsat are coming, and try to defend yourselves against annihilation."

38

Alien Ship :
Alpha Centauri :

Some days I feel my age. I know I am much older than my father was when he passed from the world. My brothers and sisters are all long gone, and my only grandson has died.

When I think about it, I can understand how many people my age start to look forward to the end. It is not that terrible a thing, passing from this world into the next. All things must end, and on the days when my bones ache and I miss my family and friends who have passed, I look to the sunset of my life with a sense of peace and welcome.

Today is not one of those days. Today I feel young and full of excitement, despite the danger to the Earth.

Following the path of the gods, standing on a structure built by the people of the stars, and meeting sky travelers from alien lands, I suddenly long for another lifespan of years.

When Ah Tabai, the traveler who shares our Mayan ancestors, invited us on board his star ship to return us to Earth, the scientist, Kenny, jumped with excitement. If I were not so old and fragile, I would have jumped, too.

As we entered the alien ship, I could feel a tingle of electricity pass through me, and I could not tell if it came from the vessel or from the wonder I feel.

Ah Tabai took us to a passenger room with seats that flow

out of the walls. When I sat down, the seat gently formed itself around the shape of my body. It felt like I was floating in the air, and I had the urge to fall asleep, but I fought to stay awake.

Our host told us it will be a short journey to the beacon, and then we will arrive in our home system a moment later. He said he will answer all of our questions when we are in our home system.

As I drift into sleep, I think about the story Ah Tabai told us, and how the gods who created the star beacons have been missing for a thousand years.

And I think to myself:

I believe I know the secret the gods hid on Earth, and I might also know what happened to them.

EMERGENCE

to be continued in *Worlds Away*...

About the Author :

Valmore Daniels has lived on the coasts of the Atlantic, Pacific, and Arctic Oceans, and dozens of points in between.

An insatiable thirst for new experiences has led him to work in several fields, including legal research, elderly care, oil & gas administration, web design, government service, human resources, and retail business management.

His enthusiasm for travel is only surpassed by his passion for telling tall tales.

Visit ValmoreDaniels.com